The Solitary Sprout

R. Chudamani (1931–2010), short story writer, novelist and playwright, was the daughter of T. N. S. Raghavan, an Indian civil servant, and Kanakavalli, an artist and sculptor. Owing to a physical disability, Chudamani was educated at home. A major Tamil writer of the second half of the twentieth century and recipient of several literary awards, Chudamani's writing eludes labels and traverses pressing existential and socio-economic issues. She has written over two hundred short stories, and several novellas, including *Pinju Mukham* (1959) and *Iravuchchudar* (1974), which was translated into English as *Yamini* (1996).

Chudamani led a simple, austere life, and left all her properties to Sri Ramakrishna Mission and other service-oriented institutions to be used for educational and charitable causes.

C. T. Indra is retired professor and head, Department of English, University of Madras.

T. Sriraman is retired professor, Department of Literatures in English, School of Distance Education, The English and Foreign Languages University, Hyderabad.

The Solitary Sprout

Selected Stories of R. Chudamani

Translated from the original Tamil by

C. T. Indra

and

T. Sriraman

Orient BlackSwan

THE SOLITARY SPROUT: SELECTED STORIES OF R. CHUDAMANI

ORIENT BLACKSWAN PRIVATE LIMITED

Registered Office
3-6-752 Himayatnagar, Hyderabad 500 029, Telangana, India
e-mail: centraloffice@orientblackswan.com

Other Offices
Bengaluru, Bhopal, Chennai, Guwahati, Hyderabad,
Jaipur, Kolkata, Lucknow, Mumbai, New Delhi,
Noida, Patna, Visakhapatnam

First published by Orient Blackswan Private Limited 2019

ISBN 978-93-5287-690-7

030194

Typeset in
Cambria 11/13.8
by Le Studio Graphique, Gurgaon 122 001

Printed in India at
Akash Press, New Delhi

Published by
Orient Blackswan Private Limited
3-6-752, Himayatnagar, Hyderabad 500 029, Telangana, India
e-mail: info@orientblackswan.com

Contents

Acknowledgements

We are grateful to Dr K. Bharathi, Trustee, The R. Chudamani Memorial Trust, for kindly granting permission to translate these stories, selected from the collection of Chudamani's Tamil stories entitled *Tanimaittalir* (2013), compiled by Sita Ravi and K. Bharathi, and published by Kalachuvadu Publications, Nagercoil, Tamil Nadu.

C. T. Indra's English translation of the story *'Senthiru Aahivittaal'* was first published with the title 'Herself' in *Indian Literature*, No. 267, January–February 2012, pp. 15–30. It is reprinted here, with slight modifications, by kind permission of the Sahitya Akademi.

Introduction

C. T. Indra and *T. Sriraman*

Virginia Woolf memorably captured the nature and textuality of modernist literary sensibility when she wrote in her classic 'Modern Fiction':

> Examine for a moment an ordinary mind on an ordinary day. The mind receives a myriad impressions—trivial, fantastic, evanescent, or engraved with the sharpness of steel. From all sides they come, an incessant shower of innumerable atoms; and as they fall, as they shape themselves into the life of Monday or Tuesday, the accent falls differently from of old; the moment of importance came not here but there ... if the writer were a free man and not a slave, if he could write what he chose, not what he must...[1]

With airy wit Woolf made fun of stolid writers who go around with a "magnificent apparatus for catching [all of] life", but end up catching it "just an inch or two on the wrong side".[2] The ironic outcome of this exercise is that "Life escapes", as Woolf pithily put it. Her classic modernist novel *To the Lighthouse* demonstrates the nature of the alternative artistic finesse that creates a reality which is at once delicate and strong:

> It was to be a thing you could ruffle with your breath and a thing you could not dislodge with a team of horses.[3]

That precisely describes the art and artistry, the subtle solidity of R. Chudamani's achievement as a short story writer.

I

Raghavan Chudamani (1931–2010) has often been identified as an early feminist among Tamil writers. That may be true, but the label by no means captures the range of her concerns and interests. She is not an iconoclast, but she is no less radical in her approach to human/interpersonal relations, larger issues touching upon institutions, identity, the class divide and poverty, to name just a few. One does not expect Chudamani to be strident, loud or muscle-flexing in dealing with any issue. But her critique of entrenched institutions and of the attitudes that go with them is no less sharp, even revelatory often. She challenges with a quiet tenacity the way society 'interpellates' or hails human beings, conditioned as they are by 'Institutional State Apparatuses', to use Louis Althusser's insightful model of analysis of subject construction. Institutional State Apparatuses, or ISA as they are known in Critical Theory, are constituted by family, religion, the educational and legal systems, all of which shape the identities and values of subjects, conditioning their self-perception and behaviour. How do we construct the identities of mother, father, husband, wife, son and daughter in the realm of family? How do we construct identities at the societal level of master, servant, privileged, deprived, teacher, taught, female companion, male lover, artist and society? Chudamani explores these questions in her stories and captures the answers in moments of epiphany which are often unconventional, challenging received images and searching for a buried stratum of truth in knotty situations and relationships. She assails conventions calmly, or to be more accurate, she calmly sets aside conventions without resort to a battering ram or verbal theatrics. She is not interested in demolishing institutional structures as much as zeroing in on the pre-nominal state of reality when a self discovers a truth about itself in and through the roles played out as mother, wife, mother-in-law, paramour, lover, father, husband, cook, maid, employer and so on. The individual in a challenging situation arrives at an insight or self-perception at the deep structural level by an intrinsic moment of enquiry, not by the route of any superimposed ideology, or facile compromising. But that moment of cognition unerringly undercuts a given existing system and calls for a serious rethinking on the part of the reader. This invariably is what transpires in a Chudamani story. The epistemological process of arriving at an experiential truth in each case, with an economy of effort, makes Chudamani a quintessential short story writer.

The situations depicted in the stories are neither extraordinary nor bizarre, but commonplace ones familiar in a South Indian/Tamil milieu. Sometimes they are located in a typical brahminical family setting, sometimes in a non-brahminical milieu, and occasionally in the interstitial spaces between the two milieus. Some stories foreground the material disparity in people's lives; no rosy utopia but an acceptance of want and alienation. In others the writer's eye turns fully psychewards to capture the fears arising from insecurity, the ensuing trauma and collapse of confidence. Sometimes the clichéd paradigm of extramarital relations is turned on its head, and all value judgments go awry; or a second marriage, for the man or the woman, is probed, making the reader reflect on what endures in a relationship, what love is.

Another aspect of Chudamani's creativity is her open and gender-neutral imagination. Not confined to male or female mental habits, it is, to use Virginia Woolf's term, androgynous.

Besides, she has the uncanny ability to enter adult, sub-adult and child consciousnesses, maternal, paternal, step-motherly, step-fatherly, patriarchal mental make-ups, their positive and their negative dimensions, the one not cancelling the other. For, in life a resolution of conflict more often takes place not through ideological abstractions but in real, experiential terms. Characters in Chudamani's stories frequently make such epistemological journeys to reach an understanding of a particular human truth. While there is no attempt to idealise any resolution so arrived at, there is always an unflinching clarity and honesty in the cognition. This may be regarded as the hallmark of Chudamani as a writer.

II

Some brief analyses of the stories and illustrations of the observations made above may be in order.

We have in the corpus of Chudamani's stories a spectrum of mothers very different from each other, yet sharing some essential aspect of motherhood. In them the reader encounters some surprising individuals and learns to reckon with their moment of self-affirmation. For instance, the poor cook in 'Karmayogi' who is neither bitter nor angry at being left to fend for herself in her gray years. She expects nothing from her sons, who remember her only when they need money from her hard-earned savings, which she readily parts with, her justification being that after all they are her sons. She stuns her employer with this essentialist affirmation of a mother. The yogic equanimity, nobility and selflessness behind the seemingly loquacious chatterbox of a woman is something the socio-economically secure and organised family struggles to comprehend. The central exchange between the mistress of the house and the cook conveys the core of the mother's perspective: in response to her mistress' righteous anger when the son shows up to ask for money, "Does he think you are a millionaire or a milch cow?" the cook quietly replies, "Neither. He has thought of me as Amma and come."

Chudamani has a penchant for depicting stepmothers and stepfathers, but they are neither stereotyped nor idealised. 'This is more important' is an instance of the remarkable dispassion with which a mother's motives are unravelled through the natural affection she shows towards her ailing son and the reserve with which she relates to her well-meaning stepson. The story also exemplifies the possibilities of transformation by means of introspection. The transformation takes place in an epiphanic moment after years of maintaining a formal and rather strained relationship. The son and the stepson play their part in the transformation; but the major shift occurs after a brief but honest self-analysis by the woman.

Mothers with a single male child are generally characterised by the trait of possessiveness, often wrecking the son's marital happiness. The insecurity of losing one's hold on the only son is proverbial in Indian society, literature and cinema. In contrast, in 'Adamancy, thy name is Amma!', Chudamani depicts a mother who insists on leaving her newly-married son and daughter-in-law to set up house on their own. Hurt and perplexed, her son fails to understand her motives, branding her as adamant. It is his mother's friend who tries to explain to him why his mother was joining a service home. For one, the mother wisely steps back from a situation where she may fall into egoistic possessiveness. The other ostensible reason is that she has nurtured her son into an adult, educated him, found him a helpmate, and now he must manage his own life. Over and above this realm of maternal duty, there is also her own inner self which must, at some point in her life, do what pleases her being. Chudamani implies that by interpellating a woman as mother and as mother alone, we fail to recognise the presence of other spaces within her psyche. Whether the son comprehends this occluded area in his mother or not, the writer makes us as readers acknowledge its existence. 'Adamancy, thy name is Amma!' is bold in theme, but at the same time only delicately suggestive of the Oedipal complex, perhaps on the mother's part rather than the son's. There is a masterly use of details, for instance, the young man's close physical resemblance to his late father, the propinquity of the rooms in the house. The quiet psychological insight comes from the mother's friend, though the son fails to comprehend its import: "At the age of forty-five a woman can become a grandma, Arun, but not an old woman..."

A similar perspective marks 'Herself'. Here we find the daughter so possessive, even mindlessly so, that she demands that her mother spend all her time with her when she comes home with her child for a month-long visit. She is shocked when her mother tells her that she has some work in the Women's Association and that she must go out, though she has kept everything ready for her daughter and the grandchild. The daughter cannot reconcile herself to the idea of her mother having a life of her own. She has circumscribed her mother in a stereotype, and is aghast that her father should allow his wife to be so independent. His doing the house chores and sharing responsibility in running the home deeply offend his daughter. He tries to explain to her that his wife is a free individual, and that he respects her individuality. Chudamani critiques entrenched attitudes in children towards their parents and suggests that it is not patriarchy and male domination alone that have stunted a woman's growth and realisation of her potential; the subliminal selfishness and sense of entitlement in the children can also deny the mother her spiritual right to be herself.

Maternal possessiveness takes a curious avatar in 'Fear and trembling', a story which almost verges on the gothic in depicting the terror felt by two childless widows who bring up their late sister's son, and their jittery responses to an unknown hostile force in the form of the boy's father who returns to claim his son. Their anxiety to hide the truth of his father's existence from the boy betrays their deep insecurity and jealousy, however much they try to give it a veneer of maternal tenderness. They are not mothers, but their subconscious claims the right of the mother. They try hard to justify to themselves why the man has no right over the boy after abandoning him as a baby, forgetting that he might be thrilled at the thought of meeting his absent father, and that his longing is but natural. At the same time, as Chudamani makes clear at the beginning, it was the boy's unexpected arrival in their midst that lent meaning and joy to their vacant lives; and so their horror at the prospect of his being wrenched away, which renders them psychopathetic, is also understandable. Chudamani's portrayal of the desperate possessiveness of the two aunts in vying with each other to groom the boy and look after his every need is brilliant in its Freudian depth and insight. The story has a slightly open ending. The father's motives in wanting to reclaim the child are not clear, but the focus is on the women.

Chudamani's treatment of patriarchy in two stories translated here is revelatory. The crude, even brutal side of patriarchal thinking is represented in unvarnished narration. The surprise sprung upon the reader, however, is that patriarchy is overcome not by confrontation but by female complicity. Not realising this secret is the undoing of the men representing patriarchal mindset and values. In 'Must prop up this crumbling edifice', we have an aged father in a lower middle-class family who blindly exercises his authority from his privileged position in the family to deny his daughters freedom of choice in any matter. As a result they are reduced to nonentities even after, and despite, securing an education and employment. When they flee and marry on their own, they are barred from the family for sullying the family honour. One by one, the parents lose their three daughters who leave home clandestinely, sinking them in a pall of gloom and inviting societal stigma. But what is the truth behind this serial escapade? That brings us to the mother's role as a 'victim' of patriarchy. Does she have any agency at all; or is she only an abject punching bag for her irascible, autocratic husband who meekly obeys his diktat, to the extent of losing her children to an inhuman paternal whim? It is here that Chudamani opens a new window on the wife and her silent agential role in facilitating the escape of her daughters, and yet remaining the unprotesting, voiceless, ever compliant *sahadharmini*. She 'defeats' her husband not by defying him but by lovingly submitting to his will. Her aim was to help her daughters find their future, and at the same time also to shield her husband from an imminent collapse of his ego. There lies the secret of her attitude to patriarchy and negotiating with it.

'Pride takes a blow' is even more powerful a representation of the typical South Indian Hindu family as an embodiment of patriarchy and its workings. It beautifully illustrates the operation of hegemony—which, as we may remember, is defined in Critical Theory as 'manufactured consent'—both at the interpersonal and societal levels. The husband, a respectable bank employee who is helpful to friends and clients, is immensely proud of his wife's complete and willing acceptance of his will in all matters. The apogee of his patriarchal power is reached early in the marriage when, following a misunderstanding with his wife's family, he commands her to choose between him and her natal family. She chooses her husband, breaking all ties with her parents and siblings. And for years, the absence of any resentment in her person allows him to believe that his will and pleasure alone matter to her.

One day, he learns of the tragic death of her dear younger brother, who valiantly fell to a bullet on the battlefront while saving his fellow soldiers. The young man—who was just a little boy when his sister was ordered to sever all her familial ties—had done his nation proud. This event somehow disturbs the husband's complacency and equanimity, and takes a curious turn when he wishes to let his wife know of the tragedy and mourn her beloved brother, and thus overwhelm her with his newfound generosity and compassion. Chudamani's artistry is brilliant in depicting this moment of the thawing of his self. But this time, he cannot manoeuvre her as he has done all these years. She withholds her innermost self from him, as also from us, so completely that he realises he can never truly conquer her, never break her pride. It is this knowledge that shatters his pride as the omniscient, omnipotent husband. He also realises how profoundly he has impoverished himself by rejecting her fullness and reducing her to an image that he has fashioned for her. The conversation between the newly compassionate husband and the placid wife—whose adroit repudiation of his moves is concealed by the most homely obedience—can bear close analysis using the Speech Act theory in terms of its *locutionary* content (the wife's silence), its *illocutionary* import (her refusal to respond to his embarrassed hints, inviting her to open up, mourn her loss and seek comfort), and its *perlocutionary* force (the denting of his male pride). Once again, Chudamani effortlessly demonstrates how a woman pulverises patriarchy by the dual strategy of surface surrender and inner self-affirmation.

The joint revolt by three women in 'No fury like a mother's' is not against patriarchy but against a harsh and mindless educational system represented, ironically, by a female teacher who, guided solely by a philosophy of disciplining and punishing (rather, disciplining by punishing), humiliates her erring girl pupils by stripping them naked in class. Incensed by the trauma that their daughters go through, the mothers of the three girls unite and tame the teacher by threatening to mete out to her the same punishment.

In middle-class Hindu society, stepmothers are more common than stepfathers, at least in convention-bound families. In 'Not a stepfather', Chudamani presents a nuanced view of a young stepfather while exploring the problems of a young widow with a child remarrying, and the stigma it brings upon the family in a conservative society. The story beautifully narrates the child's apprehensions in accepting a second father. Sensitive and wise handling by the stepfather results in his acceptance by the child, and by the rest of the family (the grandmother). The story is bold in foregrounding a young widow's right to happiness without losing her dignity and her family ties.

Chudamani thus uses a given narrative space to explore multiple relationships. Extramarital relationships are a common theme in serious as well as popular literature. Chudamani has some remarkable stories that explore this theme with sensitivity and often poignancy. A fine example is 'Forgive me if you can', which is narrated in the form of a man's interior monologue to his dead wife, crying out in contrition and pleading forgiveness for, and simultaneously also seeking legitimisation of, his transgressions. In English poetry, the 'dramatic monologue' was often used by Robert Browning to create fascinating and complex personages like Fra Lippo Lippi and Andrea del Sarto. In this story we see the relatives gathered to mourn and arrange for the rituals prior to cremation. Amidst all this activity, the husband feels lost and forlorn as if he does not belong there. Friends and relatives know of his infidelity, and treat him with scorn at the ceremony. Moreover, as the son alone has the right to perform the obsequies for his mother, the priest addresses only the son, leaving the widower resentful and further isolated. He feels alienated and alone in his own home. The pathos of it is that he does not get a moment's privacy to sit near his wife's body and grieve in solitude. He stands at a distance like a visitor and looks over people's shoulders at his wife. He could never bring himself to confess his infidelity to his wife; by the time he summoned the courage to tell her, she fell fatally ill and died. Now desperate for a shoulder to unburden himself, when the funeral procession moves towards the cremation ghat, he finds himself walking in the opposite direction in utter despair.

How does the writer, a woman, portray such a man? How do we react to his special pleading? Is the writer endorsing infidelity? If we regard the institution of marriage within a narrow conventional moral framework, we miss the finer human nuances. It is not abstract morality that Chudamani is concerned with; there is a whole psychic space here that is often not reckoned with. She creates a strange empathy in the reader's mind for the husband's predicament. It is not meant to condone his acts of omission and commission when his wife was alive, only to demonstrate how literature helps us understand human motivations and frailties, and the soul's need for companionship in sorrow. In the hands of a strident or a lesser writer, this story may well have become loud, crass and callous. With Chudamani, it becomes a poignant and soul-searching journey.

In Tamil, '*vadikaal*' denotes a channel or a medium which helps drain off the excess that needs to be filtered or given an outlet. Used as a metaphor, it implies a therapeutic function in performing such an act, thereby restoring normalcy or equilibrium in the person who makes use of such an outlet or vent. Chudamani adds the suffix '*-an*', brilliantly converting it into an agent noun '*Vadikaalan*', denoting someone who is used as a human drain or vent by others. 'Mr Outlet' unravels the subliminal libidinal space driving a physically challenged young man to vent his fury at so-called 'normal' society. Chudamani explores his thought processes, locating them against the insensitive, stereotypical views of all those who come to him only to unburden themselves of their joys and sorrows, in the guise of friendship. For some time, he does not seem to mind their intrusion into his private space, and is a willing listener. He is regarded as an intellectual or a *gnani*, a realised soul immune to the everyday material realities around him. It is therefore convenient for everyone to treat him as an outlet for what they cannot contain themselves, and almost habitually take him for granted. Chudamani highlights how we in our unconscious upholding of so-called 'normalcy' often do great violence to others and their humanity. When the protagonist falls in love with a girl, a love that he, however, cannot express simply because people do not attribute any emotional or erotic impulsions to him, the terrible irony that explodes on him is also his moment of implosion. This story is a testimony to Chudamani's profound insight into human psyche and her creative intelligence which borders on the art of Dostoevsky in a work like *Notes from the Underground*. In both this story and 'Forgive me if you can', Chudamani turns the spotlight on the social sphere and the conventional attitudes of those who occupy its middle spectrum. Knowingly or unknowingly they do violence to individuals who are different. It is that space of internal violence and hurt which she explores with admirable sensitivity.

In 'A chair and a death', Chudamani brings in several of her concerns in a spectrum of critiques. Presented here is a well-to-do family comprising benevolent-minded members of society, and the family of servants devoted to them. The intersection between the two enables the writer to explore how class divide operates, and what negotiating strategies are employed by both groups to keep transactions between them smooth and free of conflict. Though the maid and her husband enjoy the confidence, even affection, of their paymasters, they judiciously avoid crossing the invisible *Lakshman rekha* at all times. The smooth flow of life runs into trouble when the grandmother develops a fondness for the little servant boy and allows him to take liberties with the unwritten code of household conduct. The daily evening ritual of allowing the servants to watch television in the main hall with the masters—the servants sitting in a corner of the hall at a respectful distance—is violated when the little servant boy tries to climb on to the folding chair next to the grandmother's recliner. The grandmother initiates an alternative to the dominant ideology of the family by encouraging the boy to move near her—she enjoys his company as much as he does hers. But her egalitarian outlook is not shared by her family. Even so, ignoring their social prejudice and taboos, the old woman develops a happy intimacy with the little boy. However, this tentative and idyllic relationship founded on an inwardly recognised principle of equality, sharing and love is soon ruptured. Their radical and equal bond is rudely broken, and in the process both the child's innocence and the grandmother's idealism as well.

How does the writer put this delicate yet strong ideological critique of prevailing class consciousness in art form? The folding chair the servant boy is asked to sit on is the symbol of a possibility—of a happy, non-hierarchical bonding between two persons from opposite poles of society. When the boy is harshly tutored by his parents on his limits, he is too young to construe the lesson intellectually, but he does recognise that this chasm will not be bridged despite the grandmother's affectionate overtures. Both parties know the virtues of maintaining their respective limits. The grandmother's failure as a non-conformist to persuade her family to think afresh causes the symbolic death of the chair—she decides to keep it folded away in a corner once she realises that the boy will never again attempt to sit next to her. It is her way of protesting against the social inequity which she tries to challenge, but in vain. One is reminded of G. M. Hopkins's profound sonnet 'Spring and Fall: To a young girl', which mourns the death of the innocence of the young girl who sheds tears when the golden leaves of trees fall in autumn. Too young to know that seasons are cyclical in the natural world, she is lost in grief. For whom or what does she mourn? Aware that as she grows older her heart will turn colder to such sights, the poet poignantly ends by saying, "It is Margaret you mourn for",[4] meaning, it is the loss of her own childhood and innocence that she will eventually mourn. Similarly here in the story, it is the boy who mourns for himself unknowingly, and the grandmother who mourns for herself, but with knowing. When a social critique of the ideology of hegemony is offered in this way, one perceives, though dimly, the way out of such a social, class, material impasse.

III

Chudamani constantly recognises and celebrates the possibilities of the transformation of consciousness and perspective. Such transformations are brought about by people who see the world and people differently, and help others to see them as such. An old man is amused and annoyed by what he considers his wife's 'ignorant attachment' to family ties and obligations, but comes to see at the end that the bliss he finds in the *Bhagavad Gita* is the same as the joy she finds in having children and grandchildren to take care of, and he realises that 'Paths there are many'. The dying mother in 'Death, be not proud' who can see the principle of joy and beauty in everything and everyone even as she is succumbing to cancer, the woman in 'From narcissist to artist' who reinvigorates her frustrated artist-brother by pointing out that what he had been seeking was success and recognition and not fulfillment, and the eponymous grandmother in another story who infuses hope into the granddaughter who has lost a baby soon after birth (by simply admitting that she could give no comfort as she had never gone through such a loss) are all examples of such a meliorist outlook. The spokesperson for such an outlook in 'Litany' is God Himself who is also the narrator of the story. Right at the outset the speaker denies that He is omnipotent or omniscient, and the tragic and cruel turn of events striking a young widow would seem to confirm the denial. However, the end (in the form of an unexpected and kind intervention by a nephew-in-law) suggests that He has other names as well such as mercy, justice, humanitarianism. The Tamil title for the story significantly is '*Namavali*' ['Litany of the Lord's names'], with all its associations.

A common feature in many of the stories is the presence of a character, in some cases the narrator, who functions as a kind of registering consciousness through whose eyes we watch and evaluate events and characters, for instance the younger friend in 'Identity and amnesia' who gradually comes to sympathise with the older woman who writes her name everywhere in her house out of a sheer fear of loss of memory and therefore identity, or the South Indian brahmin daughter-in-law (in 'Insecurity') who is able to see the anxiety and apprehension of her American sister-in-law that she might lose her Indian husband to his roots.

The most admirable example of such a character is the mother of the sub-adult school boy who develops a 'crush' for his tuition teacher Champa in 'The young adult'. This story boldly touches on a taboo subject in Tamil middle-class milieu and handles it most endearingly by constituting the mother as an understanding and caring human being. Chudamani, in depicting the young boy's inchoate sexual stirrings, makes a brilliant foray into the genre of *bildungsroman*, which typically represents the experience of coming of age and aims to capture the growing consciousness and personality of a young person. In German '*bildung*' means education, and '*roman*' means novel. What Chudamani has done is to compress the quintessence of this Western genre into the form of a short story, focusing simultaneously on the mother's initial puzzlement, and her adolescent son's wonderment turned to bitterness. There is no moralising or preaching. What we get is a sensitive and lyrical dramatisation of the growing awareness, on the part of the mother, of her beloved son's trauma, its raptures and disappointments, all experienced in a state of innocence. There is nothing risqué here, nothing of '*virasam*' as we say in Indian languages. In 'The young adult',

Chudamani has achieved a variation of the bildungsroman from the one on the servant boy and the aged landlady that we examined previously.

A word about Chudamani's attention to settings and details within the small canvas provided by the genre, which puts her in the company of great short story writers. We have mentioned the son's resemblance to his late father in 'Adamancy, thy name is Amma!'. The contrast in 'Karmayogi' is between two women of the same age, one the mistress and the other the cook, the former lovingly cared for by her children, and the latter neglected but rising to nobility through her unconditional love. The theme of class stratification in 'A chair and a death' is introduced right at the beginning of the story when the elder mistress feels embarrassed at her own surprise at the names of the new maidservant and her husband, Sakuntala (not Muniamma or Karuppayi) and Dakshinamurthy (not Kuppan or Madasami). The artist's habitation and the weather are truly descriptive of his frustrated mental state in 'From narcissist to artist'. The sights that the American daughter-in-law captures in her camera (including her mother-in-law and sister-in-law wearing nine-yard saris on Varalakshmi Vratam day) provide an insight into the only way she can relate to her Indian connection through her marriage.

IV

One of the fascinating, often challenging, tasks in the act of translation is finding appropriate titles in English for the source texts. In the case of Chudamani, we followed different ways. In some cases the title of a story could be literally rendered into English, for example, 'A joint letter', 'Identity', 'This is important'. However, we did not always do that. Often the translator may go beyond word-for-word translation and strike at a title which would carry the inner import embedded in the deep structure of the theme and the narrative line taken by the author. Hence it was a creative journey for us to find cognate but not literal renderings. Some examples would suffice. The Tamil story titled '*Irandavadu appa*' (literally 'Second father') underscores that the stepfather is eager to assure the little boy that he is as affectionate as the late father. Chudamani, too, stresses this positive aspect. But sunk into the boy's psyche is the instinctive fear of a stepfather. We chose a title which combines the positive and the negative dimensions of the mother's second marriage. Hence 'Not a stepfather'.

In some cases our exposure to English and European literature prompted us to think of poetic, suggestive titles. The dying mother penning a letter to her son, leaving it halfway through, and the daughter completing it after her mother's death, is an interesting case. It is simply called '*Oru koottu-k-kaditham*' (literally 'A joint letter') in Tamil. We decided to use the first line of John Donne's famous sonnet 'Death, be not proud' in order to highlight the positive spirit of the old ailing mother who chooses to focus on the values of life rather than her imminent death. Similarly, instead of the Tamil title '*Kadavaiyarotattumpodu*' ('When someone knocks at the door'), we chose 'Fear and trembling', because it is a story which is at once gothic in its atmosphere and narrative technique, and psychological in its exploration of the elemental insecurity and fear of loss which haunt the two sisters. We must mention here a very special gesture that Chudamani herself extended to Indra when the latter submitted her translation of the story '*Senthiru Aahivittaal*'. Chudamani quietly gave it the compact and pithy title, 'Herself', to stress the spirit of independence that Senthiru the mother affirms to her demanding daughter. The one-word title conveys so much that the literal rendering of the Tamil title would not have. One of the arresting titles in the Tamil version is '*Vadikaalan*'. The expression '*vadikaal*' in Tamil, as we have noted earlier, normally denotes a channel or a medium which helps to drain off what needs to be filtered or given outlet. Chudamani has made it an agent noun by adding the suffix *-an*. Hence the English translation, too, places 'Mr' before the noun, and foregrounds the selfishness and crass insensitivity of people around the protagonist, who is physically challenged.

Chudamani's sleight-of-hand way of dealing with patriarchy in a couple of stories also prompted us to explore different ways of rendering the titles. For instance the Tamil title '*Kaavalaimeeri*' is ambiguous. 'Breaking free' suggested itself as a good option, for the three girls in the story do break free from the shackles of their autocratic father. But who helps them achieve it? It is their mother who accepts her position of total submission to her husband's will without demur. The aged husband with his ostensibly invincible authority symbolises an institution which is dilapidated, and it is the 'docile' wife who literally props it up. If you read deeper into the story, you tend to ask: Who really breaks free? And who is imprisoned by his own ego? The insights we got from these inquiries made us look for a double-edged rendering which would reflect at once the surface slavery and subliminal freedom of the mother. Hence the title 'Must prop up this crumbling edifice' was arrived at. We hope the altered title reflects these ideological resonances. This same paradox operates in the title of the other powerful critique of patriarchy, 'Pride takes a blow'.

The texts themselves presented several challenges in translation, given the way Chudamani's empathetic imagination works. We started this Introduction citing Virginia Woolf's remarks about the difficulty of "catching life" in art and commenting on the artistic finesse that she herself achieved in creating a reality which is at once delicate and strong. There is another observation made by Woolf which may be relevant while discussing Chudamani's language and style. Talking about the special linguistic needs of a woman writer, Woolf said:

> ... the very form of the sentence does not fit her. It is a sentence made by men; it is too loose, too heavy, too pompous for a woman's use.... a woman must make for herself, altering and adapting the current sentence until she writes one that takes the natural shape of her thought without crushing or distorting it.[5]

While Chudamani, never a flag-waving ideologue of any kind, wouldn't have proposed a specific writing style for all women writers, it is right to say that she evolved for herself a style which "takes the natural shape of her thought". Her thought, never argumentative or merely ratiocinative, always tended inward, capturing not only states of consciousness but also the subtle shifts and currents in them in moments of epiphany that make the characters see themselves, and others, in ways that are refreshingly life-asserting.

A fine example of such an unconventional vision is the way people are described in the stories, always relating the physical features to the inward psyche. We are not talking here about authorial points of view but the relative perspectives of the characters themselves. The sounds that the child makes are only lispings to the others, but to the sensitive ears and heart of the grandmother they are a song, a joy, "A lusty proclamation to the world: Here I am, look at me, look at me" ('Grandmother').

With regard to fictional descriptions of people, it has been observed, especially by feminist stylisticians, that male writers, while describing men, relate their physical features to their psychological and emotional make-up, but tend to adopt a fragmented method when describing women, reducing them to anatomical elements (for example, the famous apostrophe by Andrew Marvell with its inventory of the beauties of his coy mistress). On the contrary, women writers, it has been pointed out, always take a more complex view, relating physical details—be it of men or women—to deeper levels of consciousness and being and growth. The mother's observation of her teenage son in 'The young adult', of the changes in him after he starts going to his new teacher Champa, brings this out strikingly.

> Now there was a new glow in Vasu's eyes. He seemed to have suddenly acquired a new faculty, an eye and a mind for ever newer sights and sounds, thrilling and throbbing at its own intensity of feeling. It was as though he stood on the cusp of a mysterious stage when intuitive knowledge blossoms as if by magic and there was a new quickening of nerves, an excited opening of all portals of sense-perception, a strange exultation in the gait, clothing and demeanour. And a restlessness, too. Gomati suddenly noticed that he had grown taller than her. There had been a sudden growth in his physique like the spreading of a wild bush. He stood tall like a long line drawn, with an unfathomable fire inside springing and surging outward. Was he now a boy? Or a grown-up? It was a third state of being which contained both these within itself. Those two consciousnesses, child and adult, had installed themselves in that middle stage of a fourteen-year old, the age so full of the thrill of wonder. It was the intensity of the clash of boyishness and maturity which had caused that strange restlessness in him.

The Tamil passage is highly lyrical, but lyrical in the most organic fashion, marrying word and phrase with a process of observation, apprehension and even adoration.

> She was standing in the sacred presence of a grand transition, face-to-face with the seamless magical transformation of one being into another. Shouldn't she offer silent worship to it at least briefly?

Elsewhere in the story, too, especially towards the end, there are portions which are similarly nuanced and which depict the mother's sensitive awareness of the adolescent's present trauma—when he comes to know that Teacher is married—but also her perception that it is but a necessary transitional stage and a healthy sign of the boy's growth. We had earlier referred to the story as a variation on the bildungsroman in that it is the mother who perceives the boy's growth into adolescence and the certainty of his evolution into adulthood and sexuality. Such a perception being described in a work of Tamil short fiction written in 1966 was radical if not revolutionary, coming as it did in the context of middle-class reservations about themes of sexual evolution even among men.

But the mother's perception itself is a thought-out process, not a declamatory statement. The penultimate paragraph of the story begins with her initial shock when the boy angrily reveals that his dropping of the tumbler on the husband's toes was not accidental but deliberate. But this shock is immediately followed by a slow, almost step-by-step, understanding of the boy's mental state (*siridusirudai*: "little by little"). The paragraph in Tamil consists mostly of short sentences, with one long sentence almost at the centre which visualises the certainty of his future growth into full manhood and masculinity. The Tamil words here are all of organic growth—from *pirappu* to *valarchi*, from *salanam* to *polivu*, *idaipparuvam* and *vilimbunilai* to *muzhumai*. The evolution of thought as well as the language are telling examples of the Negative Capability of Chudamani's art. We have tried our best to capture the impact of the passage, replicating the Tamil syntactic structure in English, too. We had a slight difficulty with the word "*neettu*" (in the phrase "*siruvanaineettu, periyavanaiadaiyumparuvam*"), which can normally mean 'give up' or 'shed', but considering the transformation meant here, we decided on 'slough'. Another considered choice was 'with no stirrings of inquietude' for "*salanamatru*". Here is the paragraph in our rendering:

> Gomati stood speechless. Comprehension came little by little. This was the sorrow of a man taking a new birth out of his childhood. It was the pain of that sorrow that was making him cry. This was the intermediate stage when he had to slough off his self as a boy, and see himself anew as an adult. These stirrings, desires, upsurges that were beyond his own understanding—all these were only markers of this intermediate stage. His feelings towards Champa were but a sign of the awakening of his manhood. There was nothing else special to it. In a few years from now, when that awakening would be complete, and his growth into manhood would attain fullness, all these sorrows would vanish and he would emerge as an adult male, as the sovereign lord of his own natural empire. There was no stain attached to the stirrings that were troubling him at present. There was no flaw in the purity of his being. He was her son. And he was growing up. That was all. It was the surge and agony of the beginning of the transition that he was going through now. This was not a permanent state. It would pass. Then her grown-up son would emerge resplendent, with no stirrings of inquietude.

Another significant feature of Chudamani's narrative style has to do with the thought processes at work especially when a character, in a moment of shocking self-realisation, and an understanding of the other, recalls and evaluates the past. We have tried to render these passages as we believe the author herself did, with the use of Free Indirect Speech and Free Indirect Thought, as stylisticians have called them. An example is the succession of thoughts that pass through the authoritarian husband's mind at the end of the story 'Pride takes a blow'.

> Had he not been inordinately pleased in ordering her to renounce her people, and more so that she

> had conducted herself accordingly? Hadn't he felt proud and arrogant in the knowledge that she had no existence except that of being his wife? Hadn't he always regarded it as his victory that whatever she thought about and agonised over within herself, she never revealed it, by gesture or word, as far as he was concerned, but always hid it?
>
> His folly was now all too clear to him. It now hit him with shocking impact, weighed down as he was by the truth that she would not deign to open her heart to him even at this hour when stricken by such immense sorrow.

Chudamani's genius—the defining quality of her fictional imagination—consists in this constant attempt to enlarge the vision, the effort to see oneself and the world in a new, more empathetic light, to move towards unconditional love. The translators can only hope that this quality has not been lost or distorted in this English rendering.

References

1. Virginia Woolf, *Monday or Tuesday* (UK: Hogarth Press, 1921). Also in Virginia Woolf to Lytton Strachey, 'Modern Fiction', *The Common Reader*, First Series, available at https://ebooks.adelaide.edu.au/w/woolf/virginia/w91c/complete.html#chapter13 (accessed 29 April 2019).

2. Virginia Woolf to Lytton Strachey, 'Modern Fiction', *The Common Reader*, op. cit.

3. Virginia Woolf, *To the Lighthouse* (UK: Hogarth Press, 1927).

4. Hopkins, Gerard Manley. *Gerard Manley Hopkins*, ed. Catherine Phillips (New York: Oxford University Press, 1986).

5. Virginia Woolf, quoted in Sara Mills, *Feminist Stylistics, The Interface Series* (London: Routledge, 2004), 46.

1

Karmayogi

All said and done, fifty years are fifty years. One doesn't have the same physical strength as before. Why go on straining oneself? "*Amma*, we shall employ someone to cook. You take rest," the son had said quite sympathetically. The daughter-in-law, too, said, "Amma, isn't it enough that you toiled all these years, bearing children, bringing them up? Now you just sit back and relax." Chellam felt very proud. Not only this son and daughter-in-law, all her children bore so much affection and regard for her. They vied with each other in taking care of her. Could there be a greater joy in life?

"All right. Do arrange for some woman to do the cooking. Only a woman will stay at home and look after everything responsibly." Thus Chellam gave her consent to her son Gopalan one day. That is how Bhagirathi came into their household.

A thin, shrunken physique. Nine-yard sari patched up all over. No vermilion mark on the broad forehead, but there was calm writ on it. Peace in the eyes. A smiling countenance. The hair, strewn with dark and grey strands, looked like streaks of sacred ash from a distance.

Chellam took a liking for her. The woman could be her age or even a little younger. So she was sure to work hard with strength and energy at least for a few years.

"How much salary do you expect?"

"Whatever it pleases you to give."

"You shouldn't think of being absent frequently under the pretext of going home."

"Amma, I'll be content to remain here forever. I am a single person. There is no one that I have to go and look up."

"Are you good at cooking?"

"I can make dishes in all the forty varieties."

Chellam was taken aback. In the first place, she herself didn't know that there were forty varieties of cooking. So she quickly dropped the matter.

"I don't know about all that, but the cooking must be tasty to our palate. We don't like too much chilli. My son, daughter-in-law, and children—that's our family. And we also get lots of visitors. You must do everything with a sense of responsibility. The children may each demand a different dish at one and the same time. You shouldn't pull a face at such things."

"Not at all, Amma! Family means there will be a thousand things. Besides, I am very fond of children. I don't mind even if ten more children turn up, let them. I will happily cook for all of them."

It looked as though she wouldn't stop talking once she started! But in the way she talked and smiled, there was evident a pitiably tender wish: "I must please them; I must get this job somehow."

"All right, come with me. I'll give you directions," Chellam said and got up.

Although, right from the day she started work, they all thought that she was a bit slow-witted, everyone came to like Bhagirathi.

There were plenty of occasions for them to have a good laugh at her expense. Despite toiling nonstop for all of them—the elders as well as the children—right from five in the morning onwards, she somehow always had the time to keep on chattering. You only had to ask, "*Mami*, please get me some coffee," and along with hot coffee would arrive her instant chatter.

"Coffee, did you say? Of course I will get it! Who can say there is no coffee for you! No dearth of milk and sugar in the house, is there? Will they be depleted if I make one cup? I will bring it to you in a trice. Drink to your heart's content. And if you want more, please feel free to ask."

Should someone happen to compliment her, "Mami, today the *rasam* is very tasty," they would regret why they mentioned it at all!

"Is it tasty? I'm so happy you like it. Not only this, there are seven more kinds of rasam I can make. Please feel free to ask for whatever you wish to eat. Please don't hesitate. Don't think 'What will Mami say?' No, I never get angry. I shall make a whole lot of varieties and serve you. No trouble at all. What more important task do I have than to prepare and serve whatever it is that you desire!"

And they would each begin to worry how quickly they could finish eating and escape from that relentless flow of words!

"Have you eaten, Mami?"

"Of course I have! What is it that I lack here? Thanks to your gracious self, I have everything. Last year they sent me away from the place where I worked earlier. For a whole year I was jobless and struggled to survive. It is only after coming to your home, Amma, that I am able to eat my fill, and eat good food, too."

At the end of that nonstop chatter, always that expression of deeply-felt gratitude. Had she suffered so much?

"I'm happy that *Jaganmatha* has preserved me in this state. How can we blame others for the consequences of our own deeds? Why talk about it? Now tell me, what should I make for today's tiffin? Shall I soak *dhal* for making *vadai*? One of these days I'll make crunchy snacks which will keep for a few days, and the children can have them whenever they like. I can make all kinds of savouries, Amma. Whatever you want, please just tell me without hesitating." And she would go on and on.

Watching her running around and toiling and bustling everyday without showing any signs of feeling tired or irritable or bored, Chellam would be struck with wonder. Poor woman with no one to fall back upon, a destitute anxious to find refuge somewhere, she thought.

One day Bhagirathi came up to where Chellam was resting and sat down with a sigh, stretching her legs out on the floor.

"Mami, why don't you go and rest for some time?" Chellam suggested, absorbed in her *Ramayana*.

"I will. Resting is not a problem. Surely I can take rest whenever I like. You must do me a favour, will you, Amma? I've been thinking about it ever since I moved here. But somehow I couldn't bring myself to ask."

Chellam closed the book and looked up at her. The shrunken frame was slightly gasping for breath. In the depths of those eyes was a trace of fatigue which seemed to cloud over them.

"What is it that you want me to do?"

"You must write two postcards for me."

"Postcards? To whom?"

"To my sons."

"Do you have sons?" Chellam asked, quite surprised.

"Yes. I have. Two of them."

"Oh." For a moment Chellam could not speak. Then she said, "You had said you are single... So I thought..." and she trailed off.

A thin smile surfaced on Bhagirathi's dry lips. And for the first time Chellam saw a sadness, an unfathomable depth and a bitterness on that face.

"If there is nobody to support one, one is alone, isn't that so, Amma?"

"Where do they live?"

"The elder one is an accountant in Madurai. He has a wife and three children. The younger one is nearby, in the village of Vangur. He is quite well off, looking after the lands. He has two children."

Chellam's surprise grew as she listened to her.

"It is now eight months. Neither of them has cared to drop a line. It doesn't occur to them, does it, that the one who begot them may be anxious about them? No, I'm the one to be anxious. Amma, these are not things we have any control over, are they? We might detach ourselves, but the physical body gets agitated, doesn't it?"

Chellam was silent. Her throat felt a little sore.

"Can you write two postcards for me, Amma?"

"All right. Tell me, what should I write?"

Half closing her eyes, Bhagirathi was lost within herself as she began to dictate:

"*Chiranjivi* Pacha, Amma's *asirvadam* to you. I am well here. Do write a word about the welfare of yourself, daughter-in-law *Soubhagyavathi* Sita, and of the children, *Sou*. Jayam, *Chi*. Raghavan and of *Chi*. Muthu..."

"Why don't I just say: Write a word in reply about the welfare of all?"

"No, Amma. Only when you enquire about everyone individually by name do you feel as if you are seeing them in front of you, don't you?"

"I suggested it because I thought then we could move on to the next matter."

"What other matter? That is all. Please inform them that I am now working here."

"Hm. Next?"

"That is all, Amma. Please ask them to reply to this letter at least, and give your address on top."

"What do you mean, 'to this letter at least'?"

"I wrote five or six letters before this, getting someone or the other to write them for me. Neither son bothered to reply."

"Is that so? That is sad."

"Yes. Why would they reply." Bhagirathi looked at her calmly and added matter-of-factly without any trace of bitterness in her voice, "As I was struggling without a job at that time, I had written them a letter asking for ten rupees. That is why there was no reply."

The postcard slipped from Chellam's hand. How serenely she had spoken! What kind of detachment was this? Was it possible to accept this bitter, harsh truth with such equanimity? How was this any different from a *yogi*'s tranquillity?

"That's why I'm asking you to mention that I am earning now. Then they will reply without fear, won't they? All I want is to know that they are well."

Chellam did not stir for a while. Then, overcoming her feelings somehow, she picked up the card from the floor and leaned back.

"I'm sorry, Amma, I have troubled you. I can write in Tamil, but these days my eyesight has become dim. After all I'm getting old, am I not? Not one or two, this *Masi* I completed a full sixty years."

Chellam sat up straight in her chair with a start, suddenly feeling very guilty. Her fifty years, the physical fatigue, taking rest on account of it, cutting down on the work, the moral and emotional support of her sons and daughters—all these lanced through her heart like spears. Before her was this other woman with a body bearing the inner load of sixty years, a frame slightly gasping for breath, under compulsion to work for herself and feed her own stomach even though the children were reasonably well off. Chellam looked up at her once, and lowered her head.

Just as Bhagirathi had expected, replies arrived from the two sons.

"Bhagirathi Ammal? Is this the house?" the postman asked doubtfully.

"Yes, it's me," she ran up and received the letters. After requesting Chellam to read them out to her, she exclaimed happily, "*Appada*! Both of them are well. How nice to hear good news after a year! It's all the grace of the *Jaganmatha*."

Chellam was infuriated.

Every month, Bhagirathi would return the salary to Chellam, asking her to keep it safe.

"Don't you need money for your expenses?"

"What big expense do I have, Amma? By your grace, I eat to my fill twice a day. For other sundry expenses, it is enough if I take two or three rupees now and then."

Chellam's son Gopalan said, "I shall open an account in the bank in your name, Mami. At least some interest will accrue," and he arranged for it.

There was an influenza epidemic spreading all over town, and Chellam also contracted it. She felt somewhat embarrassed when she saw Bhagirathi closely observing her son Gopalan attending to her every need with affection and concern. But there was no envy in her eyes, only caring and approval.

Unable to contain herself any longer, Chellam said commiseratingly, "Mami, I feel sorry for you."

She expected that the naïve woman would ask, "Why?" But Bhagirathi did not do so. Smiling at her as one who understood everything, she replied, "Your womb is blessed, Amma. Let it remain so forever." The depth of the woman's heart was beyond comprehension.

After Chellam, it was Bhagirathi's turn to catch the fever. Bedridden, she patiently endured it, and was looked after with kindness by the whole family. At the same time, there was an ineffable enveloping sadness that they all felt.

"I feel sorry for her, Gopala! You write to her two sons about her condition. Let's see what they do," said Chellam. Gopalan did so. The mother and the son waited eagerly. Ten days passed, and there was no reply from either of the sons.

"What kind of children are these? She could just as well have brought forth a coconut sapling or a squirrel! Or she could have stayed barren!" Chellam fumed. Bhagirathi's wretched condition wrung her heart. Suppose this family had not cared for her, what would have been her lot? Should she become bedridden, was there no one to provide even a drop of water to this mother who had borne children? Chellam was overwhelmed by pity.

But Bhagirathi didn't seem to be thinking along these lines at all. As soon as the fever subsided, she was back on her feet and resumed her chores.

"Mami, why don't you rest for a few more days?"

"What need have I for more rest? Don't I look solid as a rock? Thanks to your gracious self and your noble deeds, I lack for nothing. I cram myself with food and top it up with coffee. If I speak otherwise, my eyes will turn blind. Please tell me, what can I make you for dinner? Don't think that this poor Mami had fallen ill, and so nothing will be cooked. I have no difficulty whatsoever. I will make curry, *keerai koottu*, chips, *pachadi*... everything. Don't feel embarrassed. Just tell me whatever you want."

The same naïve nonstop chatter. Was she a first rate fool, or a fully self-realised ascetic? One of the two, certainly.

In the end one had to regard her as a fool. It was natural to make mistakes if one was inexperienced. But it was sheer unforgivable folly if, even after burning one's fingers, one kept repeating the same mistake without realising one's stupidity. Such behaviour deserved rebuke, not pity.

One evening, when Chellam saw someone who had come searching for the house and was lingering at the entrance, the first impression that she got of him was certainly not a positive one.

"Who are you? Whom do you want to see?"

"Isn't Bhagirathi Ammal staying here?"

"Yes she is," Chellam replied, looking at him with suspicion. Impelled by the force of hatred and the incisive inner feeling breaking out, she asked him sharply, "Are you her son?"

"Yes, her second son. My name is Ganesan. I have gone all over the place looking for the house! How is Amma?"

"She was very unwell. You must have received the letter."

"Mm. Yes. Is she better now?"

"She is up and moving about somehow."

"I must see Amma. Can I?"

"You cannot see her now. She is busy at work inside. Tell me, what's the matter?"

"No, it would be nice if I could see Amma herself."

"If you come to someone's workplace at any time you like and say you want to see her, how is that possible?" Chellam sternly rebuked him.

"In that case I shall come tomorrow. Please tell me, at what hour will she be free?"

Chellam glared at him and went inside. Soon, Bhagirathi rushed out excitedly, her eyes and face surging with radiance.

"*Vaada*, Ganesa! Come! How long since I saw you! Are you well? You look a little run down. I hope there is nothing wrong with your health. When did you come? Been so long since I've seen you all, my eyes have become blurred, *da*! Are you doing well?"

Bhagirathi's eyes turned moist as she caressed her son's face and shoulders with her calloused hands, the veins bulging.

"What's wrong with me, Amma? I am fine. Thank God that you have a job now. That's a good thing."

Chellam, who was watching from the window, was furious. So he was happy that she got a job. That meant only one thing.

Her surmise wasn't wrong. Ganesan kept visiting his mother for three or four days. A day after that, Bhagirathi came and stood before Chellam.

"What's the matter, Mami? Isn't it a wonder of wonders that your son has at last come to look you up?"

"True. He has come seeking help."

"I thought as much. For money, isn't it?"

"Yes. It seems there is some problem in matters concerning the land. He urgently needs three hundred rupees, it seems."

"Does he think you are a millionaire, or a milch cow!"

"Neither. He has thought of me as Amma and come."

Chellam was stunned by that calm response which came accompanied by a smile.

"Now, isn't there roughly about a hundred and fifty rupees of my money in the bank? I told him that. Why don't you spare at least that much, he suggested. Poor boy! Such a crisis! Amma, will you please speak to your son and get me that amount?"

What incorrigible folly!

"Mami, don't be angry with me for saying this, but let that money be there for you to use in times of crisis."

"What use is that money if it is not going to be of help to my son? If it is a crisis for him, is it not a crisis for me, too?"

"Will he be grateful to you for it? Will he come to your rescue should you ever be in a dire situation?"

"No. He will not."

"When you know that so well, when you have seen for yourself how your sons have treated you, why has this ignorant attachment still not left you?"

"How are they responsible for it, Amma?"

Chellam could not take it anymore, and started speaking vehemently. "Mami, is it not the duty of the children to look after the parents in their old age? Is it not expected of human nature to show at least this much gratitude? How much we toil for them! We beget them, unmindful of our physical pain. We turn our blood into milk and suckle them. We strive indefatigably, physically and mentally for their welfare alone, valuing them dearer than our life. If the mother doesn't attend to the child, what will be its lot? Don't we bring them up with such total dedication? How much we do for their sake!"

"How can we not do it?" broke in the calm voice.

Chellam looked up and stared at Bhagirathi—there was nothing save absolute clarity of thought on her face.

"You tell me, Amma, can we remain indifferent without doing all this? What is there to feel so proud about in what we feel and what we do for our children out of attachment? Is it something that we consciously cultivate and express as love? The moment the child is born, the attachment and love are born in our mind and body along with it. It is not something willed and done consciously. It is nature's law. It is a force which our body feels on its own. Even if we resist it, we cannot refrain from doing things for our children, can we?"

Chellam was tongue-tied.

"As long as we live, we give to our children. There is joy in it for us. After all, don't we give because it brings us joy? It is up to them to feel grateful or not. Does that attachment arise with the hope that children will do things for us in return? We have no choice but to be led by that attachment." Bhagirathi's voice grew tender, "And there is no greater blessing than this either, Amma."

Chellam could not believe that this was a human being speaking before her. It sounded like the astral voice of a deity. Was this woman a fool? No. One was a fool only if one misjudged and was deceived. What do we call this state which holds only love, selfless, unconditional love as its ultimate goal and acts as a *karmayogi* without a thought for the fruit?

She asked softly, "Mami, tell me, as mothers we protect our children. When they desert us utterly, leaving us without any support, who is there to protect us?"

"Isn't there the Jaganmatha who begot all of us?"

Chellam did not say another word thereafter.

Ganesan came and left after taking the hundred and fifty rupees. Chellam felt choked looking at Bhagirathi who was, as usual, engaged in her endless everyday toil.

She would work as long as there was strength in her body. And when, bereft of all strength, unable to work, with no one to support her, slowly losing her eyesight but not her affection, she had to wander in the streets...

Would the Jaganmatha take care of her?

Originally published in Tamil as '*Yogam*',
in the magazine *Kalaimagal*, August 1963.

2

From narcissist to artist

There was no sign of the rain abating. The pitch-dark sky split asunder by the criss-cross of lightning roared with a thunderous voice. Though the door and windows were shut, the light and sound of the storm kept leaping into the room through the iron bars of the ventilators. Manikkam sat huddled in an old reclining chair. The decrepitude of age had begun to show in his frame, even the arms pressed tight to the chest for warmth. For all that, he was not even forty-five yet. The ageing in excess of the years had been caused by a combination of toil, frustration, and constant emotional agitation. The ragged clothes, the hole-ridden woollen shawl wrapped round as a piteous shield against the chill reflected this—the only thing alive in that gloomy room were the streaks of light still emanating from his rusty eyes.

As he reclined motionless and as the eyelids began to droop at last with the first signs of sleep, there was a knock at the door. Who could it be, at this time of night? He looked at the time-piece on the table. It was eleven. Could it be someone from downstairs? The landlord lived there with his family, but none of them ever troubled Manikkam. They were a cultured family who left him undisturbed, acknowledging that an artist was by nature an introvert with creative urges that sought solitude for their fulfillment.

The knock was heard again. He rose and went to the door, determined to make it clear to the unwelcome visitor that he didn't quite like his coming at this unearthly hour.

It was, however, not a 'he' but a 'she' on the other side of the door. He couldn't at once make out who it was. She stood there like a statue mounted on the pedestal of darkness in the verandah. The bits of her frame revealed faintly by the light from the room gave him no help in recognising the shape as a familiar person.

"Who are you, *amma*? Whom do you want to see? If it is the Mudaliyar family, they live downstairs. I am a tenant here upstairs..."

"It is the tenant upstairs that I came to see." Her voice, like a sweet, even musical note, interrupted him with no diminution in its gentleness. She looked at him with deep and calm eyes. The voice grew softer still. "Don't you know me?"

He stood still. The next moment, some trait of that voice, the way she stood with a mixture of friendliness and reserve, kindled his memory like a flash.

"Valli!...Valli, is it *you*?"

"Yes, of course. You can't recognise your own younger sister, Manikkam!"

"It's been quite a long time, that's why. I think you will agree. Come in!"

He stood aside. She entered the room, walking with a slight limp. He closed the door, showed her to a chair and resumed his seat.

For a while, they sat surveying each other silently, he mildly agitated, she quite composed. She observed the clothes that betrayed his indigent state, the prematurely aged body and the dilapidated surroundings. He saw and stored in his eyes her serene shape, her humble yet tidy clothes, the pale and delicate face beneath the dark crown of hair streaked with grey.

"How have you been, Valli...all these years?" There was an embarrassed hesitancy in the query.

"Quite well, Manikkam. How do I look?" She smiled. He observed that she, who once used to address him as '*Anna*' in those now-forgotten younger years, was now calling him by name.

"How did you know that I was here?"

"By sheer chance. Just heard it from someone. All right, I thought, I will do the nice and proper thing as a younger sister and look you up once."

"After so many years! Mmm."

"I just wished to know how you were doing." She looked round at the room. "And from what I can see, it doesn't seem like a very prosperous place."

"How will it when it is not."

"How much space do you have in this portion upstairs?"

"Verandah, this room, another small room next to this, kitchen, bathroom."

"That small room is your studio?"

"Yes."

"You are alone?"

"Yes."

"Marriage? Family?"

"None at all."

"Oho!" She broke into a laugh seeing the expression on his face. "Don't be alarmed, Manikkam. I haven't come to stay with you, only to look you up. I will go away."

"In this rain?" Now that he was relieved that she hadn't come with any intent to stay, a generous spirit surged from within. "Why don't you stay for the night and leave in the morning when the rain stops?"

"No, thanks. Haven't I taken care of myself all these years? I am not going to be scared of rain and storm now at the age of forty, am I?"

Was there a sharp undertone of bitterness in her words? A shade of anger stirred within him.

"Isn't it something that you yourself chose, Valli? You ran away leaving a note that you were leaving the house and that we were not to look for you. And you were just eighteen then. So young and so stubborn and wayward! There is no point blaming me now."

"I am not blaming anyone, Manikkam."

"Moreover, I did search for you, but I couldn't find you."

"It was my intention that you shouldn't find me."

"But why did you act so, Valli?" He sat up with a sudden interest. "For a long time I was keen to know why you left home. Did you want to commit suicide?" As he lowered his eyes towards her feet, she withdrew them under the folds of her sari.

"No," her voice came through serenely. "I didn't think I was unfit to live just because of a slight limp in the leg."

"That is the right attitude."

As he nodded wisely like a sage who had achieved consummate mastery of knowledge of good and evil, she couldn't keep quiet. "Thank you so much for your esteemed approval," she said with mild sarcasm.

Anger rose within him and surfaced with cruelty. "Perhaps, you ran away with some lover who didn't mind your lameness?"

"Not that either!" she laughed.

"Then why did you run away? Just to have the satisfaction of making me search for you?"

"No."

The silence grew denser little by little and appeared even more threatening with the storm howling outside with all of Nature's fury.

"I ran away only because I didn't want to be a burden on you."

He looked up. They stared at each other without speaking. For a few moments he felt quite inert.

"You...what?" he finally managed to say, uncomprehending.

She fixed her eyes on the window which shielded the room against the torrents of rain. Through a gap in that wooden frame, the sky was entering and exiting the room whenever there were streaks of lightning.

"Weren't we always a poor family, Manikkam? When father died at the work place, it was quite difficult for mother to manage the family, even with her widow's pension. So you had to take up a job. You were working as a clerk on mother's insistence. But you hated it. Because, all your thoughts, your interests lay elsewhere in your dreams. Your heart lay in those dreams you had about painting, with its colours, brushes and canvasses, and the pride and joy of creation that it brought."

"Yes! Quite true! Quite true!"

Manikkam's voice rose and quivered with intense yearning. He stood up and, pacing up and down agitatedly, he said choking with emotion, "Yes, I did dream. Art was all my love."

"Yes, I knew," her voice came through with a gentle quickening, her eyes still fixed on the window. Some of the flying insects that had gathered round the dim bulb had also lodged themselves on the window pane.

"And then mother was afflicted with influenza, and on the threshold of death. We both were sunk in grief. But in your heart, along with grief, there also lay hidden a secret feeling of relief..."

"Don't talk nonsense, Valli!"

"...If she breathed her last, there would be no one to compel you to do the job that you never wished to do. The relief rose from your desire to dedicate yourself totally to the art of painting."

He was silent, unable to contradict her.

"However, mother, on her death bed, extracted a promise that you would take care of me, your lame younger sister."

He bowed his head. She went on.

"You made the promise all right. But you also understood that it meant the same old imprisonment for you again. You hated me then. Because you were responsible for my welfare. In order to ensure a safe life for me, you were forced to take up a job which would give you a steady monthly income. You fretted over your position, that you were compelled to work as a clerk again to earn money, when your soul yearned to follow your heart's desire to steep yourself joyously in the art of painting. I understood your agony. It was to provide you an opportunity to paint, with no care for anything else, and to find fulfillment in your life that I decided to leave home, and I did so."

He stood looking at her intensely, overwhelmed by gratitude and tenderness towards the sister who had made such a big sacrifice for him. He came closer and gently took her hand.

"Thank you, Valli! Thank you so much!"

It was only when he looked at her in close proximity that he could see the wrinkles on her face and notice that her body was shivering in the cold. He removed the woollen shawl he had covered himself with and tenderly wrapped it round her shoulders. She pulled the shawl close to her with hands that had turned livid with the cold, and smiled at him.

"No one can have such a wonderful younger sister like you, Valli! Again and again, thank you!"

"Don't thank me, Manikkam. I did what I did not for you but for my own sake. I didn't want to be considered a burden and a barrier. My act of leaving you—the truth is that, rather than a younger sister's sacrifice, it was just a reflection of my own sense of self-esteem."

He rose quickly and stood apart. He didn't speak for a while. Then the words surged up and exploded in agony.

"But, Valli, do you know how it all ended? I painted and painted for years. My studio was full of my paintings—but I lacked real talent. No knowledgeable art critics saw merit in my creations. I have failed. I have failed utterly." He looked at her and spoke with bitter derision directed against himself.

"Poor Valli! I have achieved nothing. The sacrifice you made to release me ended only in failure. Now, when you have come to know this, don't you feel sorry that you left home and security?"

"No." She looked at him calmly. "We should evaluate deeds by the motives that impel them, not by the consequences. I did what I did because I felt a compelling need to do so. For my own mental peace, and to provide you an opportunity. I have no regrets."

"But the opportunity I got only ended in failure, Valli! I have wasted my whole life! All I have acquired are this prematurely old dilapidated body, this bald head, wretched poverty, and the agony of defeat and failure..."

"Is that all? Have you got nothing else?"

"Nothing. Nothing else."

"What an ungrateful wretch you are! You pursued your heart's desire! Dwelling in the clouds for countless blissful hours, filling canvases with colours. Did all that mean *nothing* to you?"

"But all that is wasted..."

"Why? Because you have not been accepted as a great artist? Because you haven't succeeded in the eyes of the world? It is certain beyond doubt that you are utterly ungrateful. How many people in the world get the chance to engage in the pursuit they cherish most? To get such an opportunity is itself a rare privilege. But I am a crazy fool to come and say this to you! The fact is that you never had any real love for the art of painting. If you had just wanted to paint, we could have called it love. But what you wanted was to succeed. You sought an outcome which had nothing to do with the joy of artistic creation. Where was love in it? It is no wonder that you are unhappy. How can there be joy where there is no love? If, as I had thought, you had truly loved art, all these years that you spent engaging in painting and all those pictures that are kept in that room wouldn't seem a waste to you today."

He stood petrified and stared at her unblinking in wonder. His heart throbbed and pulsed with astonishment at the realisation. The heartbeat ticking away like a clock seemed to play the note of an eternal truth. What intensity there was in those eyes that were fixed on him! And what love in that intensity! He looked at her and smiled gently, his face suddenly lit up by a new radiance.

"What a profound truth you have revealed, Valli!" His voice was low and gentle. He looked at her, flooded by wonder and adoration. Valli! A generous demeanour. Locks of hair pleasingly turning white. An unfathomable sadness in those deep eyes. Even the wrinkles were like soft lines painted on a pale and stately countenance. As she sat there, her very aspect and all her features seemed to convey so many untold mysteries of the pathos and expanse of life. He didn't dare ask her what she had been doing all these years for a living.

"Valli!" he addressed her gently with a lucidity of mind he had never felt before.

"Yes, Manikkam?"

"Will you permit me to paint a picture of you? I do not seek any success in this endeavour. It will take shape as a monument of love, as a symbol of our lives. That is all I want."

"As you wish."

"I am very happy, Valli!" He looked at her with moist eyes and said, "Do you know what I shall name that picture of yours?"

"What?"

"The mystery called life!"

Originally published in Tamil as '*Vaazhvenum marmam*' [The mystery called life], in the magazine *Kadir*, November 1965; the title was later changed to '*Oviyanum oviyamum*' [The painter and the painting] when the story was included in the collection *Tanimaittalir* (Nagercoil: Kalachuvadu Publications, 2013).

3

The young adult

Gomati was relieved that she had at last found a solution for the problem she was having with her son Vasu. Vasu had just turned fourteen, but he had already got his parents deeply worried over the matter of his studies. For quite some time now they had lost all hope that he would work with purpose and be a good learner. The boy was, of course, not lacking in intelligence. But what was the use if he didn't apply his mind to his studies? He was somehow managing to scrape through the annual examinations and getting promoted. He was as inattentive at home as he was at school. To make him study well seemed a feat beyond their capabilities, no matter what means they tried—entreaties, threats or inducements. He seemed to have a special aversion for the subject of Social Studies. Gomati at last decided that the only way to make him take to studies properly was to arrange for 'private tuition'.

She did so. And what a good idea it turned out to be! These days Vasu had begun to pay close attention to that subject.

His teacher's name was Champa. She was perhaps twenty-eight or twenty-nine. She lived in the next street. She had a Bachelor's degree in Arts. Though she was quite well-to-do, she had willingly taken up teaching as a hobby. When Gomati had approached her with a request, she had gladly agreed.

Now seeing the rapid progress Vasu was making, Gomati wondered if Champa was a born teacher.

One evening Vasu returned home from the teacher's house after the class. These days his talk was all about Social Studies, that is, all about the Social Studies teacher.

"*Amma*, you know what Teacher says? History and Geography are very interesting subjects! I now think she is quite right."

"Amma, Teacher says King Chandragupta Maurya couldn't have achieved anything if there had been no Chanakya. See, how interesting!"

"Amma, Teacher says I should keep all my books neat and tidy. She is quite right. I am going to cover all my books with wrappers right away."

Gomati would stand wonderstruck. How many times she had told him to keep his books in a good state! But he had never listened. And now! Champa surely must have some magic skills up her sleeve.

Now there was a new glow in Vasu's eyes. He seemed to have suddenly acquired a new faculty, an eye and a mind for ever newer sights and sounds, thrilling and throbbing at its own intensity of feeling. It was as though he stood on the cusp of a mysterious stage when intuitive knowledge blossoms as if by magic and there was a new quickening of nerves, an excited opening of all portals of sense-perception, a strange exultation in the gait, clothing and demeanour. And a restlessness, too. Gomati suddenly noticed that he had grown taller than her. There had been a sudden growth in his physique like the spreading of a wild bush. He stood tall like a long line drawn, with an unfathomable fire inside him springing and surging outward. Was he now a boy? Or a grown-up? It was a third state of being which contained both these within itself. Those two consciousnesses, child and adult, had installed themselves in that middle stage of a fourteen-year old, the age so full of the thrill of wonder. It was the intensity of the clash of boyishness and maturity which had caused that strange restlessness in him.

One evening Vasu said to his mother, "Amma, Teacher was wearing a very beautiful sari today. Do you know that you don't have such fine clothes at all?"

Gomati looked keenly at her son. The chubby plumpness of childhood had vanished from that young face. There could be seen in the jaw a masculine impulsion to break free. A thin dark line ran over the upper lip. Gomati also realised that the dots which had sprouted on his cheeks were not caused by prickly heat. Her eyes still fixed on him, she felt she was standing in the sacred presence of a grand transition, face-to-face with the seamless magical transformation of one being into another. Shouldn't she offer silent worship to it at least briefly? It was only after a few moments that she said softly, "Is that so?"

"Yes, Amma! It was a very, very beautiful sari."

Gomati had seen Champa that evening when she was standing at the entrance to her house. So she knew which sari it was.

"I, too, have a sari exactly like that, Vasu! Don't you remember? It was only yesterday that I was wearing it!"

"Were you? I didn't notice it. Anyway, it looked so beautiful on Teacher."

It suddenly struck Gomati that the shorts he was wearing no longer suited him. For an instant the memory of the time when she had taken him in her arms and fondled him stirred an inward longing, and a wonder if something had slipped through her hands.

Vasu didn't miss a single tuition class. Each time before leaving for the teacher's house, he spent half an hour in front of the large mirror. He had to adjust his clothes, groom his black-ruby hued hair into a rising wavy shape. He had to elegantly flip the shirt collars up with fingers now tinged with masculine pride.

He was all attention while the class was going on. He listened with care to what the teacher said and registered it in his mind even as he was looking at her countenance with silent adoration. The "Good evening, Teacher" spoken as he entered her house sounded both joyous and reverential like some kind of prayer. Her very proximity was pure joy. Sitting and looking at her—the very embodiment of grace—with unblinking eyes, listening to her voice, figuring out the explanations she provided, studying the lessons to her satisfaction and making progress through her instruction with the eagerness to draw praise from her—each of these things was a rare and wonderful pleasure.

Sometimes Champa would appear rather pensive. On those occasions Vasu would gently enquire in the manner of a privileged devotee putting a question all by himself to the deity, "Aren't you well, Teacher?"

"No, nothing like that, Vasu," she would say and smile again. And that would be like a spray of radiance on him.

"What is that cut on your finger, Vasu?" Champa asked one day and, with the sympathy and consideration that an elder sister would show, held the finger and inspected the cut. A study table always stood between them and they didn't sit close to each other. Now Champa's touch, which had arisen as a gesture of sympathy, sent a sharp thrill down Vasu's spine. In an instant he was sweating and shivering all over. He couldn't speak for a while. Thoughts and feelings sprang and spiralled within him. But there was no clarity in them. It was all an eddy of imprecision, a pleasure which was three-fourths pain.

"What is this cut, Vasu?"

"Nothing, Teacher..." The words came haltingly. "Well ... this afternoon, when I was sharpening my pencil, the razor blade just cut my finger."

"Tsu, tsu! The cut is quite deep. See, it is bleeding. Did you show it to your mother?"

"No. She didn't notice it either. She is not like you." He paused. Then the words dropped like petals, "She is not smart like you, Teacher."

"All right, all right, don't try to flatter and sidetrack me. That won't do. This needs immediate attention. Wait for a while." Champa went in and brought some medicine and pieces of cotton and cloth. As she cleaned the cut, applied the ointment and bandaged the finger, Vasu was sitting on the edge of the chair, his eyes lowered, his muscles tensed and his blood vessels quickened as he was transported to a world of bliss. He of course had lots of female relatives—his mother, sisters, aunts paternal and maternal, cousins—but *she*, she appeared the very image and wonder of femininity. He felt that miracle within him, but without comprehending what it was, a confused rapture which was beyond thought and knowing. The feeling made him her vassal and gave him fulfilment. She was deity, and he devotee. He asked for nothing else.

"Ah! Done! How does it feel now, Vasu? Does it hurt?"

"No, Teacher!" The rapture of adoration glowed in his eyes.

Vasu kept the bandage on his finger for a week even after the wound had healed fully, as if cherishing some sacred relic. It was doubtful whether he would have taken it off even then if his mother hadn't scolded him and his father hadn't mocked him for being a wimp.

That evening he went to the teacher's house as usual. The class on Social Studies was going on. As she was talking, suddenly Champa started hiccupping.

"Vasu!"

He looked up. His eyes shone with ardour even before he could articulate his query, "Yes, Teacher?"

"Can you please go to the kitchen and get me some water to drink? This hiccup—ahuk!—is terrible."

"Right away, Teacher!" He ran inside. These days he was a familiar figure in the house. He went to the kitchen, got water in a stainless steel tumbler from Champa's mother and returned quickly to their study room. Suddenly his legs halted. There was a stranger standing near Champa's chair. They were laughing together. Did that man's hand rest on Champa's shoulder for a minute?

"You brought the water, Vasu? What a relief! Thanks very much! Give it to me. You know who this is? My husband. You wouldn't have seen him. Our wedding took place six months ago—before you started coming here for the tuition. There is no proper housing facility where he works. That is why I am staying here with my parents. He has come on leave for a week."

None of the details that she gave in the midst of her hiccups registered in Vasu's mind. There was only one fact that sank in: Teacher was married! His dear teacher had a husband!

The pain, agony and sense of emptiness that tore from the roots of the heart struck at the core of his being with an elemental force which was beyond the realms of reasoning. He could comprehend nothing. All he could sense was that a stupendous sorrow, beyond all bounds of speech and explanation, was gripping him.

"Hand me the tumbler, Vasu! Why do you keep staring so?"

He stepped forward slowly and stretched out the hand holding the stainless steel tumbler. Maybe his sweating and trembling hand didn't move in the right direction; instead of reaching her the tumbler hit against the arm of the chair, slipped out of his grasp and fell with a heavy thud on the man's foot. He cried out in pain, "*Ammadi*!"

"Vasu, what is this!" There was a touch of sternness in Champa's voice. "Couldn't you be more careful? ... Ey, Vasu, why are you running away? Come back! It's not the end of the world! It's okay if the tumbler slipped out of your hands. Come along, Vasu, come back! Shouldn't we continue with the class?"

Vasu did not look back. He ran all the way home, threw himself face downwards on his bed and started sobbing inconsolably. The grief, unidentifiable and inexplicable, pierced through the tiniest corners of his being and shook him violently. It was a grief unaccompanied by any other emotion, a grief without any knowable origin.

His mother, who had got to know about the matter, rushed to him. "What is this, *kanna*? Champa says it is nothing. She says you are not to feel bad about it. Should you feel so heartbroken that the tumbler fell on her husband's foot? It just slipped out of your hands. Don't cry."

Vasu continued sobbing into the pillow. His voice came through the sobs, "I am not feeling bad about that fellow. Serves him right. He is Teacher's husband! I dropped the tumbler on his foot on purpose."

Gomati stood speechless. Comprehension came little by little. This was the sorrow of a man taking a new birth out of his childhood. It was the pain of that sorrow that was making him cry. This was the intermediate stage when he had to slough off his self as a boy, and see himself anew as an adult. These stirrings, desires, upsurges that were beyond his own understanding—all these were only markers of this intermediate stage. His feelings towards Champa were but a sign of the awakening of his manhood. There was nothing else special to it. In a few years from now, when that awakening would be complete, and his growth into manhood attain fullness, all these sorrows would vanish and he would emerge as an adult male, as the sovereign lord of his own natural empire. There was no stain attached to the stirrings that were troubling him at present. There was no flaw in the purity of his being. He was her son. And he was growing up. That was all. It was the surge and agony of the beginning of the transition that he was going through now. This was not a permanent state. It would pass. Then her grown-up son would emerge resplendent, with no stirrings of inquietude.

Gomati looked with pity and affection at the figure that was lying face downwards on the bed. She sat down near the bed and stroked his head comfortingly.

Originally published in Tamil as '*Irandinidaiyil*' [Between the two], in the magazine *Karpanai*, April 1965.

4

This is more important

The pain gone, the face was now in deep slumber in the comfort of fatigue. Gazing upon that sleeping face with tearful eyes, Vedam quickly turned away, mildly troubled by the thought that even a mother might cast an evil eye upon her child. After how much apprehension and how many prayers his life had been restored!

She felt goose pimples all over her body. She looked down at her hands. Needle pricks marked the spot where her blood had been drawn to be transfused into his veins when he was oscillating between life and death—the seal of her love. Luckily her blood group was 'O' positive, which could be donated to anyone, and so she had given it to her son in this crisis, thereby becoming a mother who was blessed to give him life a second time.

Gopu woke up.

"When did you come, Ma?"

"As usual at five. How are you, *raja*?" She drew the chair closer and stroked his hair. "How do you feel today?"

"Much better, *Amma*."

"Raja, after you come home, we must go to Tirupati once. I had taken a vow that, if you survived, both of us would walk it to the hills."

"Done!"

"It is all the grace of that deity."

"No, no, it is what *this* god has bestowed!" he smiled, pointing at her. "How can even Lord *Yama* come anywhere near me when you, who are like a goddess, agonise for my sake?" he laughed.

There was no need to find meanings behind those words. These were just the expressions of a heart deeply moved.

"Here, I've got some oranges. Shall I peel one for you?"

Her heart swelled as she peeled an orange and dropped the pulp segments into his mouth one by one. Every small act performed for her son gave her joy a newfound meaning.

"You, too, have some, Ma!"

"I don't need it. You are the one not doing well."

"Won't you have just one, Amma? Please...aren't you my golden Amma?" the eighteen-year old lisped like a baby. How could she deny him?

"Sankar also brought me three oranges. I ate half of one, and the remaining I gave away to the nurses and the sweeper boy."

"Was Sankar here?"

"Yes, in the afternoon."

"No office for him today?"

"It seems he had a touch of fever in the morning and had taken leave. By the afternoon he was feeling better, I believe, and so he thought he might come and see me."

"Not bad. At least he remembered you."

"Why? Sankar has always been fond of me, hasn't he, Amma?"

"Who said he hasn't."

"He is quite affectionate to you as well, isn't he?"

"Are you suggesting that I haven't treated him well? Do you know how harshly every other woman treats the children of the first wife? I for one have always treated him with some fear."

"Why should anyone be afraid of Sankar when he is such a good person?"

All said and done, it was a blood relationship. Would it not assert itself? It was true that Vedam did not hate her stepson. However, it was a bit irritating to hear her son, in his present state of health, singing the other's praise just at this tender moment when he was sitting close to her and basking in her maternal love.

"All right, *da*, don't strain yourself too much by talking. You will tire yourself out. Did you like the fruit, raja?"

Gopu did not reply.

"Why? You didn't like it?

"I did, Ma! But didn't you ask me not to speak?"

"Tut, tut, you wicked fellow!" She stroked his forehead tenderly.

"I'm tired of eating oranges. I feel like eating apples. Will you get me some tomorrow when you come?"

"Of course! Why didn't you tell me earlier, *kanna*? I would have got them today itself."

"That's all right. Sankar said..."

"Don't you have anything else to talk about, raja?"

"Fine. I won't say it."

"All right, all right! Say what you wanted to. Why should you have that grouse?"

"Sankar said, '*De* Gopu, you are going to have a *manni* soon!' Is that true, Amma?"

Sankar's maternal uncle was looking for alliances for him. Last week when Vedam had spoken to Sankar, he had said that his uncle had picked a couple of alliances and was pursuing them.

"Yes, I heard there were a couple of suitable alliances. After seeing the girls, they will discuss other matters and decide on one of them."

"I will get fully well before his wedding, won't I, Amma?"

"Of course you will, *kannu*," she said softly.

The nurse attending on Gopu brought him his bread and milk at 5.30 in the evening; the delay was because Gopu had gone to sleep earlier. Then the doctor came and examined him. His regular words of assurance, "You don't have to worry at all, Amma," brought cool comfort to Vedam's heart. Even the slight touch of fatigue she had been feeling for the last few days vanished. After the doctor left, she sat up again.

The twilight of dusk was fading and it was slowly getting dark.

The nurse came again, fed the patient, and left after attending to his needs. After having her dinner from the 'tiffin box' she had brought with her, Vedam spread out her *jamukkalam* on the floor to sleep on. She was allowed to stay with Gopu in the nights because she had admitted him in the 'special ward', even though it had meant taking a loan. When Gopu's condition was serious she had spent day and night at the hospital. That routine had changed only in these last ten days when he had started showing improvement. Every day she would come in the evening and stay for the night. At dawn Vedam would gaze at her son and fill her heart with that sight—that was her *surya darsanam*. Only after that she would start for home.

The next morning, after reaching home, attending to all the household chores, as she reclined wearily on the ancient cushioned chair, her eyes roved across the photographs hung on the wall opposite. In all the four, there figured the one who was no more. His enlarged solo picture occupied the central place. Even now she couldn't look at it without her eyes turning moist. In another picture it was he and she together; in the third, the two of them, with Gopu in-between. In the fourth, the proud father stood at the centre with the one-year-old Gopu held in his right arm, and his left arm around the eight-year-old Sankar.

Sankar!

Her mind wandered confusedly for a while. She had learnt from Gopu that Sankar was feeling feverish yesterday. Shouldn't she go and enquire how he was? But the thought that had appeared tentatively vanished even before it could take shape. Didn't Gopu also say that Sankar was better now? Then why worry?

Vedam's relationship with Sankar had never been spontaneous. For his part, he had been quite attached to her, calling her "*Chitti! Chitti!*", but in her heart, the sense of aloofness and distance she had felt towards him had never gone away. Of course she was never remiss in taking care of him. She had never spoken a harsh word to him nor made an angry gesture for the world to censure her as a cruel stepmother. Even so, there was always this inexplicable unease in the very thought of his relationship with her.

When her husband had died, the twelve-year-old Sankar's maternal uncle had taken him away to his house. After that, Sankar would often come and chat with her whenever he visited them. He was very fond of his younger brother. Vedam, too, conducted herself without violating the grammar of external civility. Even so, there was always a strain and unease in that relationship, not the natural sense of ease and comfort which one feels with one's own kin. Sometimes she would chide herself over this. Was it not wrong on her part not to have treated that boy with affection? The heart melted at the very thought of Gopu; but that was not so in the case of Sankar, was it? Should she not feel the same affection towards him as well?

As she was about to get up from the chair, she suddenly felt as if her head was reeling. She quickly leaned back and closed her eyes.

It had been like this for the past four or five days, this whirling of the head. An extreme fatigue as if the whole body had grown light as gossamer. Was it because she had donated blood? Or was it the consequence of keeping awake for long hours over this past one month, drowned in anxiety, thinking of the son's condition? Whatever it was, she realised fatigue seizing her. Affection might strengthen the heart, but the body was after all a physical burden, wasn't it?

She opened her eyes cautiously. The dizziness had subsided, but not gone. She panicked at the very thought that she might fall ill and not be able to visit Gopu in the evening. Just to prove to herself that she was indeed strong enough, she slowly got up and walked up to the veranda near the front door. Thank God, there was no dizziness now!

She went back inside and was about to sit down, when she heard footsteps behind her and turned. It was Sankar.

"Come in," she welcomed him without any feeling of affection inwardly.

He came in and, sitting down on a chair, enquired, "How are you, Chitti?"

"Me? I am perfectly well."

"You have grown thinner since I saw you last time."

She didn't say anything.

"Yesterday I dropped in to visit Gopu. He was talking quite cheerfully. His condition has improved a lot, hasn't it? The face looked quite bright."

Vedam stiffened inside. She decided that the first thing she would do when going to hospital that evening was to take camphor and light it and circle it round the child to ward off the evil eye.

"Chitti, you must do something for me."

"What is it that I can do for you?"

"This evening..." Sankar spoke a little hesitantly, laughing sheepishly, "I understand we have to go this evening to 'see' the girl. *Mama* has made all the arrangements. Please, you also come with all of us, Chitti."

"Why me?"

"What do you mean? To see the girl, of course! Shouldn't I know whether you like the girl or not?"

"How does it matter whether I like her or not? You are the one who's going to marry. Moreover, what is it that I am going to say by way of advice which your Mama and *Mami* can't give?"

"Is it enough that Mama and Mami see her, Chitti? After all, aren't you also like my mother?"

Vedam couldn't respond to this at once. However, she didn't feel like agreeing, though somewhere in the corner of her mind, a sense of guilt rankled. The fact was that she could not evince interest in this matter to that extent.

"People like me should not step into the forefront in auspicious matters like this."

"I don't believe in such things. I will be happy if you come."

"When do you have to be there?"

"Six o'clock in the evening. I will myself come down and take you. Will you come, Chitti?" he asked with great enthusiasm.

Six o'clock. In which case there was no point in leaving for the hospital before that. It might take at least an hour to return from that place. That would mean that the time she could stay with Gopu would be reduced by two hours. Even that was okay. But, given the state of her health today, suppose she got weaker because of the strain and caught fever and couldn't stir out of the house till she was well, could she remain without seeing Gopu for a couple of days or even more?

As if to frighten her further, the sudden dizziness again swamped her. Feeling rattled and agitated, she closed her eyes and leaned back in the chair.

"No, *appa*, I won't come. I am not feeling well at all today. Just feel like lying down and resting and doing nothing else."

"What's wrong, Chitti? Why didn't you tell me in the first instance? Shall I take you to the doctor?" Sankar asked with concern.

"*Chhe, chhe*, no need for all that. Nothing serious. Ever since Gopu had that accident, we were all put through a lot of strain and worry, weren't we? All that didn't agree with me. That is all. I should be all right with a little rest."

He looked at her face intently for a few minutes and said, "All right, Chitti, then you needn't come. Take rest," and got up.

"Hope you do not misunderstand me, appa?"

"Chhe, chhe, no, not at all, Chitti!"

"If I had felt well, I would have surely come. Please forgive me."

"You are my elder, Chitti. How can you say 'Forgive me' and all that...to me! Then, shall I take leave?"

"All right. Do come and tell me everything in detail after seeing the girl. I pray that everything should work out as you desire."

"Thanks. I'll see you later."

"Will you have coffee?"

"Chitti, why strain yourself now? Just take rest," he said smiling and left.

Vedam felt somehow uneasy within. Why did this fellow have to come and disturb her peace of mind? But then, why should her peace of mind be disturbed in the first place? After all, didn't she say what was proper?

The photograph on the wall in front of her pierced the eyes: in the middle, the father, flanked by Sankar and Gopu. Both his sons. She turned away.

Fatigue pressed down on her body, but it brought her a kind of consolation. Her health was really not all right. And there was nothing wrong in telling Sankar that. She could go to the hospital in the evening only if she rested through the day. She spread the loose end of her sari on the floor and lay down. With the midday heat pressing down on the eyelids, she soon fell fast asleep.

When she woke up with a start, it was quarter to five. It was not just the feeling that it was time to leave, there was also something else that had roused her and made her sit up—some thought interwoven with the undying lamp of affection that impelled this mother through layers of consciousness even in her sleep. Oh, how could she have slept so carelessly! By what lapse of memory had she mistakenly thought that she could rest till evening and only had to go straight to the hospital on getting up? Wasn't there something else to be done? Hadn't the child said yesterday that he wanted apples today? The market was quite some distance away, and she hadn't taken into account the time it would take her to get there!

She didn't have the patience to comb and do her hair. She picked up the cloth bag, put on her sandals and stepped out, forgetting to lock the street door in her hurry.

The heat of the summer day had not abated even at that hour. But surprisingly she hardly felt the heat or any fatigue either when travelling in the packed bus, or jostling in the crowded market, moving from shop to shop, bending down to pick up good pieces, one here, another there.

"*Appada*! Good stuff, although costly. Gopu will love it."

What a strain it had been, running around all this distance today! But she had felt nothing, not even the thought of fatigue, when setting out to buy fruit for Gopu—her son. But when Sankar came and invited her...

She froze, as if the very thought had been chilled! Why was she suddenly enveloped by this delusion that she was standing before a faceless judge with a thousand fingers pointing at her?

Didn't she refuse to accompany Sankar because of the apprehension that her health may weaken, unable to withstand the physical strain? But when she remembered she had to buy fruits for her son, no other thought crossed her mind, not even the faintest idea that it might be tiring for her. It was true that in the morning she had felt dizzy and weak. However, because she was unwilling to strain herself for the sake of Sankar, she might have exaggerated those feelings, even to her own consciousness, without knowing it.

She didn't *want* to act for the sake of Sankar—and that was the truth.

Fatigue had intervened, making it impossible for her to be with Sankar even on an important occasion. The physical body was not all right. But when it came to her own son and his cravings, however trivial, how was it that at once strength of body and ardour of spirit arrived from nowhere?

One might of course feel an excess of affection towards one's own blood-begotten son. That was but natural. In nature there could be nothing wrong. But as for her relation with the other boy, why did she forget that he, too, had the same measure of right over her as Gopu?

She did not have to chide herself for not feeling any affection towards Sankar. After all, love was not an obligation laid on one. But then, when one discriminated, upholding one law for the son and another law for the other's son, wasn't the sense of justice being destroyed? Love could not spread to all places. It was a small entity. But justice was something which could take a cosmic form as a single principle common to the whole world and spread everywhere, wasn't it? It was not just a fine feeling like maternal love common to all creation. It was not begotten of blood. Sense of justice was an expansion of self that went beyond all limitations of the body. It was the essence of all the supreme ideals arising from a cultured mind. It was the nectar that emerged from the milky ocean of humanity.

In a fraction of a moment, it became clear to Vedam what raised man higher and distinguished him from other creatures.

In the middle, the father. On the sides, two figures. Both were his sons.

She shrank in an intense feeling of shame.

Quickly the eyes turned towards the tower clock. Five-forty p.m. Didn't Sankar say they had to leave by six o'clock? If she left now, could she reach in time? Yes, she could, if she managed to catch a bus at once, and if they hadn't already left a little earlier.

When he saw her, Sankar's eyes widened in surprise and joy.

"Chitti!"

"Since I rested all through the afternoon, I feel better now, Sankar. That's why I have come."

"Very happy, Chitti! Shall we leave? We are all ready. What do you have there in the bag?"

"How can we go empty-handed when we go to see the girl? I bought some apples."

She looked at the apples she had in her hands.

Wouldn't Gopu be waiting for them? It didn't matter. This was more important.

Originally published in Tamil as '*Iduperidu*'
[This is important], in the magazine
Ananda Vikatan, 29 December 1968.

5

Forgive me if you can

Look there—that is a corpse.

When that thing was a 'she', that 'she' was my wife. I mean to say, until dawn today.

Even when her life was ebbing away at the hospital, I did not quite comprehend that this was the end. I had always thought that those who were about to die would be in an unconscious state, or looking around with eyes wide open or fixedly staring above, or talking inarticulately and generally appearing in all kinds of bizarre positions as we often read in books. It was only when the doctor told me that I learnt that Mythili had, after remaining lucid and smiling until the end, just closed her eyes and slipped into death. Just as you mix pigments in a painting, her life and death had fused together.

How quickly the news had spread even while I was standing there, dazed! All the bustle, the arrangements, the methodical one-by-one steps in preparation. By the time I could compose myself, Mythili had been brought home and kept in the front hall in ritual fashion. What a crowd there was around her! Relations, friends, acquaintances and strangers. My brother-in-law said that our son Nanu, who worked in Madurai, had been informed by telegram. I was still in a state of shock. Keeping myself to a corner, as if I were a stranger who could not go near the crowd, I kept craning my neck and peering at Mythili again and again from a distance. Someone was weeping. Now, at this evening hour, the wails had increased, as had the crowds.

With the telegram reaching him, Nanu had taken a bus and arrived, and all at once he had become the most important person. It was to him that the priest conducting the obsequies was speaking and explaining all the procedures. It was he who, after the ceremonial bath, was busy performing the rites near his mother's corpse, uttering the *mantras* with teary-red eyes, wearing a wet dhoti and a fresh sacred thread.

And me? What about me? Am I the one who has to be kept out of this crowd? They just passed a lamp from Mythili's hand to mine and indicated, without telling me so, that this was all I had to do. Having nothing to do, I was standing idly by myself, keeping aloof. Was there to be no connection between Mythili and me hereafter? I who took on the status of her husband from her fifteenth year, I who lived a life together with her for thirty years—was I now suddenly to be relegated to the background the moment she died? And was he the only one who mattered now? All the rituals were meant only for him.

In between, a medley of voices fell on my ears.

"Mythili was in fact recovering. No one ever thought that things would suddenly turn this way."

"Astrologically, the time must have come for Nanu to perform the obsequies. Who can stall that?"

"That's true. After all, isn't he the *kartha*?"

"Here, Nanu, place this over your mother's body..."

Nanu...Nanu...Nanu! Does a woman become her son's possession the moment she dies, after having been her husband's all her life? Is this the subtle punishment that a wife finally hands out to her husband as a revenge for all the resistance, resentment and rage that accumulates in the course of her conjugal life and lies submerged within her consciousness without her even being aware of it?

The crowd had gathered around Mythili. I had to admit that I could not approach her. Even if I did manage to go near her, would it have been possible for me to show her my emotions in front of so many?

The weeping of a few intensified the moment they saw me. Some came up to me and conveyed their condolences and sobbed. "Poor man! You are the one left to suffer. People say, to lose one's wife after growing old is a misery which singes without a fire," some said pityingly. Others said with empathy, "What more could that fortunate woman have asked for? She is truly the blessed one, having died with the auspicious turmeric and *kumkumam* intact. There is nothing she lacks. It is only your condition..."

But I knew that most of them were actually saying to themselves, "Why pity this man? He would hardly be in grief that she is no more. After all, isn't he the one who gallivants with another woman?" I also knew that just the looks some of them gave me did convey this.

Many would surely have thought, merely looking at my face, that I was undoubtedly a hard-hearted man. Because I did not break down or put on a disconsolate face. Resolving not to reveal what the heart felt, I deliberately wore a harsh, hard look. How could I, effacing my individual private self, just stand amidst this herd and look at Mythili, making an exhibition of tender feelings and a broken heart? Wouldn't it be the greatest injustice to our married life?

"Look Nanu, now as you keep uttering this mantra..."

Nanu...Nanu...Nanu!

Was that an ant creeping over Mythili's face? Someone flicked it away. Thank God!

I kept peering at her from the far edge of that crowd.

How absurd! Why should the entire town make a bee-line and crowd here the moment my wife, who was 'she' until this morning, died and became 'it'?

My wife.

Why does it not strike anyone that I may want to be alone with her for some time? Not even my son!

My son, did you say? But isn't he my prime adversary today? Isn't he strutting about as the hero of the day, pushing me behind at every step as he moves closer to her, his eyes proclaiming that he alone is the one who has obtained the right to utter the mantras for her and to lead her soul on the path to liberation?

No, I shouldn't say "My son." Today, he is my adversary, the rival who has snatched my wife away from me.

I was moving about directionless like a child who had lost his way, like a stray dog not owned by anyone.

Loath to join the others as one among the many in the chorus of lamentation, when I moved towards the front of the house in search of a secluded corner, I could sense, from everyone's countenance, their murmurs, "See! He doesn't even come near her but has moved away to the entrance! Hard-hearted man!" But whenever I went close to Mythili and stood near her, none of them was sensitive enough to leave us alone even for a moment. They bathed her, draped her in new clothing, garlanded her, adorned her forehead with vermilion—all this they did standing in a crowd, a pack of evil-doers!

"There she goes in regal splendour, like Goddess Mahalakshmi, turmeric and vermilion adorning her!"

You wretches! Since I am the cause of the turmeric and vermilion adorning her, if only for that reason, can't you leave me alone with her for a while? Can't you allow us some privacy considering that if she had lost those auspicious marks, I would have been the cause of that, too?

Oh, how I longed to hold that corpse tight and sob and wail my heart out!

As long as Mythili was alive, I never had the courage to tell her about Aruna. Sometimes, quite accidentally, encountering a certain look in Mythili's eyes, I would think, "She knows!"

When all kinds of people in the town had come to know of it, how could it not have reached her ears? To think that she knew even without my telling her would give me some peace of mind—that I was relieved of that responsibility. The relief would be doubled, so would the joy, to think that despite knowing, she continued to live with me, and that therefore it also meant that she had forgiven me. But, on other occasions, when in her eyes and on her face I could only discern the familiar old expression, I would think, "No. She doesn't know yet." In such moments I would agonise and yearn to confess my weakness and seek her forgiveness. But I would not be able to summon the courage. I kept putting it off for days. Later, when she developed the liver problem and was admitted to hospital, the thought, "At least now I must confess" and the counter-thought, "I shouldn't add mental agony to the physical" would clash in my mind. Before this struggle could be resolved, the stage arrived when, after the surgery, her condition deteriorated, and she died.

From that moment this morning until now, I was filled with one sole yearning: to cling to that corpse and cry my heart out saying, "Mythili, please forgive me!"

Is there anyone who doesn't deserve this privilege? Is there anyone in the world who doesn't need to ask for forgiveness? I believe that when someone dies, people very close to that person must each be left alone to be with them for some time, and that this was a basic humanitarian gesture on the part of others.

Bearing the agonising weight of that unfulfilled longing and the grief of her loss, I just stood there looking at her from afar like an utter stranger.

The wails grew louder. The moment for carrying her body out had arrived. I noticed many pairs of eyes casting searching glances at me, eyes which asked: was I crying? Was I breaking down?

I went near Mythili. That face was closed like an eternal mystery. I should have confessed much earlier. But how could I? How can a man say to his wife, "I am betraying you"?

I reached out a hand and gently touched the lock of hair near her forehead. Dark hair which had started graying. My fingers felt leaden. The whirl of emotions within the heart did not gush out on the face and the frame. In front of so many people, I could only remain like that.

Why don't all of you go away from here? The one who lived as my companion for thirty years is about to be reduced to a handful of ashes. Before that I must tell her all that I have to say. I must pour my heart out to her. Won't you give me that opportunity? Why don't all of you get lost? In fact, what business do you all have here? Why do you come between husband and wife?

My heart was screaming. But I stood silent, my eyes anchored to her face; not one teardrop fell. Within, the heart was breaking into pieces. Withdrawing my hand from her hair, I stepped aside. They all looked at me with anger and contempt, as though I had failed in some examination.

The bier was brought inside. The keening reached a crescendo. All manner of loud laments and wails were heard.

"Stop...Stop! Don't take my wife away just yet! I must speak to her alone. Our chapter is not over yet!"—my heart cried out. But the hand, which had raised itself involuntarily following the heart's cry, was withdrawn. Lying on the bed of palm fronds borne on the shoulders of four men, Mythili had already set out. Nanu walked in front, holding the pot with the live coal pieces, his briefs visible through the wet dhoti, leading her on the path connecting this world and the next. The crowd followed suit. I came out to the porch and stood forlorn and bereft like an orphan as I saw her leave. The crowd, certain that I, too, would follow, turned to look at me once and moved on.

Suddenly, I started walking in the opposite direction. Why should I go with them? No one gave me a chance to spend a few moments with her to grieve, to mitigate my sorrow. And now there was no hope of such a chance. The son who had the right over the body had taken her away. He would put the final stamp of his rights by setting her alight. Even the little intimacy I had with Mythili all this while was now gone. What had I got to do with them hereafter?

"Look at that man—instead of coming with us to the cremation ground, he is going somewhere else! Outrageous! Doesn't that wretch have a heart?" When I heard these words spoken by my brother-in-law, I rapidly walked further away from the crowd so that their voices wouldn't reach my ears. I was treading a path different from theirs.

A palpable darkness enveloped my heart and weighed it down. Mythili, Mythili, Mythili!

Do you really mean to say she is no longer alive? Was she gone with daybreak today? Will Nanu light her pyre in a short while?

What gumption he has! Does this fellow in his arrogance think that he will write 'The End' to her life story? *De* Nanu, what do you know about her? I am the one who has known her in all her joys and states. I am the one who has witnessed the fullness of her being! Her story will never end as long as she lives within me. Ignorant of the true nature of this epic, you have ventured to write 'The End' to it. What an idiot you are, Nanu!

Even so, my Mythili has become his possession ultimately, hasn't she?

"Has the telegram been sent to the son?"

"In any case, we can't move the body until he arrives."

"He will probably take a bus. Hope it doesn't rain."

But don't *I* mean anything to you, Mythili? This world which laid down that your living body belongs to me has denied me the right to be alone with your lifeless body even for a few minutes, hasn't it? How terrible that I could not ask your forgiveness.

Please forgive me, Mythili, please forgive me.

Yes, I have another woman. Yes, I am indeed such a person. But I have always loved you, Mythili. You have always been dear to me. I swear on our only child, I love you, Mythili. But I yielded to temptation. Please forgive me for it. Just because I have behaved like this, it doesn't mean I am an entirely wicked man. I am a little wicked and a little good. No one in the world can say anything beyond this about themselves. If you can understand me, that is enough for me. You will forgive me, I know. All I need is this forgiveness. Had I been able to embrace your corpse and cry out, 'Forgive me!' my mind would have been at peace.

Where am I heading? Where are my legs taking me seemingly of their own volition?

Was that crowd right in judging me a hard-hearted man?

Even before the wife's body is consigned to flames, here I am hurrying towards the other woman's place?

But in my heart there is no feeling of guilt or wrong-doing. My grief is pure, and so is my memory of Mythili which is the nucleus of my grief and which I carry within me. Therefore, where I take it now is also pure.

It is a crowded locality which does not boast of wide roads, clean surroundings or any such markers of a city. Houses jostle each other without porch or compound wall. The entrance door opens right onto the street, and standing there you could see the entire length of the house through to the end.

A small boy was trying to pump water from the bore well at the end of the street. A little distance from there was the wall of a house which looked as if it had been painted ages ago. Through the grill at the top of the front door you could see a towel hanging as a roll on the corner of a clothesline in the rear portion. I pushed the door open, entered the house and went into the room next to the hall. A forty-watt bulb without a dome burned with a dull light.

The anguish I was carrying within would now have become visible on my face. For there was now no need for me to wear a mask to conceal it from anyone. I could be just myself.

What would Aruna think to see me thus—my hair and clothes in total disarray, my mien utterly pathetic in the pale, humid evening of six o'clock, not having sipped even a drop of water since dawn, my peace lost in the endless mental agony?

"What's the matter? What has happened to you?" Her query didn't quite betray the shock she must have felt, I thought. As she stood there staring at me, I leaned on the wall behind, struggling to catch my breath, overcome by mental and physical fatigue. "Are you all right? What has happened? You don't look normal..." She rushed towards me, visibly agitated.

I went and stood near the window. On the other side of the street, on the roof of the house opposite, a white cat was sprawled out luxuriously, suckling its two white kittens.

"Today, in the early hours ... she died."

Behind me, I could hear Aruna drawing her breath in, shocked.

"Wh...What!"

"She is gone."

"Who? Your...?" Aruna was always deferential and discreet about using the word 'wife' or 'Mythili', for, to her sensitive and refined sensibility, it would be an insult.

"Yes, of course, my Mythili. She is no more, my Mythili."

Before Aruna, I could be my natural self and I could openly say "My Mythili," melting in agony. In the presence of this beloved, I could feel free to talk about my wife lovingly, movingly. I could speak intimately to her of my innermost feelings. That was the measure of Aruna's nobility and generosity. When she and I were together, we were not just lovers, not just man and woman; we were two friends, and more than that, two human beings. As for age, she was just thirty-two. However, for that unsullied humaneness which dwelt naturally in her, there was no age. There was no trace in her of any gross calculation.

"So suddenly? Didn't you say sometime back that her health was somewhat better?"

"That was sometime back. Of late, it was all downhill. Finally, today..."

"I am sorry," she gently empathised.

"As soon as she passed away, everyone gathered around her. I couldn't say anything at all to her at the end ... I couldn't. I couldn't even keep her head on my lap one last time to soothe my heart, Aruna! They did not leave her alone with me even for a moment and quickly carried her away to the cremation ground."

"And ... instead of going there, you ... here?"

"True."

I turned to face her. How much empathy there was in that countenance, how much compassion! She understood why I was here. She understood that my anguished heart had, without betraying the trust of affection, come seeking refuge in the place where affection dwelt, and her kind smile revealed this.

I had locked myself in hard and tight before the crowd which had looked at me in a spirit of hostility, scrutiny and condemnation. All that hardness now melted and flowed away in the presence of this empathy. All the anger and anguish that had filled and choked my heart now burst forth in a deluge of tears and drowned me. Unable to bear it any longer I slumped down over a table, holding my head in my hands, and started sobbing. All the pent up emotion that had kept me yearning and fuming silently inside since morning now poured out as a flood as if I had gone mad, forgetting that the scene had now changed.

"Mythili! My Mythili, please forgive me! Forgive me, Mythili, Mythili, Mythili, my Mythili ... Please forgive me!"

At that moment, Aruna came up to me. Did she comprehend my need? Was she the only one who could understand? She who had refrained from even mentioning Mythili's name openly because it was not proper, she who had always maintained a respectful distance now herself became Mythili for the sake of my solace and comfort. I felt her arms enfolding me with compassion. Her voice sounded softly in my ear, "I have forgiven you, please don't cry. I have forgiven you."

Originally published in Tamil as '*Mannippukkaha*'
[For forgiving], under the pseudonym 'Kanakamani',
in the magazine *Kalaimagal*, February 1972.

6

Pride takes a blow

Vimalai was standing near the window, looking at the sky, engulfed in thought. During the day, given its mechanical functioning, the mind has no space to raise its head. But come night, the memories break free as so many stars that seem to fall off the moon like petals.

Memories.

Memories which had been surging within for seventeen years as joy, sorrow, attachment, yearning.

Appa! Amma! Velu!

Velu. Vel Murugan. Her little brother...

As she kept looking up at the sky, she was overwhelmed by emotion.

"Vimala!"

She turned. Kathiresan was looking at her.

"What are you thinking about?"

"Oh, nothing."

That "nothing" was an acknowledgement of his triumph. What else was it if not his triumph that she should in all matters go along with his words and his state of mind, without revealing any of her own thoughts or feelings or ever crossing him, as though she had absolutely no individuality of her own?

"Well, I was just curious because you were standing very still and watching the sky. That is why," he said deliberately, just to confirm his sense of triumph.

"Today the sky is very clear. So many stars are visible. I was just watching that."

The blatant lie added polish to his sense of victory. Self-satisfaction flowed within him with a gentle warmth.

It's been seventeen years since Vimalai's ties with her people were broken. Vimalai's father had said something disparaging about the autocratic ways of Kathiresan's widowed mother once. That was the cause of the enmity. Raging against her whole family, Kathiresan had thundered at Vimalai, saying, "If you feel you want me, you will leave with me right now, and cut off all ties with these people once and for all. Never again in this *janmam* will you even look at their faces or say that they are your father, mother, and little brother. If you agree to this, come with me. Or else you may forget me, and stay with them all your life." Vimalai had come out with him, following that voice of command. Did she do so fearing the social stigma of a woman living apart from her husband? Whatever her reasons, the victory was his.

Now Vimalai is forty-one years old, a mother of grown-up children, holding herself with dignity in society as a teacher in a high school. To date, she has never opened her mouth and said that she must visit her people. Can we therefore say that she could live without remembering her natal home or her parents, or for that matter her brother who was just a boy of six when she left? Can we say that she never pined or grieved for them in her heart of hearts? Well, if she did, she did not express it. There was never any mention of them in this house. If you ask why, the answer is: because that is what *he* would like. His will is what sells here. Because he nurtured enmity against her family and cut off all contact with them, his is the last word as far as she is concerned, too. His word is law; and her silence, in not voicing her thoughts, her emotions, is an endorsement of that.

Kathiresan came and sat at the dining table with obvious pride. Vimalai, too, came and sat with him. He didn't ask what the menu was. He knew there would be some dish which he liked. Was there ever anything other than what he liked in this household?

"The boy's name is Vel Murugan. He is in the Punjab. I even saw his picture. He is of course quite well-built and handsome. Twenty-three years of age. He is a good match for our Madhavi. But how could we go ahead with it? The boy is a lieutenant in the army. I rejected the proposal. Death may come when you are six or when you are a hundred, but when it concerns the army you still feel apprehensive, don't you?"

This was part of the response a friend gave to Kathiresan when some friends were visiting on a Friday evening. Kathiresan asked him, "You have been looking for an alliance for your daughter. Did anything click?" Among the various alliances mentioned in the course of their talk, the name Vel Murugan also featured. From the information about the boy's parents and other details that his friend mentioned, Kathiresan at once realised who the boy was, although his friend did not know the truth. None of Kathiresan's friends had any idea that Vimalai had a younger brother or a family. In his circle, there was no place for anyone related to her.

Kathiresan's eyes widened. This...this Vel Murugan...he is Vimalai's younger brother, no doubt about it. Is he serving in the army, then? Will Vimalai be shocked? He watched her furtively. But even he was surprised that she should appear her habitual self and not show the slightest change. Wouldn't she, too, have understood who that boy was? Then why was she so calm? Had she perhaps already heard about his joining the army? Or was this just a continuation of her conduct of obeying his command that she should utterly renounce her family? Although that obedience on her part all these years was something he had grown quite accustomed to, the present scene now, as always in the past, renewed his pride as it was yet another testimony to his absolute power and authority over her.

After the visitors left, he looked at her searchingly. As ever, with an impenetrable face, she asked him, "What would you like to have for dinner?"

"That can wait, Vimala. But did you hear what that man said about the alliances he has considered for his daughter?"

"I did."

"It was interesting, wasn't it?"

"Yes."

"What do you think of it?" he asked with deliberate probing intent.

"It strikes me that it will be a very good thing if a good match is soon found for his daughter and the marriage is also conducted."

Kathiresan smiled to himself.

"Our marriage has been a huge success, hasn't it, Vimala?"

"Yes."

"You have lacked nothing in your life, am I right?"

"Yes."

Again that cruel satisfaction in pricking her, and as much in her not betraying her hurt.

December 3rd 1971, midnight. All over the nation, people were glued to the radio. An important announcement by the Prime Minister was being aired.

"Pakistan has, without any provocation, suddenly attacked India on many fronts. Emergency has been declared all over the country..."

In the next few days, the anxiety and panic over the intensity of the war had filled every nook and corner of India. Those who could not directly engage in the war effort did whatever they could to support it in various other ways. Internal divisions disappeared and all over the country, there was a surge of patriotic feeling and righteous indignation. There was intense fighting on both the western and eastern fronts. Although India was triumphing and marching ahead, the losses were quite considerable—especially in the western sector.

Two weeks went by with reports of fighting, valour, sacrifice, courage, death and achievements. At the end of it, India attained a glorious victory, which had been accomplished by admirable political and military leadership, and the sheer heroism and courage of the soldiers, marvelled at and applauded by the whole world. The war ended.

Days went past.

When Kathiresan returned home from office one evening, he saw his old friend coming out of the house.

"Hello, sir! Leaving? Why don't you come in?" Kathiresan said as he got out of the car.

"I came quite some time back. Your wife invited me in saying that you'd be home soon, and was talking to me. Since it was getting late, I told her I'd come back tomorrow and was just about to leave. I had come to you for some help," said the friend.

"What kind of help? Why don't you come inside, sit down and tell me?"

"My daughter Madhavi's marriage has been fixed. You must help me arrange for a loan by a mortgage on my house through the bank you work for. I wanted your assistance in this matter."

"Oh, that isn't a big thing. I'll do what I can. Give me the details."

They sat in the hall for about a quarter of an hour and discussed the details. Then he got up and folded his hands by way of taking leave.

"So I take your leave, Mr. Kathiresan. Thank you so much."

"Please be at the bank by ten o'clock tomorrow. I shall stand surety for you and arrange everything. It is a happy thing that your child's marriage has been fixed with a good alliance."

"Marriage is by divine will, sir. Just look at it, somehow it just struck me that we should not give our girl in marriage to that army man. And, as if to prove me right, I heard that the boy died in the recent war with Pakistan."

Kathiresan stared at him. "That boy ... Who? ... You'd mentioned one Vel Murugan—do you mean him?"

"Yes, the very same. It seems he died on the Chhamb warfront. By God's grace, luck was on Madhavi's side. What is there in our hands, sir? This is what I was also telling your wife just now."

"Oh! Did you also tell her that the army boy died?"

"Yes. Why do you ask?"

"What did she say?"

"She just got up suddenly, saying, 'I shall get you some coffee, please stay', went inside, and came back a little later."

"Oh!"

"Shall I take leave now, sir? You, too, have just come home. Have a wash and have something to eat."

The friend left. Kathiresan stood alone.

That young man, Velu—Vimalai's younger brother—was dead.

Kathiresan was never the one to be thinking of Vimalai's people. It was not only that he didn't have any special feelings about separating her from them, but he had never felt remotely disturbed in his mind over it even for a moment. However, now when he heard that the young man—the grown up image of the young boy whose face he had forgotten, forgotten the very existence of Vimalai's brother—had died, something did trouble him.

Vimalai must be deeply grieving! She who had suffered all these years within her heart—how was she going to bear this terrible shock?

Today he must allow her to speak, poor thing, let her speak out her sorrow and get relief, why not?

He went in with soft steps and stood at the entrance to her room.

Poor Vimalai.

Was he guilty? Was he the one to blame? Was it not cruelty on his part when he ordered that she should never see them or communicate with them at all? Now, even if he permitted her to look up her brother, she couldn't. Would Vimalai forgive him?

She wasn't in the room. With a dryness of throat he had never felt before, he gently called out, "Vimala!"

"Coming!"—her voice sounded from the backyard. A voice with no trace of trepidation or agitation, the wonted everyday voice.

Vimalai emerged from the bathroom, her face wet, strands of hair curling and sticking to her face near the ears and droplets falling from her nose and chin on to the floor.

"It was very humid. I was just washing my face. It took me some time. Have you been waiting long?" she said, pulling out a towel from the cupboard and wiping her face. She applied some talcum powder below the eyes and nose. Then turning to face him, she smiled at him as usual and said, "Shall I bring your coffee?"

Her voice sounded heavy with a slight nasal tone as if she had caught a cold. He realised that the sudden cold had been caused by weeping. Kathiresan was stunned to see her stand before him talking as naturally as ever, ignoring the cold, removing all traces of tears by washing her face and touching it up with talcum powder, being for him his wife and nothing else.

"Vimala...Vimala..."

"Yes?"

But how would he ask her? What would he say? What right did he have to say anything at all!

"Vimala...I mean...He...you know that friend of mine, he said he'd been talking with you."

"Yes. His daughter's marriage is settled, I believe. Isn't that happy news?"

It was then that he understood. She was not going to talk about it. She was not going to bare her heart to him even now. It was he who had ordered that she cut off one part of her life permanently. She had kept herself tightly bound within that forbidding knot. And she was not going to loosen it now even when confronted with the death of a dear one. She was not going to talk to him now and give existence to a relationship that he had annulled.

Kathiresan was deeply distressed. "Vimala! Do please talk to me about it, won't you? Won't you open up and cry and weep your heart out and say, 'Do you know, my younger brother is gone!' If you wish, you may lessen the burden of your grief by even chastising me to your heart's content for separating you from the one who was going to die like this..." Thus his mind lamented.

"That's all right, Vimala. He...Didn't he say anything else?"

"Of course he did. He was saying that he was going to ask you if you could arrange for some loan. He had come just for that. Did you meet him at the entrance? Or had he left before you arrived?"

Vimala! Vimala! Will you still hide yourself? Won't you speak? Won't you talk about it at all?

Singed by the permanent sorrow of being uprooted from her natal ties, Vimalai had been hurt beyond words. All these years she had concealed this hurt and anguish from him and lived on. In doing so, she had held on to that very concealment as what was left of her self-esteem. This he suddenly realised.

Wasn't she now, with her usual smile and talk, simply brushing him aside as if to ask, "You asked me to turn my back upon my people. Now what have you got to do with my sorrow?"

"I'm not asking about that, Vimala..." He halted, unable to proceed further. When she had not mentioned the matter, how could he broach it? And as a continuation of what?

"He said he has his house to pledge in the bank as security," Vimalai continued.

Had he not been inordinately pleased in ordering her to renounce her people, and more so that she had conducted herself accordingly? Hadn't he felt proud and arrogant in the knowledge that she had no existence except that of being his wife? Hadn't he regarded it as his victory that whatever she thought about and agonised over within herself, she never revealed it, by gesture or word, as far as he was concerned, but always hid it?

His folly was now all too clear to him. It now hit him with shocking impact, weighed down as he was by the truth that she would not deign to open her heart to him even at this hour when stricken by such immense sorrow.

How impoverished he was! An utter bankrupt who had spurned her fullness of being as something that he did not need.

Kathiresan did not speak. Looking at her face curtaining her sorrow, he stood there as if in a daze, silent, filled with a new yearning and despair.

"Please go and change. I shall bring over your tiffin and coffee," Vimalai said as she left hurriedly, not letting him see her face.

The minutes moved on, but he did not stir. He was lost in the agony of coming to terms with the realisation that he had been subjected to a profound loss, that he was the one who had been rejected.

Originally published in Tamil as '*Perumaiyinmudivil*'
[At the end of pride], in the magazine *Kalki*,
Deepavali Special Issue, November 1972.

7

Death, be not proud

Dear *Chiranjivi* Rajagopalan,

Your *Amma*'s *asirvadam*.

When writing 'Chiranjivi', something strikes me today—who is truly a chiranjivi in this world? Every day we see people dying. I don't mean to speak of it as Dharmaputra did in the *Mahabharata*; I don't regard myself as such a noble soul. Even so, won't this thought strike others, too, at some moment or the other just as it had occurred to him? After all, isn't human nature common to us all, the high and the low? All the people in the world are not saints, but they are the descendants of saints. That, too, should mean something after all.

What was I trying to say? When the pain increases, everything slips from memory. I am gulping down medicines, no doubt, but the disease is also gulping me down... Yes, Chiranjivi. Despite witnessing deaths everyday—why? Despite carrying this body like a tree which has sprouted and grown from the seed of death, if you can call someone Chiranjivi, doesn't it sound odd? But in fact, it doesn't. It doesn't sound false, does it? And if that is so, I think that 'Chiranjivi' points to something permanent, something beyond the life and death that we see. And *that* supreme thing is what every mother out of love blesses her son with when she addresses him as 'Chiranjivi'.

You are laughing, aren't you Rajagopala? I, too, feel like laughing. Why is it that today, suddenly I am...? I have been writing letters to you ever since you got a job and went away. I have been writing a letter every week without fail. Even when your father was alive, the job of writing letters was always mine. And I always begin every letter with 'Chiranjivi'. But today for the first time I seem to be researching that word in this manner. These days, I don't know why, all kinds of scenarios and meanings present themselves and seem to become visible beyond what one sees. As though one has acquired a new pair of eyes. Yesterday, for example, I happened to look at our maid Anjalai while she was sweeping the central hall. Well, haven't I known her for quite a while? She has been working with us for five years now. But yesterday, for no apparent reason, I was suddenly stunned when I looked at her, and I thought, is our Anjalai really such a beautiful woman? The same form, the same eyes, the same limbs—but everything seemed new. Pleasing features just seemed to have arrived from somewhere and sat upon her. These days it is often like this. Whatever I see, whatever I think of, the impressions are new, just like this. Is beauty born only out of pain? Why should the whole world look so different even as the pain in my stomach goes on increasing, I wonder? Does death turn every one into a poet? I seem to be writing strange things, don't I? Perhaps you are thinking, Amma is a complete nut, aren't you? I did not myself think that I was going to write things like this. I put the pen to paper and let it take its own course. It keeps writing, making me wonder whether what is inside it is ink or thoughts. I just keep following it.

It pains, Rajagopala! These days it pains very much. But then why should it not? When Ramakrishna Paramahamsa and Bhagawan Ramana could go through pain, why shouldn't the worthless Thangamma? It is not thoughts alone which make the high and the low part of one human community, but pain and death, too.

Charu takes very good care of me. She guards me vigilantly as though I am her child, not her mother. Of course she cannot take my pain, but she does everything else. Not only does she take me to the Institute for the electric treatment every alternate day without in the least complaining, she goes to work only after giving me the medicines exactly as prescribed, and locking the cupboard carefully and stationing Anjalai next to me. She is apprehensive that, unable to bear the pain, I might deliberately consume an overdose of the sleeping pills! Fool! She doesn't know that I would not disdain any stage of life. If disease and death are a part of life, let them arrive as they please at their chosen time, and take hold of me by force. I have enjoyed so much happiness in this life. Should the same life now bestow disease upon me, will I avoid it and run away? Even in my childhood I had never called it quits in the middle of a game just because I was losing. Now when I am old and have understood that beauty is not only fair-complexioned but can also be dark, will I flee at this age?

But poor Charu, how do you expect her to know this? She is shielding me in sheer fright that something untoward may befall me. She is trying to stop the moon from waning, holding it with both her hands. But it defies her vigilance and wanes a little more every day. One day it will disappear altogether. This does not mean that her care and attention are any less valued. After all isn't she professionally a nurse, too? If only I could be born a child in her womb and render service to her in return for all the care she is taking of me as an affectionate daughter, and as an efficient nurse ... But will that ever happen? The moment you mention marriage, doesn't she fly into a rage? Her mind is quite set in this regard. I wonder if some auspicious thing will happen to her before I close my eyes forever. Even if she marries later, it is perfectly all right with me. It is you who must look for a good match for Charu.

Just as you are fortunate to have a good wife, she, too, must get a good husband. Imagine what will happen to the quality of the world if good people don't marry and beget children! If elephants don't multiply, only pigs will. If you tell her this, she doesn't listen. You remember that young man who came and 'saw' her three months ago? Charu agreed to their visit at my insistence. That boy is still intent on marrying her and in fact insists that he will marry none but her! Or else, it seems he is not interested in marriage at all. Since she refused, I believe he has not 'seen' any other girl. How nice it will be if she changes her mind! Rajagopala! The pain pricks like a needle inside the stomach. Added to the pain, the burning sensation of the radiation makes it worse. I am trying not to mind it. I think Lord Siva burned all the directions just by smiling only to make us realise that we should endure all suffering with a smile. Earlier, it was easier. Now it isn't. The pain is just unbearable. In such moments the whole world slips away.

Let us put aside my ills. After several years, recently your *Atthai* visited us one day. Don't you remember Sulochana Atthai? She made enquiries about all of you. Poor woman, she is suffering a lot.

I seem to be writing all kinds of stuff without asking about you, my child! Are you well? Even if I enquire like this every week I don't feel satisfied. You keep saying "Amma, I am well", which is celestial music to my ears. Charu teases me, saying, "For you, the son is dearer." Is that the truth? Are you dearer to me, Rajagopala? Just look at the way I address you! I have never liked to call you Raju, shortening your name as the others do. I do shorten the name Sarada to Charu as do the others. But you are always Rajagopalan for me. When that name lingers so long in my mouth like that, it is just like the way my womb expanded to hold you.

It was only last month that you came down to see me. Still, I feel like seeing you again. How greedy of me, how selfish, not bothering to think what will happen to your job! But my eyes don't listen to my words! When will you be able to get leave of absence again? I heard it is pouring in Bombay now. Take care not to get wet. When you go out, don't ever forget to put on the raincoat. Here, too, this month there is good rain. In our garden, the flowers are in full bloom. When I see them, I think of all of you. One flower is Rajagopalan, another one is Charu, yet another one is my daughter-in-law, another one is my grandson, yet another one is my future son-in-law, another one is your late father, another one is again Rajagopalan ... It looks as though Charu's charge is valid!

Take care of your health. Is your wife well? Is she getting her periods? How is the little fellow? Give him a kiss from grandma. Yesterday, when I had snake gourd milk *koottu*, I remembered that you liked it very much. When will you be coming again, Rajago...

Amma has slumped down in pain. She could not hold the pen and write any further. Therefore I continue the letter. What a prelude to a profound change this change of handwriting is! Amma's health has gradually deteriorated, the pain aggravating so badly that she is unable even to write letters—yet another stage in the worsening of this disease. I wonder if Amma can ever write again. This might be her very last letter to reach you, but without her signature. I wonder how long she is going to be with us after this, *Anna*! There is no improvement even with the cobalt therapy. Very soon she may have to be kept under morphia.

Amma is well aware what kind of disease she has become a victim of. She knows whither this pain is dragging her. She does not delude herself into thinking that she will survive. But the smile on her face hasn't changed one bit, Anna! The features of her face ... the eyes, the ears, the cheeks, the chin, the forehead, the nose, the mouth, the smile. When one is ready to die, is it all smiles then? Do those who grow mentally mature die with a smile, though, like all of us, they were born with a cry?

Did she ever need a reason to laugh? Do you remember, Anna, when you were here last time, you had said to me, "Both of you had better come with me to Bombay, Charu. We can get even better treatment for Amma there. In case it is not available there, I am ready to take her to any place in the world where you have effective treatment for this. The expense doesn't matter." When Amma came to know about this, do you recall what she said? "Rajagopala, I believe you have found some place in this world where *Yama* cannot enter to take me!" And saying so, she laughed, do you remember? No one can laugh like her. Always the same laugh, the same bloom of joy. It is only in recent times that the laughter fails her now and then. When the pain aggravates, she moans despite herself. But that is only for a moment. Amma pulls back the runaway laughter, holding it by the ear. The disease has disfigured her. Even though she is not all that old, she has become an old woman. But even when the disfigurement spreads like a shroud, when the mouth contorts in pain, when the eyelashes twitch and shrink, what peace there is in that face! Where does that peace come from—the peace that disowns any connection with the pain?

This is what I don't understand. What kind of state is this? How can someone die little by little with so much peace? In the beginning I feared that she might commit suicide, unable to bear the pain. Even now I keep the drugs under lock and key; but that is out of habit. Now I know she won't do any such thing.

It looks odd for me to express my thoughts about her in a letter which she has written to you. It feels as though I was opening the door and barging in while both of you were conversing.

But to tell you the truth, Anna, I don't mean to intrude into your 'privacy'. Do you know, I didn't read what she has written. I just sat down to continue the letter noticing that the last word was left unfinished. I did not open the door. You are her favourite child—don't deny it; it is futile!—I shall not come between the two of you.

The reason why I am sitting down to write this letter like this under the circular light of the table lamp in the peace of the night after attending to her needs, and as she sleeps in a stupor, is to share with you an amazing thing about her.

As death is closing in on her, there is, instead of darkness, forever a new beauty, light and joy growing in her mind. Anna! The face shrinks in pain. The very next minute she is exclaiming in delight, "See how the stars are shining so bright today!" This happened the night of the last new moon day.

When I stay near Amma and attend to her, I don't nurse a patient, I witness a miracle, just being with her. I feel as though I am looking at a new race of humanity.

Being a nurse, witnessing disease, loud lamentations and death in the hospital day in and day out, life tasted bitter for me. My aversion to marriage is also because of that. How quickly beauty vanishes from the faces twitching in pain! It is because they all regard pain as an act of injustice meted out to them, and resist it. Do you know how many people have complained to me, "Sister, I can't bear this! Will I survive? Is there any hope for me?" For all that, what they really experienced was only a passing pain.

They are diseases from which, even if one writhes in pain for a hundred days, on the hundred and first day one recovers and sits up. Is Amma's case the same? No. There is no relief for her pain. It is the threshold of death. They say a condition without hope is verily hell. Cancer—that is why it is hell, not because it consumes life at the end.

Suffering from such a disease as she does, how effortlessly Amma is happy! Even in the darkness of the new moon, she notices not the absence of the moon, but the presence of the stars. She has led an impeccable life. But she never complained,

"I have been a good human being, why should I be afflicted with this?" as do the majority of my patients who cannot put up with sufferings which are just ordinary as compared with this.

All the time looking at people who desperately cling to life proclaiming, "I won't die! I won't die!" and wailing, "My life," "My family," "My possessions" even as they die, I am filled with derision and bitterness towards the whole brood of humanity. But Amma simply says, "How bright that star looks!" and sets me thinking. She impels me to rid my mind of all thoughts about death and such things, and to think in a fresh way.

Four days ago, our Atthai had suddenly come on a visit. I wonder what gumption she had to step into this house. In those days, I believe she was the one who turned *Appa*'s mind against Amma by telling cock and bull stories about Amma and advising him to discard her and marry again. It seems that listening to her, even Appa behaved unreasonably for some time. Thank God, everything eventually became all right. Imagine, what would have happened to Amma otherwise? Without any compunction of conscience Atthai now arrived and entered the house. Shouldn't she have at least some hesitation at the thought that all contacts have been lost for all these years? Humph, she came in as if she was a blessed one! When she asked, "*Yendi*, Thangam! How are you keeping?" I felt like slapping her. Do you mean to say that she wouldn't have heard that Amma was dying? How are you keeping, indeed! What insolence! If I had been Amma, I wouldn't have let her set foot on the doorstep in the first place. But just look at Amma! She welcomed her with a smile, saying "Come, Sulo!" For once, I was furious to see that smile.

Atthai camped here for a whole day. She enquired about us all as a mere formality. "O, this is Sarada? So big she has grown!" she remarked, sizing me up. Did she really think I'd be the same little girl that she had seen twenty years ago? What nonsense! Then she asked about you. But she didn't pay any attention to any of the replies.

The real reason for Atthai's visit was to speak about herself. She sobbed her woes out to Amma. It seems that her children don't take care of her and, in fact, they have thrown her out. No wonder! What else would they do but drive her out if she created a rift between the sons and daughters-in-law as she did between Appa and Amma? Now she is living with a brother-in-law as a dependant, I gather. They feed her stomach half as we say, and that grudgingly. She was talking about her trail of woes; but not once did she say to Amma, "How sad that you are so utterly reduced." But Amma didn't mind in the least. On the contrary, she consoled Atthai, wiped her tears and cheered her up. She fed her to her fill morning and night, not to mention the coffee and snacks. Not stopping with that, when Atthai was leaving, Amma gave her fifty rupees and reassuringly said, "Don't worry, Sulo. If you have no one to fall back on, I shall tell my children that they should take care of you for the rest of your life. They won't go against my word." Anna, I was beside myself with rage! Left to myself, I would have taunted Atthai with hot words. But do you know what happened then? Atthai suddenly fell at Amma's feet and cried, "*Manni*! Please forgive me!" Then she left without once turning back.

That night I didn't sleep at all. I don't think Arjuna, too, would have slept the day he had the vision of Krishna's cosmic form.

"Show mercy to the enemy." Anna, I have learnt this not from books, but here at home, and so palpably. How is it possible for Amma to conduct herself so nobly even while she is so close to death! Amma has gone far beyond the state of death. Now when death actually comes to her, it will have no meaning. That is why she will not commit suicide, I know for certain. For her death is a mere trifle, no worthier than a blade of grass. Why would she attach so much value to it and invite it?

It seems everything is becoming clearer in my mind. Amma is teaching a new lesson to me—I who am fed up with life, constantly witnessing disease and death. Amma is showing me that beauty and meaning issue from our own thoughts.

Those patients moan because of their lack of strength. What makes Amma turn even death into something beautiful is the sense of beauty which dwells within her. There is nothing out there, is there? It is we who impose our own nature upon the world. This lump of clay can be shaped as we please, depending on our own deftness. We receive but what we give. I now understand that the feelings roused within us by scenes outside are but mirrors which reflect us for ourselves.

Now I see the whole truth, having seen all these days only half of it. When I realise that, in this world, there are not only those pitiable patients, but also beings like Amma, then my bitterness gradually begins to dissolve.

The letter has turned very serious, hasn't it, Anna? Perhaps you will burst into laughter, won't you? But I felt like pouring out to you whatever surfaced in the mind. That, too, continuing Amma's letter...! There is a special satisfaction in it. With her son, her favourite son ... No, no! I won't repeat it, don't get angry!

How are you all doing? I am as usual fully occupied with work in the hospital. There is always such a big crowd, making one wonder whether there is any healthy human being at all in this Madras city! One day, there was among the visitors to the patients someone in particular who lingered hesitantly on seeing me. "How are you?" he asked. It surprised me that he hadn't got angry with me. It was only later that I heard that, after me, he didn't 'see' any other girls.

Who knows? Perhaps I may ... Amma will be pleased.

What! Is it two o'clock? Let me stop with this, Anna! I must go to bed now. Amma is also sleeping soundly. With sleeping pills, of course. Even so, when she moans aloud in her sleep out of pain, she doesn't wail Ayyo! Appa! "*Easwara*" is the word that slips through her mouth. What a heritage we are heirs to, Anna!

It is very late. If I don't go to bed now, I won't be fresh for work. Love to the children.

Your affectionate sister,

Charu

P.S.: Call this a letter? It is pages and pages, like a story! I should send it by parcel post!

Originally published in Tamil as '*Oru koottu-k-kaditham*' [A joint letter], in the magazine *Kalaimagal*, September 1976.

8

No fury like a mother's

Would the child recover at all? Even the fever, raging unabated for four days, had not brought the blood back to her face—it was the same pallor as it had been the first day. Had all the blood drained away? Forever?

"*Kannu*! Lata ... Latamma!" She remembered how terrified she was the other day when she saw the shattered child sobbing endlessly and hiccupping. Now she longed to hear the child cry. That would at least be a sign of life, an end to her silence. If only there was some little movement in that frame which was now lying like the sea where all the waves had ceased...

"Lata, open your eyes and look at me! Say '*Amma*'!"

As she recalled how on that day, when the child just stood at the threshold, burying her face against the wall, her frail frame trembling over with ceaseless sobs, crying, "Amma... Amma..." and sunk in a sorrow which seemed to have no beginning or end, doubt and fear gripped the mother whether this little bud of life would ever come out of this state at all.

She heard someone knock at the entrance door. She adjusted the ice pack on the child's head, rose and went to open the door.

There were two women standing at the door, neither of them known to her.

"Whom do you want?"

"You ... Isn't this child Lata's house?"

"Yes."

"How is the child now?"

"She is in the same state."

Only then surprise registered. "How do you know she is not well?"

They looked at each other. Then one of them said, "Our children are also in the same class. My daughter Mary said Lata is down with fever and has not been coming to school for the last few days."

Lata was ill with fever. Was it just a case of the child getting wet in the rain or roaming around in the hot sun and contracting fever? "Amma... Amma..." The tender body tossing up and down. The monstrous terror that held sway over her and destroyed her young world. Terror, shock, degradation ... above all, humiliation...

"Hasn't the fever come down even a little bit?" asked the one who spoke first.

"Not so far."

"What does the doctor say?"

"He asked us to give her the medicines and keep the ice pack over her head. If the fever doesn't come down by tomorrow, she has to be given an ice-bath."

"The Divine will protect her, don't worry. Aren't you Lata's mother?"

"Yes."

"We actually came to look up the child. Can we?"

Lata's mother didn't say anything.

"Our children, too—her daughter Mary, mine Kayalvizhi—were in a similar situation once. That is, the same punishment, the same humiliation, and fever. They were not bedridden. Still, the sobbing and the agony they went through... So we do understand how your Lata feels. We couldn't bear it when we heard how, unlike our children who recovered after suffering in distress for a couple of days, your Lata has been taken seriously ill and is in bed. That is why we thought we would come and look up the child and you."

She looked up at them. Faces full of concern and sympathy. "Please come."

Lata was lying down eyes closed, just a line under the sheet with hardly a shape. The two women stood still, gazing at the child's pale, motionless face. Except for biting their lips and swallowing their saliva they said nothing. But in those gestures Lata's mother found in the women two friends and well-wishers. With the tenderness that this kindred feeling provided, she took off the ice pack, emptied the water, filled the pack again with large ice cubes and placed it on her daughter's forehead. "Lata! Latamma!"

How she had cried out distraught in the delirium of fever! "No, Miss, I will write the lessons properly hereafter... Please leave me Miss...Please no...Please no...I won't...You shouldn't do this to me... Amma! Amma!" Screams that froze one's heart. But at least she could hear her voice then! The silence and prolonged stupor now... How far had the child gone? Would she ever come back?

"At first she went on crying in feverish delirium. Then everything stopped."

One of the women gently placed her hand on her shoulder. The other kneeled beside the bed and closed her eyes. The lips moved silently. After the prayer she bowed, made the sign of the cross and opened her eyes. "*Karthar* is merciful. He loves children dearly. He will certainly save this child. Don't worry."

Lata's mother made them sit in the next room, keeping the doors open so that they could keep observing the child. The three of them remained silent for a while.

"What is the point of hiring people who should supervise concentration camps as school teachers?" Lata's mother burst out all of a sudden.

"We came to know that even the other teachers don't like the things that this one does. They do speak out, objecting to it. But it seems that one of her uncles is in the Education Department. So both the Headmistress and the Correspondent are afraid of pulling her up. And she doesn't care what the other teachers say and does as she pleases."

"But behaving this way? Teachers do scold children if they don't study well. I won't fault the teacher if she deals them a blow or two if they get uncontrollable. But how can anyone have the heart to inflict *this* kind of punishment? Should she crush and humiliate tender minds in this fashion? Does she have no children of her own?"

"She is a frustrated woman! Who else would act like the devil and mete out punishments like this?" said Mary's mother.

"If she is a frustrated woman, should our children be the victims?" said Kayalvizhi's mother.

"Lata ... Lata is a very delicate child, excessively shy. Even when I give her a bath with oil and soapnut powder she would feel terribly shy and embarrassed. She would cover her body with her hand and not let me scrub. I would shout at her saying, 'What is this, acting shy with your mother?' push away her hand and give her a bath," said Lata's mother suppressing a sob.

Even now she felt as though her entire frame was on fire when she recalled how on that day Lata stood cowering against the wall and crying, how she gathered the child in her arms, placed her head on her lap and tried to comfort her, how the child breathlessly kept sobbing "Amma... Amma..." and how finally, in the midst of sobs, stammered out what had happened.

"Is there no one to question that teacher? How many more children will she torture like this?"

"When she punished Kayalvizhi in this way, I went to the school to lodge a complaint. I couldn't get to see the Headmistress. The class teacher of the seventh standard saw me and asked what the matter was. I told her. She felt very sorry. She said that, like her, the other teachers, too, didn't like this teacher's doings, but that, regardless of what they said, she never paid any heed. It was also then that she told me about the support this teacher had from the Education Department. The class teacher then suggested that if the parents got together and made a complaint, saying this was not the first case of its kind, the management might find that there was no other alternative but to dismiss her. It was after this that my husband and I went to Mary's house and introduced ourselves to her parents. Now, when we came to know that there was yet another case, we two came to see you."

"Our three families must now make a joint complaint and somehow drive that teacher out. Otherwise, our children and many more will have no peace."

The mother looked beyond the door and looked at the tiny figure that was lying on the bed like a shadow. Those delirious screams that evening—"No, Miss, I won't do any wrong hereafter, don't take it off, don't take it off ... at least let the panty stay ... *Aiyo*! No, miss ... everyone is looking ... how can I stand like this? Aiyo! ... Amma! Amma!"

"Oh, my God," Lata's mother covered her face with her hands. The other two went and sat close to her and stroked her shoulders and back.

She was sitting in the staff room with a triumphant glow on her face, eating from her lunch box.

Three other teachers came and stood at the door. On seeing her, one of them, the seventh standard teacher, simply passed by without entering the room. The other two hesitantly entered, took the two chairs beyond where she was sitting, and silently started eating. After some time another teacher came in, sat at the other end of the room and opened a newspaper.

Normally, there would be a lot of people in the staff room during the interval. While having lunch they would discuss threadbare matters relating to the school and the home. Some others would talk about public issues. On this day there were only those four. More in number were those who peeped in and went away to the outer verandah.

The teacher with the triumphant glow was laughing within herself as though enjoying the silence that prevailed in the room and the disapproving countenances of her colleagues. She deliberately made a lot of noise while eating to make it clear that she didn't care about what they thought. Then she asked in a loud voice, "Why are you all silent? Have you suddenly decided to observe a fast of silence for a day in the week? Isn't anyone going to congratulate me?" and pouring the buttermilk into the glass drank it up noisily and smacked her lips.

The two who were eating raised their heads and looked at her. The one sitting in the corner didn't take her eyes off the newspaper.

"What is there to congratulate you on? Wasn't the outcome expected?" said one. Behind the words was the suggestion that there was nothing surprising about the victory of someone who had an uncle in the Education Department.

"Quite expected, wasn't it? Then why couldn't you people have told those three families that there was no use making a complaint against me?"

They didn't speak. Leave alone stopping those three families, hadn't they in fact been praying that the parents' plaint should succeed?

With an expression that showed she knew what they had done, she went on with a laugh, "Poor things! Aren't you all very sad that their complaint had no effect? Who knows how many of you, like the seventh class teacher, incited those parents to make such a complaint? Poor things, you would have celebrated my dismissal with *payasam* if it had taken place. But I am not going to provide you that satisfaction!"

They didn't look up.

The parents of the three children, Mary, Kayalvizhi and Lata, had lodged a complaint against the teacher. They had alleged that when their children had failed to write the lessons correctly, the teacher had, in the presence of the entire class, stripped them and made them go round the classroom naked and then stand up on the table for half an hour. The parents had objected to such a cruel punishment and requested that the teacher be dismissed from service. However, neither the Headmistress nor the Correspondent had the courage to take action against the teacher. It was a school being run with grants from the government. The teacher's maternal uncle was an official in the Education Department and quite close to the Minister. Reluctant on that score, when the Headmistress half-heartedly summoned the teacher and enquired about the complaint, she denied the charge and called in the other pupils in the class as witnesses. All those children said that the teacher had not given any such punishment. So it was concluded that those three children had used their skills of imagination and concocted the story. The Headmistress then summoned the three pairs of parents and advised them to take their children to psychiatrists, and fully cleared the teacher of the charge.

"Poor children!" That was the thought that now ran through the minds of the two teachers. Not only the children who were subjected to the punishment, even those who testified, how terrified they must have been! Should people take up the noble profession of teaching to terrify children like this? And should such cruel-hearted people go to teach innocent, sweet-spoken children? What could those tiny little things possibly do against the demonic power wielded by adults?

It is a teacher who can create in tender and radiant faces an ardour for learning and fill their eyes with wonder, thrill and pride at discovering ever newer and ever more marvellous realms of knowledge. Should she instead create fear and fright in them? This particular teacher, a frustrated woman who had a barren life with nothing to live for—what a treasure of joy and fulfillment she could have obtained from the blooming of the kids under her care! Did she even realise what she was herself losing when she thus abjured love and chose cruelty instead?

"No one wants your dismissal. But at least hereafter if you treat children a little gently, it will be good for the school. After all, if it is known outside that there was a complaint like this, the name of the school will be tarnished, won't it?" said one of the teachers.

"Is it just the school's name? It is mine, too! What gumption those children must have had to go home and make a complaint like this about me! Wait, just wait. You will see what I will do to them... I will... I will..." As she spoke these words gnashing her teeth, her countenance turned ugly. The others were startled.

"*Chhe, chhe,* what is this? Is it proper for us to engage in wrangles with children? Just ignore them as innocent kids," said one.

"Innocent kids? Venomous snakes! Is it right for them to say things like this? They open their mouths only to lie. Will they ever come to any good? I never gave any such punishment to anyone, you know that, don't you?" she said and looked around at them sharply.

They did not reply immediately. After a while one of them said, "Be that as it may. But it is our duty to nurture children's intelligence and shape them as good citizens. True or false, is it right for us even to let them entertain such a thought? I think you are excessively strict. Poor kids! They are in class one, and what do they know! It is we who have to walk the path with them and tactfully teach them. It is very important to treat them with love. Do you know how they will attach themselves to us if we show them a little love? In the last parents-teachers meeting we had, the mother of one of my pupils said to me, 'You know, when we say something wrong at home, my daughter says: What you say is wrong, Amma. That is not what our teacher has taught us'."

Said another, "We have taken up this profession to give our students the most precious time of their entire life, not to make them cry. Even more importantly, when we are dealing with these tiny kids in the primary section, we should treat them with gentleness and understanding. Otherwise their hearts will be shattered. Do you know what a great reward it is when we conduct ourselves and instruct them properly, and their knowledge grows and they utter something very bright! It is then that our occupation really becomes a service."

"I am not interested in service. Occupation will do for me. If teachers act in a namby-pamby, pussy-footing way, where will discipline come from? The kids who get admitted to your class for the first time follow you about, crying all the time. Once I saw one of them crying and waiting outside the rest room when you had gone in and, the moment you came out, holding on to your sari-end once again. Why must you pamper them like this? Shouldn't you rather give them a slap or two and bring them round?"

"Why should we slap them? When very small children come to school for the first time, for a few days they will see their mother's image in the teacher. Is it any wonder that they do so? If we treat them gently and reassuringly during that period, they will gradually get over their fear, shyness and hesitancy. I am indeed quite proud that my students love me."

"They will get normal sooner if we don't give in to them in everything and act tough instead. School is not the place for crying and fooling around and sitting on the teacher's lap. It is the place for learning obedience and studying properly. Children will come to good only if they understand that they will get punished if they don't behave." She looked towards the one who was sitting at the far end and said, "What a racket the children in your class raise! I don't know how you can keep quiet."

That teacher turned and looked. Then, folding the newspaper, she said, "They learn their lessons well. So what is wrong if they speak with a loud voice when they ask questions or answer them? Is the teacher a tiger or a demon for them to be scared of her all the time?"

"No fear, no discipline."

"My students lack nothing by way of discipline. They are spirited children and talk loudly in their excessive enthusiasm."

"Then they will turn impudent and you can never control them. 'Spirited children' are they? You were saying that you had to take leave for a week to go home to look up your sick mother, weren't you? Won't I be going to your class during that week to teach Social Studies? You will see if I don't break their spirit then." It was scary to see the frenzy in her as she said this.

"In any case, for your own good it is better to deal with children a little gently," said one.

"No one can lift a finger against me. If those three devils act smart with me again...," she paused, panting, "It was not enough to strip them naked..."

"Only two children, Kayalvizhi and Mary."

"Why, what happened to Lata? She has recovered from fever, hasn't she?"

"Yes, but she is quite weak and is in fact a nervous wreck. We don't know how long it will take for her to return to school."

"People will have to suffer if they make complaints against me."

The three gazed silently at that countenance so full of hate. Then they left the room. She, too, came out for the afternoon classes. As each one of the teachers who were around looked away on seeing her, she felt both anger and derision.

It was in the same state that she went home after the classes were over that afternoon. It was a small house, but independent. She didn't like living in a tenement, sharing space with others. A maid came twice a day. For the rest of the time, it was all her imperial realm. She was not scared of living alone, being now quite used to solitude. Unable to get on with her parents, she quarrelled and left home. A single woman even at the age of thirty-five. The early longing for a husband, children and things like that had eventually turned into a hardness and frozen her inside. As time passed, the hardness itself became a comfortable feeling, and her fulfillment lay in feeding it.

It was five in the evening. She heard the clock strike the hour while she was correcting the school notebooks and gleefully marking them low. She closed the notebooks and rose. It was her usual time for a cup of tea.

There were some shadows moving at the doorstep of the room. She looked up and ahead. There were three women standing on the other side of the doorstep. The faces looked slightly familiar, but she couldn't recognise them. "Who are you?" she said in a sharp tone.

They made no reply but kept staring at her.

"Who are you all? Did you come to ask for someone's address?" she said, the tone rising.

"We have come to the right address," said one of the women.

"So? Do you know who I am?"

They mentioned the name of the Girls' Higher Secondary School she worked in and her own name, and said, "Aren't you the teacher for Class One?"

"Yes. Have you come for some admission? It is quite a long time since admissions got over and school started. You may go," she said and made to shut the door. But they coolly pushed her hand away and stepped inside.

"We haven't come for admission. It is you we have come for."

Their very tone struck a jarring note. And when one of them shut the door and bolted it from inside, a certain panic touched her. What resulted first was a burst of anger.

"What nonsense is all this? Why do you close the door? What kind of behaviour is this, barging into someone's house and making trouble? Who are you?"

"Don't you know us?" The three stood immobile like a rock before her.

"I am Mary's mother."

"I am Kayalvizhi's mother."

"I am Lata's mother."

For some reason their steady, unwavering gaze sent a slight chill down her spine. Those children's mothers—why have they entered her house? And why bolt the door?

"Oho. I see. That's all right. First of all, go and open that door. What have you come for? You and your husbands made a complaint about me to the school, didn't you? But you also know, don't you, that when the Headmistress enquired into the matter, it was proved by the evidence given by the other children that what your daughters had said was a lie. What more do you want? Do check your children a bit and teach them to speak the truth. Go!"

The three did not speak. They just stood still staring at her. She suddenly starting sweating all over.

"Why do you keep standing here? If you don't like that decision, complain to the Board of Directors. Don't come to my house and trouble me! Go!"

They neither moved nor spoke.

Her tongue felt parched. Why were they staring at her like this?

"What is the matter? What does it mean if you keep your mouths shut thus? What did you come here for?"

"You made our children stand naked in front of the whole class, didn't you?"

"No. Not at all. That's an utter lie."

"Shouldn't you know how they would have felt, shrunken, degraded and humiliated, what agony their hearts would have gone through?"

That steady voice seeming to rise in unison from all the three presences—what was that voice saying? What did those words mean...?

"Now it is you we are going to strip naked. And drag you naked into the street. The people in the street will crowd round you and gaze at you. Just as you and the other children gazed at our children."

Her heart instantly froze. Terror-stricken for a moment and incredulous, she looked at their faces and jumped back as though she had stepped on fire.

"What nonsense are you talking? What is all this blabbering about? You had better leave. Have you escaped from a lunatic asylum? I'll call the police! Get out!"

They started moving towards her.

Her eyes instantly seemed to pop out in terror. "No! No! Please don't! Don't do anything to me! I pray to you with folded hands. I will never do such a thing hereafter. Can a woman commit this kind of cruelty on another woman? Please, show pity, leave me, leave me..."

"Yes, but on one condition."

"What condition? I'll accept it whatever it may be. Just leave me...!"

"You must resign your job."

"Aiyo! That's my occupation! That is the only occupation I have qualified myself for."

They went close to her again. One of them caught hold of her sari-end.

"Aiyo...Please don't, please don't! Don't do anything to me. I will resign."

"Do so. Right away. Right here and now, sit down and write your resignation letter."

She wrote it.

"Put it in an envelope and write your Headmistress's address on it."

She did so.

One of the women snatched the envelope from her and checked if the address was right.

"We are taking this straight to the mobile post office and posting it right now. If you play any tricks and withdraw the resignation later..."

"Remember—the second time we will show you no mercy."

"Have you understood?"

The three opened the door and went out.

Originally published in Tamil as '*Thugalseythukidattuvalthai*' [The enraged mother will beat and lay you flat], in the magazine *Deepam*, November 1977.

9

Herself

What a relief! How pleasant it feels when the village breeze caresses the body! It'll be a veritable heaven if there is also mother's cooking to add to it.

For Nitya, it seemed at first to be a perfect holiday, coming to these open fields in the lap of nature in the rustic spaces of her native village, far from the din and bustle of Bombay. She had brought Suresh along with her, but that was no problem. Mother would look after him. Father would play with him. She wouldn't have to take any responsibility. Staying at her parents' place for a month, she would herself become a child. She had come with the definite aim of finding release and enjoying herself in the comfort of her parents' care. She had in fact told her husband: "I shall just drop a letter when I reach there. And another to tell you the date of my return. I won't write a line in between. I'm on holiday! I'm going to enjoy the pampering of my father and mother like a child, forgetting for the time being that I am married, and a mother!"

Her father Chokkalingam had gone all the way to Madras Central to receive her. "My little fellow, Suresh! Do you remember me? I am your *Thatha*! Here, take this," and giving the three-year old a box of sweets, he lifted him up and kissed him, though the boy was trying to wriggle out of his embrace.

"Hope you had a comfortable journey, Nitya? How's your husband? I wish he, too, had come over for a few days." Her father kept talking with affectionate concern.

"He couldn't get leave, *Appa*! Moreover, how'll he spend the time in a village? As for me, a month will fly like a minute in the loving company of Appa and *Amma*," said Nitya. She added, "Even for you, Appa, it must be difficult to spend the time in the countryside. Why didn't you settle down here in Madras after retirement?"

"I do manage to keep myself engaged. I arrange to get books from here. What, little fellow? Why so restive? Frightened of Thatha's beard, are you? Don't worry. I shall shave it off as soon as we reach home."

"We have to catch the train at Egmore to go to Kanchipuram, don't we, Appa? Is there a train or bus from there to the village? Or do we have to travel by a bullock cart?"

Chokkalingam laughed. "Don't you worry! There is a bus. But I have arranged for us to go straight to the village from here by bus."

"Good, we are spared an extra break in the journey. Why didn't Amma come, too, Appa? Isn't she eager to see us?"

"Your mother couldn't make it. She's busy."

"Busy did you say? What's this sudden engagement that she has, I'd like to know?"

Without saying anything, Chokkalingam first took her to a coffee stall.

As soon as she got down from the bullock cart in front of the house, Nitya felt as if a breath of freedom swept over her. She was amused to see Suresh looking at the strange surroundings in wonder. The house was small. Although a tiled house, it was simple enough not to be very different from the neighbouring hutments. It looked like an *ashramam* in the midst of thickly grown tamarind and peepal trees. In the space adjoining the house, enclosed by spiky bamboos, one could see a kitchen garden with supports for creepers and plants and plant beds. What! Is Amma growing vegetables at home now?

It'll be a great combination—home-grown vegetables, and the flavours of Amma's cooking!

"Amma!" Before Nitya could move a step forward, Senthiru herself emerged out of the house.

"Welcome, Nitya! Keeping well? You little fellow!" Senthiru lifted up the child. "Oh my God! He's become a big boy, I say! In jeans and 'slack' shirt. Hm! Good, good! It's been two years since we saw him, isn't it? He's grown quite tall. Come on in. Why do you keep staring like that? I'm your *Patti*, little fellow! Look! He closely resembles our *mappillai*, doesn't he?"

"He does very much," remarked Chokkalingam.

"Come in, Nitya!"

Nitya followed her mother into the house. Amma, the same sweet, affectionate appearance. But then, isn't there a difference somewhere? In the old days, Amma would be absorbed in the chores at home, not caring to adjust her sari or even keep her hair neatly combed. Her face oily, sweat dripping down, she would buzz around smiling, offering to comb Nitya's hair or saying, "I thought you'd like *adai*, so I've soaked the dal." One felt like rushing to hug her. Today, the simple cotton sari Amma is wearing looks elegant. Her hair looks neatly combed. Above all, there is a new vital energy in her bearing. Doesn't it almost create an illusion that she has grown younger! The woman who greeted her grandson saying, "I'm your Patti, little fellow!" hardly looks like a grandmother.

"Here's your coffee." When her mother handed her the coffee, Nitya's flow of thoughts was interrupted. Surely the mother who handed her the coffee herself is the same old Amma.

Having taken a sip, Nitya indulgently said, "There is nothing to beat your coffee, Amma! Where does one get coffee like this in Bombay? But come on, Amma! Is there nothing to go with the coffee? There would always be some dish for breakfast. Don't we have anything today?"

"Why not?" said Senthiru. "Today we have *idli*. I have had breakfast. The batter is kept ready. Your father will show you the kitchen. Please go in and make breakfast. Serve him and yourself. If the little fellow takes idlis, give him some as well. The oil and the chilli powder to go with the idli are there on the mesh shelf. If you prefer coconut chutney, do make some. The broken coconut is there near the grindstone. I shall be out for a while."

Nitya couldn't comprehend. "Going out?" she asked mechanically.

"Yes, to the Association. I have to give tailoring lessons. I must hurry up. I'll tell you about it in detail when I return. So you'll take care of everything, won't you? I'm leaving," Senthiru called out to her husband and, stepping into her footwear, she briskly walked out of the house and soon vanished from sight.

"Appa, what's all this?" Nitya asked, her eyes wide open.

"Nothing, dear. Your mother Senthiru has now become herself. That's all," Chokkalingam answered casually.

"What does that mean?"

"In the past, she was just a mother to all of you, wasn't she? Now, she has found an identity for herself."

"What is this 'Association' that she is going to?"

"There are a number of women's associations in this village neighbourhood."

"You mean, like the 'Ladies Club' in the city? But even when we were in Madras, Amma always stayed at home; she never joined any Ladies Club, did she? Then why all this new practice here?"

Father smiled gently, looking at Nitya as if she were a strange object. He didn't make any comment.

"What does Amma do in this Association?"

"To begin with, she started helping in whatever way she could as a 'voluntary' worker. Teaching the village girls modern hygiene, helping to cook meals in children's homes, writing accounts for illiterate folks on special festival seasons, accompanying people to the Primary Health Centre in case of an emergency and so on... When she was doing such odd jobs, on one occasion, she had to help two girls in the tailoring class with 'cutting' when they were struggling with it."

"I didn't know Amma had that much skill in tailoring."

"So you see, even you had no idea. I wonder whether Senthiru herself was aware, while bringing up all of you, that she had some other special talents."

Nitya flushed, feeling that her father was blaming her and her siblings in some way, making fun of them. "All right, so she helped them learn 'cutting'. And then?"

"Obviously, the *Gramsevika* had seen that your mother had skills in that field, and she made a note of it. When one of the seamstresses of the Panchayat Union was suddenly taken ill and gave up her job, the Gramsevika spoke to the Union Commissioner about your mother. As a result, your mother has been working as a permanent tailoring teacher for the last five months."

Nitya was silent. So her mother coming out to the front of the house was not just out of eagerness to receive her daughter who had just arrived, was it? Was it more a part of the briskness of the tailoring teacher adding one more item to her agenda on her way out to work?

An inexplicable disappointment reared its head in Nitya's heart. She had come all the way from Bombay. Amma had just said "Come," and gone out immediately. Far from making idlis for her, letting her relax and chatter away, Amma had actually gone out instructing her to make breakfast for herself, and eat it! Wonderful!

"What, Nitya, you are stunned, are you? I'm hungry. Will you come and make the idlis, or shall I make them and serve you, too?" asked her father.

Around two in the afternoon, Senthiru returned home along with another woman.

"This is my daughter Nitya. She is married and lives in Bombay. Where's the child, Nitya? Sleeping? I brought this lady over to introduce both of you to her. She is the Gramsevika for this Block, Mrs Devamani Velayudam. When we moved in here, I was eager to grow a garden. I approached her when I was told by the neighbours that she'd be able to give proper advice. It was then that we came to know each other," Senthiru spoke animatedly.

The stranger must be upwards of fifty. More or less her mother's age. A peaceful and cheerful face. But even while greeting her, Nitya was watching only her mother. Truly, now Amma was the stranger!

"I'm very happy to meet you! What, Senthirumma! Is she your only daughter?"

"No, no. We have five children in all; two boys, three girls. She is the youngest. Please be seated. I shall fetch a glass of buttermilk for you. Nitya, did you and Appa have lunch?"

"We did. It was Appa who suggested that we eat, because you would be late in coming back," Nitya responded, not showing her anger at losing the privilege of being served food by her mother the very first day of her arrival.

As Senthiru went inside, Devamani spoke about her with great enthusiasm. "You must be very proud of your mother. How eagerly she toils for the Association as well as in her own life! After she joined, the standard of the tailoring class has indeed gone up. Besides, she also helps by participating in the adult literacy programme. She and I have become great friends."

Nitya remembered the old days. Amma would be at home. Nitya would bring her friends over and introduce them.

One of them would say, "Your daughter's composition was really first rate. Today the lecturer read it aloud in the class, Mrs Chokkalingam." Now, everything is topsy-turvy.

"Please, have this."

After drinking the buttermilk brought by Senthiru, the Gramsevika stayed for a while, asking Nitya about life in Bombay. When Senthiru finished her meal and joined them, she took leave of both of them.

"Come, Nitya. Come and sit by my side. There hasn't been time since morning to chat with you," Senthiru said.

"Chat, you said! I thought you had no time even to look at me!"

Laughing, Senthiru drew her daughter close to her. "Naughty girl! Did you think that I was home and yet didn't pay you any attention?"

"For that matter, why can't you remain at home? You have no affection for me, I dare say, Amma. You could have also come with Appa to Madras to pick me up."

"I very much wanted to. But I just couldn't manage. Nitya, there is hardly any break from the Association work. If we undertake any job, mustn't we discharge it well? But really, Nitya, how keen the members are to learn things! That's a reward in itself for all the labour. You know, there's a girl called Mangamma. Must be your age. How quickly she picked up embroidery, you'll be surprised to know!"

"Enough, Amma! Must you carry all this with you even after you come back home? I have come all this distance to see you, remember."

"That's why I say we shall now sit and talk at leisure. Tell me, how are you, Nitya? How is our son-in-law? Little Suresh is really sweet—have you put him in school?"

As her mother started enquiring about her and her family, Nitya felt quite pleased. And gradually, she, too, became cheerful. When Suresh woke up, Senthiru lifted up her grandson and petted him. Grandpa and grandma vied with each other for the grandson's affection. In the evening, when Nitya undid her hair, her mother combed and plaited it. Nitya's sense of contentment was full. Doesn't it all sound as sweet as the old days once again! This is the Amma I know. She rested her head on her mother's lap and indulged herself awhile in her affection. When Amma brought hot milk for Suresh, when she cooked dinner and served her and her father, Nitya nodded approvingly.

"Shall I serve you some more? Why are you nibbling at the food? Eat well. By the time you leave here, you must become plump beyond recognition, so much so that our mappillai should wonder, 'Who's this?'"

Nitya was swimming in joy, finding herself in the very heaven she had expected and hoped for when her mother warmly attended to her and fed her with food which carried her special touch and flavour.

After dinner was over, they spent some time chatting, and then Nitya went to bed saying she was tired. She couldn't fall asleep at once. She dimly heard her parents talking to each other in the outer verandah. They spoke about her for some time. She was pleased. Then father enquired about mother's work at the Women's Association today and other things in general. Mother enquired about the books he had brought from Madras, and about the subtle points in the volume of modern poetry he was reading currently. This exchange was quite irritating for Nitya. Finally, she felt somewhat pacified and fell asleep only after her mother had gently shaken her and handed her a glass of milk.

The next day when her mother made breakfast in the morning and served them all and then started preparing lunch, a young voice at the door called, "Senthiru Amma!"

Before her mother could answer the call, Nitya peeped out. A little girl, of about seven or eight, was standing there with a notebook in hand. "It's you, Vasuki. What is it?" so saying, Senthiru came out.

"Tonight all of us at home are going to the next village for a wedding. So, will you teach me the lesson right now?" asked the little girl somewhat shyly.

"I'm busy right now," Senthiru hesitated for a moment. But Chokkalingam said, "The child has come all the way. Don't send her back. Go and take the lesson." Senthiru washed her hands, wiped them with a towel, took out the *sruti* box and went to the verandah.

"Sit down Vasuki. We shall finish that Hamsadhvani *varnam* today. You've practised whatever has been taught so far, haven't you?"

"Oh yes, I have!"

"Come on then. Sing."

As Senthiru operated the sruti box, the little girl started singing, striking the *talam* with her hand.

"What's all this, Appa? Does Amma give music tuition, too?"

"Just for the pleasure of it. About ten children come over three times a week to learn. It's all free," her father explained, continuing with the cooking from where his wife had left off. Nitya stared at him for some time. Then suddenly she remarked, "I never thought Amma would change so much for the worse."

"Changed in what way?"

"Where is the need to teach music to strangers, leaving the husband to cook? Why all this unnecessary bother? Can't she be content looking after you and the house?"

"And the children she brought forth, you mean!" her father said, laughing. Nitya's face turned red. Even so, she couldn't say that she relished this new incarnation of her mother.

"Your mother has discharged her duties by all of you without any room for complaint. Having done that, what's wrong if she relates herself as an individual with those not belonging to her family and with the society at large?"

"Even so, it doesn't look nice that she should create an interest for herself while leaving you to do all the chores, does it? Do you mean to say, Appa, that *you* like it?"

Chokkalingam gently brought down the bronze rice pot, tied a piece of cloth around its mouth and slanted the pot slightly to drain out the water. He then looked up at her intently for a moment, and said in English, "I am a highly self-respecting man. I feel more proud when a fully developed, independent human entity, rather than my slave or my shadow, loves me."

Nitya stood there not knowing what to say by way of response.

Chokkalingam suddenly started laughing.

"Why are you laughing now?" she asked, annoyed.

"Our roles have reversed, haven't they? Thinking of that, I laughed. It is I who should say, my wife must be just a machine slogging for me; and you who should ask, why, isn't a woman a human being, too? But what has happened here is the opposite. How true it is when they say, women are the enemies of women! How funny!"

Nitya chided him, saying, "For you, everything is funny!" and moved away to the front of the house. Senthiru was teaching the last part of the varnam after writing it down in the girl's note book. How sweet her voice is! None of them even knew that she could sing! Amma knows tailoring, music and what not. Good Lord!

When the lesson was going on, Suresh was glued to the place, listening. Little rascal! How quickly he had developed an attachment to his grandma! Right from the morning, he had been chatting with her in broken Tamil.

When the lesson was over, Senthiru closed the sruti box, latched the hook, and put it away in a corner. Then she lifted Suresh up and seated him on her lap.

"Did you like the music, Suresh?"

"Oh I did!" he lisped.

Laughing, Senthiru pressed his face against hers. Then looking up, she said, "Do you know who this is, Vasuki? My grandson. Come from Bombay."

Eyeing Suresh jealously, the little girl said, "Even so, Senthiru Amma, you are *my* teacher, not his, aren't you?"

Patting the student affectionately on her cheek and sending her off, Senthiru came in with her grandson, and Nitya remarked, "Amma, you seem to have become quite a big shot in this place. What other jobs have you undertaken?"

"Nonsense. Nothing of that kind. Is it such a big thing to teach a couple of people a few things we know?"

"Have you formally learnt music, Amma?"

"I did, long back. These youngsters are not going to sit for an exam after all. They learn to sing just for the love of it. My music would do for that. I managed to get some music books and brushed up what I had learnt. I have bought the compositions of Thyagaraja and Sivan with notations. Those of Dikshitar alone are not yet available. Bharathi, Kavimani, Gopalakrishna Bharathi ... all of them are here."

"Why all this unnecessary trouble?"

"Trouble? Do you know how happy I feel when the children learn so eagerly? Take this Vasuki, for instance. Such a bright child! Because of her interest, she has finished the lesson in the morning itself since she won't be able to make it in the evening! She has an elder sister called Kamakshi studying nursing in Madras. Whenever she comes down for vacation, she, too, would be here for learning music! Then..."

"That's all right, Amma. Appa has finished the cooking. Will you be here at least today to serve?"

"But I can come only when the tailoring class is over, Nitya."

"Why don't you apply for leave till I'm here?"

"What an idea! Are you a small baby for me to be with you all the time? I attend to my work; I also find the time to chat with you."

"You don't love me at all, Amma."

Senthiru turned to Chokkalingam and said, "You finished all the cooking? Many thanks!" and she hurriedly left for the tailoring class. Later, after returning home, she gave herself to the family for some time. They all took a stroll along the green fields for a short while. In the evening some half-a-dozen little boys and girls landed in the house to learn music. When she finished the class and got up, it was past seven in the evening.

"I suppose there's no music tuition tomorrow, is there?" Nitya asked sarcastically.

"No."

"Thank heavens!"

The next day, at noon, Nitya suggested, "Will you soak dal for adai, Amma? We can have tiffin in the night."

"Oh, sure, I will. You're very fond of adai, aren't you?"

"It's long since I tasted it, Amma."

Senthiru set about preparing the ingredients for adai. In the evening, Nitya watched with great satisfaction as her mother cleaned up the grinding stone. Then her mother said, "Nitya, you get it ground. I'll be away for a brief while."

"Good God, Amma! When you said there was no music class, I thought you'll be free this evening. I asked you to make adai only because I thought you were going to be home."

"I've offered to help in the adult literacy programme, Nitya. Two evenings a week. Today is one such day. I'll be back soon. Shall I get going?"

When Senthiru set out, her hair neatly put up, wearing a bright, clean, simple home-starched sari, carrying some books in her hand, Nitya swelled with anger. Then, when she had to grind the batter for adai, she couldn't contain her tears. With what hopes she had come to her parents' place, to be petted and pampered! But how sad that she was toiling at the grindstone, while her mother went out without a care!

Nitya recalled the old days. When their parents were in Madras, neither she nor her elder sisters, nor, for that matter, her elder brothers would do any work whenever they came home. Amma would take all the responsibilities upon herself. She would never go out; they would all be out gallivanting, going to movies, shopping, leaving the children at home, asking her to look after them. Even when they returned at ten o'clock in the night, Amma would have set the plates and would serve the food hot. She would have fed the children and put them to sleep. As soon as they returned home and changed their clothes, she would fold the new saris and trousers neatly. Even if they came back after watching a late-night film, she would keep awake and let them in with a smiling face. After doing all this, Amma would ask, "What would you like to have for breakfast tomorrow?" and in the morning, she would individually prepare for each one of them what they liked and serve it to them. She would hand them their glasses of water and cups of coffee.

That is what a mother should be like! How come she is so completely transformed now?

At night, however, the sight of Senthiru feeding her grandson rice and milk and putting him to sleep was somewhat comforting for Nitya. Then Senthiru made Nitya and her father sit down while she made the adais, and served them on a plate with butter and jaggery. Nitya relished every bit of it.

"It's superb, Amma! Why don't you make me one more?"

Senthiru did so.

Then she made one for herself, brought it over on a plate, sat down and ate it at leisure.

"My stomach felt full and I thought one would be enough. Now I feel like having one more. I'm so tired, Nitya. Will you please make an adai and bring it for me?"

Nitya glared at her mother in anger—should she slog for her mother? How unjust! Most unwillingly she got up and made one more adai, and even as she was serving it on her mother's plate, she burst out in fury.

"Why won't you be tired? You asked for it! Keep to your home and your housekeeping, and you will have the energy.

Whoever asked you to take upon yourself all the affairs of the village? Which other women do so? Why for you alone this needless burden?"

Senthiru looked at Nitya for a fraction of a moment. Then turning towards her husband, she said, "I'm thinking of going as far as the next village along with Devamani Ammal tomorrow. I'm going to find out if I can pick up anything new there about the methods of teaching adults."

In ten days' time, Nitya got used to her mother's new routine. And as the days went by, she somehow came to accept it, although grudgingly. It was not as though her mother was not spending time with her chatting or, for that matter, indulging her. She cooked, served whenever possible; every Friday she applied oil to Nitya's hair and washed it. Whenever there was no other work, Senthiru looked after her grandson. During the time that Nitya stayed with them, on two Sundays her parents took her and their grandson out on excursions to Kanchipuram and Tambaram. Even so, during the nights, lying next to Nitya and listening to the account of her life in Bombay with great interest, her mother would suddenly make a remark like, "You know, that Mangamma's embroidered tablecloth sold for twenty-five rupees. You know how beautifully she had done it!" And Nitya would be put off by a feeling that her mother's world now included a whole new dimension within itself. For a moment she would find her mother a complete stranger, and be puzzled.

A few days after her arrival, because of something that her mother said, Nitya's puzzlement became worse.

There was a letter for her mother from Nitya's elder sister at Mangalore. She had written that she was saddled with a very young child and an infant baby, and was finding it difficult to manage both. Hence it would be a great help if Amma would go over and stay with her for about six months until the baby grew up a little.

After reading that letter, Senthiru laughed. "Why do you laugh, Amma? Poor *Akka*! How moving to read her letter! I'm sure you'll go to help her, won't you?" asked Nitya.

"She might as well employ a nanny to help her. I'm not required to be there for that."

"Amma, how could you speak so heartlessly?"

"Look Nitya! To this house, all are welcome, be it my daughter, son, daughter-in-law, son-in-law or grandchildren. It is indeed their house. I'm ready to welcome them at all times. I shall help as much as I can, do all that I can. Suppose some great calamity befalls any of them, I'm even prepared to drop everything and rush to their side. But, for petty difficulties, to imagine that mother alone is obliged to toil, that is not acceptable to me.

"Don't I have my house to maintain? Am I an errand boy to be at everyone's beck and call? Now your sister wants me there, only to be an *ayah*. Do you mean to say that she doesn't have the means to employ a maid? Does her mother strike her as someone who is just there anyhow, and whose services must therefore be used?"

Nitya was stunned. For a couple of days she walked about the house not talking much, keeping her head down. Observing this, Senthiru put her arm tenderly around Nitya one day, thinking that the girl must be feeling ashamed for having spoken without understanding her mother. "Don't feel bad, dear! Will I ever mistake you?"

Nitya eagerly lifted her head. "So Amma, you didn't really mean what you said, did you? You are going to Mangalore to help Akka, aren't you?"

Overwhelmed by surprise, Senthiru stared at her. That night, she bitterly said to her husband, "It seems children will always think of their mother as being devoted only to them, slaving only for them, and they wouldn't like to see that mother in any other light."

"Why children alone, Senthiru? How many adults can see someone as an individual without relating them to oneself? Just leave it at that. That is all they know. Don't let this matter hurt you any further. Go and sleep." So saying, Chokkalingam patted her on the back comfortingly.

At the end of a month's stay, Nitya left the village. This time, the visit to the parents' home had been a mixed experience. Appa was his old normal self. It was Amma who had changed. Wasn't she affectionate as before? She was—there wasn't an iota of doubt about the affection.

Even now, when Nitya was leaving, how many of her favourite sweetmeats Amma had prepared and stacked in a basket! "So the day of your departure has finally come, has it?" Amma said in a rather choked voice, stroking her head lovingly. But despite all this, somewhere in a corner of her heart, there was a touch of discontent in Nitya.

Amma accompanied Appa to put her on the train at Madras. She carried her grandson right until the train was about to leave. She got biscuits for him. "Take care of yourself, Nitya! Drop a line as soon as you reach home," she urged. "The house will be empty without you and the child," she repeatedly lamented. Nitya leaned back against the seat, feeling somewhat pleased.

When the whistle blew for the train to depart, Amma handed her grandson to her daughter quite reluctantly and said, "Be careful Nitya. Don't sit by the window. Be watchful when you go to the toilet. Have an eye on the child." She gave several such pieces of advice. The train started moving.

"See you, Amma. See you, Appa. Suresh, say 'Ta-ta' to Thatha and Patti," said Nitya.

Suddenly, she saw her mother running alongside the moving train. Why is Amma chasing the train? What does she want to say?

"Nitya! Nitya!... I forgot to tell you something!"

"What is it, Amma?"

What else could it be: don't forget to take the milk from the flask at night, that's what it must be, Nitya smiled to herself smugly.

"You'll have lots of women's magazines available in Bombay. If you find any new embroidery design in them, do cut it out and send it to me...!" Senthiru called out breathlessly as she ran.

Originally published in Tamil as '*Senthiru aahivittaal*' [Senthiru has become herself], in the magazine *Kalaimagal*, February 1978.

10

Not a stepfather

When she returned home with her husband after their honeymoon, Madhu, who was waiting at the entrance, rushed out calling "*Amma*!" and hugged her.

"Madhu, my *raja*! How are you, *kånna*?" Greeting him, she gathered the child into her arms and pressing him close, was lost in ecstasy for a while.

"Don't speak! Why did you leave me for sooo many days?" The voice came out muffled from the face buried in the mother's neck.

"I won't hereafter, kanna. Hereafter, Amma will not go anywhere leaving Madhu."

"Promise?"

"Promise!"

"Amma... Amma..." Madhu was uttering that word again and again as if he were tasting all kinds of riches. Anjugam patted him on his head and back to her heart's content. Then she lifted up his face and caressed it; running her fingers through his hair she kissed him on the forehead. Then she hugged him again. Tears welled up in her eyes.

"Madhu... my Madhukkanna..." Somehow controlling the rush of emotions, she softly asked him, "Did you go to school every day?"

"Oh, I did!"

"Did you go without crying?"

"Not a day did I cry."

"That's my good boy! I hope you didn't give trouble to *Patti*."

"Never."

"Very very good boy, Madhukkanna! Do you know what I have got for you?"

"What is it Amma?" His eyes widened. "Is it a ball? An aeroplane?"

"No..."

"Cowboy 'dess'?"

"No..."

"What is it then?"

She was silent.

"What else, Amma? Why don't you tell me?" The little hands shook her shoulders.

"An ... *Appa*."

Madhu blinked, unable to comprehend. Anjugam turned her head and looked behind her. As if waiting for that signal, Senthil stepped forward.

"Don't you see, Madhu?"

"Who is this?"

"Your Appa."

"Umhhum. No, he isn't."

"Yes, I'm your Appa," said Senthil smiling.

Confusion spread over the child's face. "My Appa has gone to *Swami*. Patti has told me."

"That's the old father. I am the new father."

"Hm?"

"Do you know what Appa has brought you? All that you had asked for."

"Ball?"

"Ball, aeroplane..."

"You are not my Appa."

Madhu stuck close to his mother. Anjugam looked at Senthil once and went inside the house with the child.

"Amma, I'm back, Amma! How are you?"

"What will befall me? I am quite well. Isn't it fated that I should continue to live solid like rock after bearing witness to all disgusting things and putting up with them?" replied Thangammal. Senthil, who was about to follow his wife into the house, abruptly halted at the entrance itself.

Anjugam glared at her mother in anger. "So this is the courtesy you show those who come home? If you entertained so much hatred, you could have replied asking us not to come when I wrote you a letter saying that we would arrive today, have a wash, eat and then leave. Why didn't you do that?"

"How could I say no? Whether I like it or not, you were born in my womb, weren't you?"

"Much you care for my happiness, your daughter born of your womb!"

"Anju!" Senthil's voice sounded from outside. Anjugam went out.

"Anju, why do you talk like this, losing your patience? She is your mother. However angry she may be, she is one who bears concern and affection for you. If you can't endure her words, how are you going to face and put up with the society at large?"

Anjugam came inside. "Amma, please forgive me for talking back. We shall leave right away and take Madhu with us."

"What? Take Madhu with you, did you say? What nonsense are you talking?"

"What is nonsensical about it?"

"Imagine Madhu staying with you!"

"A child must stay with its mother, where else?"

"That man..."

"Hereafter, he is Madhu's father."

"As far as I am concerned, it is not so."

"That's your will and pleasure. As far as we are concerned, it is so. Madhu will only live with us. All these things we already decided."

"Is it at all practically possible?"

"Don't the first wife's children live with the second wife?"

"How could you compare the two things? Anju, I cannot send the child. He should not grow up in your shade."

"Madhu dear, come, let us pack your things."

"What? What? All right, all right. Now have the coffee. We shall talk about it later."

"No, Amma, we are leaving."

"I am asking both of you to have coffee, believe me! As you wrote, you can have a bath, eat and then leave. But, where are you going, if I may ask you?"

"To a hotel. We will stay at the hotel while we look around for a house, and then move in."

"So his people, too, I suppose, refused to admit you into their family?"

"What is so surprising about it when my own people take such an attitude?"

"Should you have at all entered into such a marriage, antagonising the families on both sides?"

"You said you'd get us coffee?"

"You answer the question I asked. You call this a marriage? It is nothing but utter selfishness. You didn't have any consideration for the child, did you?"

"Haven't we debated all this a thousand times already, and settled it?"

"No, we haven't! It is not a matter that can be settled either."

"Then why speak about it at all? That, too, after the wedding is over?"

"I'm not able to face anyone outside. Everyone keeps asking me, 'What a shame, Amma! How could your daughter do such a thing?'"

"What did your daughter do? Commit a murder or a robbery?"

"*Pavi! Pavi!*"

"Madhu dear, come! Appa, Amma and Madhu will go to a hotel and have coffee there."

"Wait, *di*! I'll bring over the coffee! So quick to take offence you are, as always!"

"Are you going to keep your *mappillai* standing at the threshold and serve him the coffee there?"

"My mappillai is there, hanging on the wall as a photograph."

"No, he is standing at the entrance."

"All right, all right! Bring him in here and ask him to be seated."

Senthil entered the room, but before he could complete saying "*Vanakkam*," Thangammal had turned her face away and started to go inside. Anjugam's face hardened. Senthil said to her with a conciliatory smile, "Take it easy."

"Senthil, please remain seated here. I shall go inside and be back soon."

"Don't fight with Amma."

"As though I have nothing else to do!"

After she left, Senthil surveyed the room. Where was Madhu? When did he slip out? In a corner of the room, on the wall, there hung a framed bust-sized photograph of a young man about thirty years old. Senthil went and stood in front of it, keeping his hands clasped behind his back.

It looked like a picture that had been taken out of a group photograph and enlarged. A bright countenance, a radiant smile lighting up the entire face. What kind of dreams were bubbling up from the depths of that smile? Youth, wife, child, life just beginning. Was the curtain brought down abruptly at that point? As if the book-binder had by mistake placed 'The End' at the beginning of the book itself? How did all those life impulses pressing inside, all those wants steaming within, all those longings allow him to die?

Don't worry, I will fulfil all of them. That would be doing justice to you, and to her, too.

"Coffee."

Senthil turned to look. Thangammal, having placed the tumbler on the table, was going back inside. Did she bring her grandson along only to announce to him that the coffee had arrived?

The child, looking up at him for a moment, was about to follow his grandma inside.

"Madhu, why don't you stay for a while?"

Fright in the young eyes.

"I won't harm you. I just have to ask you something. Why don't you come here?"

The fright hadn't gone yet. Madhu shook his head in a no, keeping himself to a corner.

"You don't even have to come near me. You can stay where you are."

Uncertainty for a few seconds. Then Madhu lingered hesitantly. "What?"

"You like looking at this picture, don't you?"

"Oh, very much!" came the prompt and enthusiastic reply.

"I like it, too."

Madhu did not respond.

"Shall we both look at it together?"

Again the shake of the head in a no.

"You don't like looking at this picture, do you? All right. You go. I shall look at it alone."

He turned his back to the child and stood there looking at the photograph. After a while, he looked to his side through the corner of his eye—there was no one there. He looked again. When he looked the third time, Madhu was there. Looking at the picture, now and then glancing at Senthil suspiciously; there was jealousy in the child's eye.

"Why do you look at this picture?" asked Madhu.

"Because I like it."

"You needn't look at it." Madhu was silent for a moment. "Do you know who this is? My Appa."

"Yes, like me."

"You are not my Appa."

"I am your Appa. New Appa. There in this picture is your old father. I am your new father."

"No, not at all. You are just an uncle."

"Did you take a look at the things I brought for you?"

"Ball? Didn't you say ball?"

"Yes. And an aeroplane, just as you wanted. And a book with pictures of all the zoo animals."

Madhu's eyes filled with curiosity. But he checked himself.

"You haven't really brought all these things. You are just bluffing."

"Of course I have. I will show them to you. Won't you come?"

"I don't want any of those things."

"All right. If you don't want them, be it so. I shall give them all to another Madhu who is here."

"There is no other Madhu here, is there? I am the only one."

"No, no, there is another Madhu who eagerly says he wants all the things I have got for him. I am not talking about you. You of course don't want any of them."

Senthil went out to the verandah and brought in a leather suitcase. He opened it and took out a multicoloured ball, a train which would run on a track to be assembled, an aluminium aeroplane, a teeny-weeny tractor, a crane, a big book with thick wrappers, and spread all these on the floor. Without turning towards Madhu, he said aloud, as if to himself, "I also brought a cricket set for the good boy Madhu, didn't I? Now where is it? Have I kept it in another suitcase or what?"

Madhu walked up gingerly to stand a little closer and looked at those objects. Each one of them caught his eyes. On the front cover of the book was an elephant lifting up its trunk beautifully. Aeroplane, ball ... he had seen this kind of toy train in his LKG class friend Suresh's house. His hands were itching to make it run. What were those other two beautiful things? A road engine? What was the other? If he asked this uncle, would he tell him? And there seemed to be a cricket set, too. All ... *all* of these things for him?

"Who ... who are all these things for?"

"I told you, didn't I? For that other Madhu."

"Who is this other Madhu?"

"Ask your Amma. It was she who told me there is a very good boy here called Madhu, and that he will take the toys I have so lovingly brought him."

"But there is only one Madhu here, and that is me."

Senthil didn't say anything. Madhu, too, was silent for some time. Then he looked at Senthil from the corner of his eye. Can I trust this uncle? For a split second his eyes darted towards the inner quarters. He could see Patti hiding behind the door. Not too far. If this uncle behaves badly, I can quickly run to Patti.

"There is no other Madhu here."

A brief silence.

Then, "All these things are ... for me, aren't they?"

"So you are that good boy Madhu!"

"Hm."

"Then they are all for you."

"Promise?"

"Promise."

Madhu slowly came forward and touched all the toys one by one.

A little later when Anjugam came out after a bath, she stood stock still. On the table the coffee brought for Senthil remained unconsumed, lukewarm with a film of cream on top. The multicoloured ball was lying in a corner. Madhu must have kicked it there after playing with it. Madhu and Senthil were sitting on the floor, completely absorbed in assembling the pieces of the railway track. Nearby were the crane, the aeroplane and the tractor; and the book lay open with the picture of a lion on one page and two rabbits on the opposite page.

The railway track, now fully assembled, formed a huge circle. Senthil showed Madhu how to wind up the train and set it down on the track. The train started running round and round on the track. Madhu clapped his hands in joy. "The train is running! My train!" His eyes, too, ran around with the train. Senthil kept watching him with a smile. Anjugam silently withdrew from that scene.

Madhu was absorbed in the running train for some time. Then he flew the aeroplane. Then he kicked the ball from corner to corner. He looked at all the pictures in the book, open-mouthed. He had forgotten the whole world while playing. Suddenly, remembering what his teacher had taught him, he turned to Senthil and said, "Thank you, uncle" in the accents of a grown up.

Senthil gently corrected him, "'Thank you, Appa'."

"Umhhum, you are not my Appa."

"Of course I am."

There was confusion spreading on the child's face. Looking up at Senthil once, he walked towards the corner wall and, looking up at the photograph, said, "*This* is my Appa. My Appa has gone to Swami. Patti has told me."

"True..." said Senthil and went and stood behind him. "Your old Appa has indeed gone to Swami. That is why he cannot come back, can he? And won't it be difficult for Madhu without his Appa? Therefore, he has sent me to you to be your new Appa."

"Is it my Appa who has sent you?"

"Yes."

"Are you my new Appa?"

"Yes."

"Promise?"

"Promise."

Madhu stood there uncertainly, looking up at him, his face betraying an expression which was a mixture of joy and confusion. For the first time, Senthil touched the child and gently caressed his hair, saying, "Why else would I have brought all these toys for you so lovingly, my dear Madhukanna?"

Joy bubbled over the child's face. Then immediately protesting, now rather weakly, and drawing his head back, he said, "Umhhum, nothing of the kind. You are not my Appa, go."

"*De* Madhu, you mustn't talk like that. From now on, he is your Appa." Hearing the voice, both of them turned. Anjugam had returned. But it was not she who had spoken. It was her mother who was standing behind with tears welling up in her eyes.

Originally published in Tamil as '*Irandavadu appa*'
[Second father], in the magazine *Muhangal*,
15 April 1980.

11

Fear and trembling

If they were to describe their affection for that child they would have to create a new language.

"*Periamma*!" It was sheer joy to hear Gopi's voice. Joy to get him the things he needed. Joy to cook for him, to feed him, get him ready and send him to school, to wait eagerly and receive him when he returned, give him his tiffin and Bournvita, fondly stroke his hair while listening to all the news about school with their gaze fixed on him, to take him out somewhere, help him with his homework, to put him to sleep at night and lovingly watch the sleeping boy—everything was sheer joy, not only for Nilamani but for Vasanti, too.

Except for the evenings and nights, Vasanti wouldn't have the time for this service. She was a working woman. But even there, it was thoughts about Gopi which permeated her inner being and illumined her work, her responsibilities and skills. How much this little fellow had managed to score in his last test in science! So intelligent! So like Radha in brains! Didn't he say his sandals had become worn out? Should take him to Bata this evening itself.

And he had said that when he grew big, he would either be an aeronaut or a marine engineer. *Adeyappa*! How many dreams in that little head of his!

"*Akka*! We will fulfill whatever it is that he may desire," Vasanti would say. Nilamani would vigorously nod her endorsement. There was no question of any of Gopi's desires going unfulfilled so long as they were alive.

These two childless widows had reconciled themselves to a meaningless life and were spending their days mechanically when, all of a sudden, they got Gopi as a ray of light in the void and, since that moment, his happiness became the goal of their life. They had found a purpose in keeping themselves alive.

Even today their hearts would thud when they recalled how they had come by this fortune. Their younger sister Radha, heartbroken on account of her husband's extremely suspicious nature and cruel words, had committed suicide. When Radha's husband forsook the six-month-old child, saying, "That *saniyané* is not my child, throw it out!" the baby had found refuge in their affectionate fold. Their ardent wishes and blessings that their younger sister should enjoy everything that they themselves had lost in life—all were burnt out in that disappointment and agony. Tearfully, they had gathered the baby and held it close. But very soon, the child became an antidote for their sorrow.

When he would come running, calling out "Periamma!" whoever it was that came out responding, "Yes, my dear *kanna*," be it Nilamani or Vasanti, there was absolutely no difference in the affection expressed. The word "Periamma," connoting tenderness, concern and soothing comfort, was common property, going beyond the physical difference of the two faces. If his own mother were alive, he would have received the affection of one woman. Losing her, Gopi received the love of two mothers.

"Periamma, today the P. T. master thoroughly broke our backs! Periamma, today a new boy from Hyderabad joined our class. The school took a donation of five thousand rupees!"

Then one day,

"Periamma, today my *Appa* had come to school."

The faces on both sides of the boy were shocked.

"Wh...What, Gopi? What did you say?"

"Appa was there to look me up. My Appa."

They looked at him intently. On his face was a new excitement. Appa, he said?

That rogue had deserted the little child long ago, hadn't he? Where did a father spring from all of a sudden now, in the ninth year of the son, after the two of them had told him that his mother was dead and his father had gone missing, and they themselves had been the two parents to him, creating a new fullness of life for him so that he wouldn't feel the lack?

It was Vasanti who first managed to recover from the torrent of thoughts that burst forth.

"What are you saying, kanna? Who was it that had come? What happened...?"

"Today, during the last hour when the class was going on, the Headmaster came to my classroom. Someone who called himself my Appa had come to see me, he said. He took me to his room. There was a stranger sitting there. When he saw me, he got up and came to me. Periamma, he was tall and handsome and looked like Amitabh Bachchan! Smiling, he stroked my hair. 'So you are Gopi, kanna? I am your Appa, Somasundaram,' he said. 'But my Appa has gone missing, hasn't he?' I said. 'But you see—I am found now!' he said, patting my shoulders, 'You look grand!'"

The boy was surely under the spell of some extraordinary experience. There was a new thrill in those fluttering eyes, in the smile.

"He held out a pack of eclairs and said, 'Take it, Gopi, it is for you.' But the Headmaster intervened and said, 'No, not here in the school.'"

Oh, he did a good thing. That *pavi* is quite capable of even mixing chocolate with poison.

"Appa said to me, 'I have come after making enquiries about your address, your school, and many more things about you. Tell your Periammas that I will drop in at home one day. I would like to speak to them'. Before leaving, Appa hugged me and patted me."

"What is all this Appa, Appa, Appa! What do you know of Appa? After so many years some wastrel comes to the school and visits you, and you are jumping up and down saying Appa! He could even be a kidnapper, for all I know. Hereafter if any stranger comes like this and says he wants to see you, say no...!" Nilamani was shouting hysterically.

Vasanti pressed her hand and said, "Akka, control yourself a little, please, not before the child..."

"Yes, child—*our* child! That's what everyone should know..." Nilamani drew the child to her with passionate rage and held him tight. Somewhat frightened by the fury and the grip, Gopi slowly freed himself and, with his eyes downcast, said, "Is tiffin ready, Periamma? I have assignments to write after eating."

It was Vasanti who took him away and gave him the tiffin. Then, after setting him up for the lessons, she joined her sister. All this while, Nilamani had not stirred. She was just sitting there, staring at the floor. There was shock and consternation in Vasanti's heart, too. Even as she moistened her lips and tried to speak steadily, the tremulous voice betrayed what was inside.

"Don't worry, Akka..."

"What right does he have? Where did he surface from? Are you sure it is him? Or was it some imposter? Where was he all this while? Why has he come back now? Why should he go to the school to look up Gopi? Why should he send word saying he will visit us here? What has he got to do with us?"

"Akka, Akka!"

"Vasanti..." Nilamani looked up with panic-stricken eyes. "Here ... to talk to us ... why does he want to come here?"

"Just to enquire about his son's progress perhaps,.." Vasanti said, trying hard to believe her own words. "Perhaps, he's ashamed of his earlier behaviour; that's why he wants to see Gopi and us..."

"Perhaps..."

That night after the child settled down in bed, the two of them sat on either side. Looking at him lying there with closed eyes, a ball of fire rose from the pit of the stomach and seized the life-spirit. Overwhelmed by surging emotions, Nilamani bit her lower lip and quickly rose and left that place.

After a brief while, Gopi opened his eyes sleepily and looked up. Seeing that only Vasanti was there, he softly called, "Periamma!"

"Yes, kanna?" Vasanti patted his forehead and gently ploughed his hair.

"How does Appa know that I like eclairs?"

For a moment Vasanti was taken aback. She was struck by the eagerness in his voice, and felt a sudden fright.

The sisters spent the whole of the next day in sheer terror. In the morning when the school bus arrived to pick up the child, they walked on either side of him up to the bus as if they didn't want to let him out of their sight. They stood looking at him when he boarded the bus and as the bus turned the street corner and disappeared from sight. When Vasanti returned from work in the evening, the faltering steps her sandals took betrayed fear: would there be some news? After sending Gopi to school, Nilamani kept looking anxiously at the entrance till evening. Would Gopi return home? Or would some news arrive, saying, "Somebody has kidnapped him"? And when Gopi jumped down from the school bus, she hugged him with a yearning as never before. She patted his face. She stroked his hair.

"What is it, Periamma?"

"Today ... I hope no one came to school today to see you."

Gopi lowered his head and said, "No..."

Appada! She took him inside, keeping an arm around him. When Vasanti returned home, she occupied the other side of the boy. A guard on either side, at the centre a treasure.

They bolted the entrance door. Still, the eyes and ears were again turned in that direction. Did they hear the sound of a taxi, or an auto, coming and halting outside the house? Was there someone knocking at the door? Was there some male voice calling out "Gopi"?

They helped the boy with the homework, served him dinner and put him to bed. They felt some relief only after eleven in the night. No one would come after that hour, would they?

Restless for long, they went to sleep only after two o'clock, and got up around five in the morning. Again the ears and eyes circled only around the entrance.

After Vasanti left for office and Gopi for school, Nilamani was standing at the entrance, when the postman delivered an envelope to her. An envelope addressed to her name.

Nilamani felt a sudden shudder in her heart. Her hands shook. She stared at the letter. Who was it from? Normally there were hardly any letters either for her or for Vasanti. There were very few people known to them.

Coming into the room, she sat for a long time looking at the envelope without opening it. Then with trembling fingers she tore it open and pulled the letter out.

Although the envelope bore only her name, Somasundaram had addressed the letter to both her and Vasanti. He now deeply regretted the way he had behaved towards Radha, and for washing his hands off the child, and was asking for their forgiveness. The experiences of the last eight years and more had brought him maturity and taught him true values. He had become a new man now. He had come to realise how much he loved his son. He had come to Chennai on transfer. He wanted to keep Gopi with himself hereafter and bring him up as an act of expiation of the wrong he had done him. He had married again, and had a three-year-old son. His second wife was a good woman; she, too, very much wished that Gopi should be with them. It was his duty now to give Gopi a proper home and family with father, mother and a younger brother.

"The two of you have brought him up, and I will never forget all the good you have done. I will forever be grateful to you. You have discharged, in fact, what was my duty. From here on, I release you from that responsibility. I am even ready to compensate to some extent the expenses you have incurred all this time in taking care of him. Very soon, when I come to meet you and talk it over, we shall decide on it after due consideration. I do hope you will not refuse to hand over Gopi to me. After all, he is my son..."

"But you cast him away, saying he wasn't your son, and left! Now all of a sudden where has this new relationship surfaced from?" shrieked Nilamani, forgetting that she was alone.

Throughout the day, the dazed state of mind did not clear. There was no thought of eating. She wasn't even conscious of the body. What should they do now? They could not part with the child. There was no question of sending the child with that man. And what right had he to demand so...? Should they run away somewhere out of this town, taking Gopi with them?

She sat down, got up, wept, stared at the closed door at the entrance, paced the room up and down, sat down, got up, banged on the table raising her hand and bringing it down again and again. She sat down, covered her face and cried. In the evening as soon as Gopi came home, she hugged him and wept silently, her body racked by sobs.

"What's all this, Periamma? Let go of me. Periamma, please, why don't you let go?"

When Vasanti came home from office and stepped inside with trepidation, Nilamani ran up to her, thoroughly shaken.

"Vasanti, Vasanti, just read this letter! Thunderbolt has struck, *di*!" She slumped down into the chair, drained of all energy.

Vasanti slowly took the letter from her and read it. Her face turned pale. For a while she stood stock-still, unable to move. Then she stumbled to a chair and sat down, the letter burning the hand. She stared at the floor and, without raising her eyes, reached out a hand and held her sister's. At that touch, Nilamani's sobs gushed out. Then, gradually containing them, when she looked up, Vasanti, too, turned towards her. Their eyes met, dazed and terror-stricken. They remained so, like two orphan girls sitting and holding hands, looking at each other.

Nilamani burst out in anger, "He is thanking us it seems, and will compensate us with money. *Chhi*! How else will that brain of his think? What right has he to snatch away the child from us?"

"He is his son, Akka," Vasanti said in a dead voice.

"How is that possible? How, I ask? Gopi is our child. We brought him up. We are the ones who have lavished affection on him, holding him dearer than life. The fellow who said without any compunction that the six-month-old baby wasn't his child and who went away—why should he come now and claim a right?"

Vasanti did not speak. She was struggling with something that seemed to be choking her throat.

"No, impossible, impossible," Nilamani shook her head vigorously. "We can't hand over Gopi to him at all. He is ours..."

"Periamma, my uniforms needs pressing," Gopi said, coming out of the room inside.

"Gopi, my dear, come here kanna," Vasanti's voice called weakly. He came.

"Your Appa ... your Appa has written a letter, Gopi. He wishes to take you with him. You ... how do you feel about it?"

Even before her last words were spoken, Gopi's eyes suddenly widened and flashed with enthusiasm. Nilamani, who was intently watching his face, her eyes and lips quivering, shrank back for a moment as if she had been dealt a blow. Then she got up like one possessed and shook him by the shoulders, saying, "Surely you won't agree to it, will you? Surely you won't go away with your father, leaving us alone, will you?"

"What's all this, Periamma? Take your hands off my shoulders; it hurts." The boy extricated himself from her and hurried away from there.

Nilamani kept staring after him. She turned to look at her sister, wide-eyed. "Do you see the injustice, Vasanti? We thought he was our whole world. But does he have even an iota of love for us? The moment we said his father was calling him..."

"Don't blame the child, Akka. Why do you take it that he has no love for us? Who knows what he yearns for in his heart of hearts? His classmates might have perhaps teased him, asking, 'Where's your father?' He has never said anything to us, no doubt, but who knows what goes on in his mind? If that is so, whatever is happening right now might be, as far as he is concerned ... good for him, might it not?"

Nilamani shrank into the chair. She covered her face with her hands. Vasanti was bent low over the letter. Every now and then a huge sigh escaped her, leaving her all atremble. As she kept holding the paper in her sweaty palm, the characters on it got disfigured and seemed to turn into blue puddles.

They heard a knock at the door. Startled, both of them lifted their heads. Eyes widening in fright, they looked at each other. Vasanti got up slowly. Her legs had gone limp. Stumbling, she went to the door. She hesitated for a moment. The heart fluttered; the hand trembled, unable to grip. Somehow she managed to release the bolt and open the door. Outside, there was a man standing.

"I've brought the gas cylinder, Amma. You are the one who had booked it, aren't you? The address wasn't very clear."

It took Vasanti some time to find her voice and say, "No, not this house."

Bolting the door again, breathing heavily, she went inside looking for Gopi. Both the sisters felt somewhat relieved. Of course, the relief would only be a temporary one ... until there was another knock at the door.

Originally published in Tamil as '*Kadavaiyarotattumpodu*' [When someone knocks at the door], in the magazine *Kalki*, Deepavali Special Issue, October 1984.

12

Adamancy, thy name is Amma!

He didn't think that *Amma* would so stubbornly set out to leave. When one day last month, Devanai said to him, "Arun, I'm thinking of moving to a working women's hostel," he didn't take it seriously. "Don't tease me, Ma! As if you would ever leave me and go!" he laughed cooingly. Then he completely forgot about it.

Now he understood that Amma was not teasing him. She was seriously engaged in making the arrangements. She had approached a friend at the Social Welfare Board for help, it seemed. All the payments had been made. She was going to leave on the first day of the next month. Just twelve days more.

But why? Why?

There had always been a cordial relationship between him and Amma. She was married at the age of eighteen. He was born when she was twenty. She lost her husband to brain fever when she was twenty-six. It was a great achievement for a mother to bring up an only, fatherless son without spoiling him!

His mother accomplished that. While she poured all her love on him, she saw to it that his individuality was not affected. They were not only mother and son but very good friends, too, he firmly believed. Why then was she insisting on leaving? How could she bring herself to leave him?

"Why should you leave, Ma? What has happened to you all of a sudden?"

Devanai laughed. "Nothing has happened, *da*! What's all this? Why are you so worked up over this?"

There was always something especially beautiful about Amma's laughter. Her smile, revealing the neat and bright array of teeth, would spread all over the face, except perhaps the eyes.

"Do you think this is an ordinary matter? I can't go on without you, Amma!"

"You are talking like a child, Arun. You are a grown-up person, holding a job. And now you are married, too. You have a companion!"

"Does that mean that hereafter I don't need the mother? Had I known that you would act this way, I would never have agreed to marry at all!"

"What a fool you are! Don't say such things. Do you know how I brimmed with joy to see you with a wedding garland around your neck? Not even when I brought you up after your father breathed his last, and educated you and saw you as an engineer; it was only when I finally saw you in the wedding paraphernalia and becoming a householder, it was only then that my responsibility and duty ended. I felt as though my heart was full because someone who would light the lamp in this house had arrived."

"You mean to say, don't you, that you will wash me off your hands and hand me over to another person and become carefree? All right, all right. You don't love me at all."

"Ridiculous! You are whining like a baby," Amma said, stroking his head. Could there be any bliss like that? He caught hold of her hand.

"Arun, do I have to tell you that I love you?"

"Then why do you want to leave me?"

"You see, our house is rather small. This new flat is good enough only for two people to run a family. Look at this ... If I enter the kitchen, Malli has to come out; if she goes in, I have to be out."

"Come on, Ma! Don't try to offer lame excuses ... Aren't there countless small houses where a whole battalion of people—mother-in-law, father-in-law, son, daughter-in-law, brother-in-law, sister-in-law—live?" Seeing his wife emerge from their bedroom after adjusting the shape of her *bindi*, he got up and, putting an arm around her shoulders, added, "What do you say, Malli? Am I not right?"

"For shame! Can't you be quiet?" said Mallika, squirming in embarrassment.

"Why should I feel ashamed in front of my mother of all people?"

"Wonderful!" said Mallika extricating herself, and went and sat next to Devanai on the sofa.

"*Atthai*! Do you wish me to be branded the daughter-in-law who, as soon as she arrived in the family, drove out the mother-in-law?"

Devanai stroked her hair. "Who will say so, Malli? I'm also going to be in the same Madras. We are going to meet each other every now and then. There won't be room for anyone to say anything, my dear! Don't worry."

Amma was resolute.

It was just three months since Arun had got married, and the sheen of a newly-wedded groom had still not worn off. The honeymoon visit to Bangalore, for which he took leave of absence from his office, lasted only ten days; but even after returning, the honeymoon continued as far as he was concerned. Mallika would be taking out a bedsheet from the bureau in their bedroom; and that was the time he also had to brush his hair in that room! She would be in the kitchen making coffee; that is when he also had to go in there and ask, "Where have you kept the 'mixture' we bought yesterday at Annapoorna?" When having a bath he had to keep calling out to her, "Malli, where's the soap?"; "Malli, bring me the towel!"; 'Malli, not this shirt, bring my blue shirt!"

Even in the front hall, and in the presence of others, when there were occasions that he might have something to say to her, he would go near her, touch her on the shoulder or the head and start speaking to her, saying, "Look, Malli!" Only then was he satisfied.

But then, even though he had so much love for his wife, his bonding with his mother had not lessened in the least, had it? Didn't Amma know it? Wasn't it true that Amma and he were friends, and would that truth alter now that he was married? How could he exist without Amma?

That night when he retired to their bedroom with Mallika, his mind was still on Amma ... On the other side of the wall was Amma's room. He could sense her moving about in her room. Her movements were always soft and gentle. However, through the thin partition wall even very light sounds could be heard from one room to the other. He could hear the sounds of Amma shaking the pillow free of dust and placing it on the bed. He heard her switching off the light. She switched off the light and lay down. Then again the sound of a switch. The rustle of the pages of a book being turned. Good god! Had she started reading now, switching on the table light as she lay down?

"Amma? Are you still awake and reading? Switch off the light and go to sleep. If you keep awake like this, won't it be bad for your health? On top of it you get up so early in the morning...!" Arun called out to her from their room.

"Don't worry about me, *appa...*" came the reply from the other room.

"If I don't worry about you, who will? Perhaps you are indifferent to what I feel and are busy packing..."

No reply.

"Hum! Too adamant a woman! If you fall ill staying alone, it is only this son of yours who must rush to your help, isn't it? Will you say no even then?"

No reply. Arun moved his eyes away in fury. Mallika was dusting and laying the bed linen on their double bed. That sound and that sight captivated his mind. When he started speaking softly, Mallika laughed gently, and he forgot about Amma.

Another two days, and Amma will be leaving.

It was a little late in the evening when he returned home. Even at that hour, Amma was not at home.

"Malli, where is Amma?"

"She said she would visit Kapaleeswarar temple and be back."

"Why today? Is there any festival at the temple? But then, Amma is not the traditional type of devotee. Why this new practice of a temple visit?"

"Maybe her mind is disturbed, poor thing."

"Nonsense! Her mind is much stronger than ours. By the way, are you going to bring me something to eat, or is it that you are confident that just by looking at you the stomach will get filled?" and so saying he moved closer to his wife.

When the door of the hall suddenly opened with a bang from the outside, both of them hurriedly moved apart, startled and blushing. Visalam *Mami,* who was about to enter, also abruptly stepped back, but after Arun's welcoming, "Come in, Mami," got over the momentary embarrassment and came inside. Visalam Mami was a long-time friend of Amma's.

"Have a seat, Mami! Will you have some coffee? Amma has gone to the temple. She will be back anytime now," said Arun. The feeling of embarrassment was still lingering in his mind. *Chhe*! Why didn't I bolt the door? ... If it was Amma, it would've been all right. But Mami is an outsider all said and done, isn't she?

"I'm also coming from the temple. I met your mother there. Both of us were walking back here together. On the way we saw a vendor selling fresh vegetables from a basket. Devanai said, 'I'll buy a couple of them, you carry on.'" Even as she spoke, Mami abruptly stopped and looked at him, it seemed, in amazement.

"What Mami, what are you looking at?"

"For a moment, I thought I was looking at your father."

"Ad nauseam I have heard that I resemble my father! And I'm sick of it. Tell me something new."

"Has Devanai made arrangements for leaving for the hostel day after tomorrow? I came here thinking that she may need some help with the packing."

"What Amma is doing is very wrong—don't you think so, Mami?"

"What are you referring to?"

"Moving to the hostel."

"What is wrong with it?"

"You are no good, Mami. You will only support your friend, won't you!"

"So you know it. Then why complain to me?"

"Don't try to skirt the issue. Why should Amma leave from here? If you ask me, I'd say, she can resign her clerk's job and stay at home in peace. Then she can't possibly speak of going to the Working Women's Hostel and such things, can she?"

Mami laughed. "A very good point, indeed!"

"Am I one of those sons who regard the mother as a burden? Or for that matter does Malli belong to the kind that regards the mother-in-law as unwanted? I am Amma's only son—in fact her only child. Is it right for a widowed mother to say that she will go away from the son and live by herself?" His voice trembled slightly. "What is Amma's grouse against me?"

"No grouse at all. On every occasion she showers praise on you and Malli, saying you are such a golden-hearted pair."

"But what's the point of praising us and then leaving us?" Arun burst out. "I must say Amma is a little too stubborn!"

"Mami, you please explain to her. If you say it, Amma will listen to you. What she is doing is not proper. Why should she leave at all?"

"Your mother may have thought, let the young couple have a nuclear family and enjoy themselves, mayn't she?"

"But Amma is no hindrance to our enjoyment."

Mami gave him a look that was somewhat strange.

"Moreover when we ourselves don't propose to have a nuclear family, what is it that bothers Amma? There is some other reason, I am sure..."

Mami was silent.

"Mami, many a mother—especially those with an only son—will not let him grow at all. They would pet him as if he were a baby on the lap. But my mother is a rare person; she has always treated me as an individual. For as long as I can remember she has been with me as a friend, giving me the status of someone equal to her ... I can't afford to lose that friendship!"

The room became absolutely still. Visalam Mami's eyes stared at the wall. It seemed as though, going beyond the wall, the mind was moving away in some other thought zone. Then slowly she turned her eyes on him. She was about to speak, but for some reason, halted. Then she said:

"Arun, your mother may have treated you as an individual. But *you* have not seen Devanai as an individual woman, although you claimed in a highly progressive spirit that you regard yourselves only as friends; that is what I think. Please take her away from that relationship, hold her at a distance from it, and see her as a person."

"I don't follow."

"Then drop it. Well, how are things? How are you? Did you two go to any movie? Mallika, how do you spend the time during the afternoons?"

"Mami..."

Even as he interrupted her, Mallika, who was looking out at the street through the window, said, "There she is, Atthai has come..." and she got up to meet her.

"Tell me, Mami, what did you mean? If I failed to regard Amma as a person, what then did I do? Did I treat her harshly like cattle?"

"Don't get angry, Arun ... Don't I know of the attachment you have for Devanai?"

"Then what is it? Why should Amma leave?"

"This house is small..."

"Is it?"

"You and Mallika are a newly-married couple..."

"I didn't know that, are we?"

"You exactly resemble your father..."

"This is the umpteenth time..."

Mami was silent for a while. Then, "Arun, what I'm saying is ... A mother is someone who has known us, been with us, developed a familiarity with us, and someone we have got used to since childhood. Hence we take her and her existence for granted. Besides, when we say Amma, it is an 'image'—that is all! That image has certain traditional features. One who pours maternal love on us, one who attends to our needs, one who is the recipient of our love and respect, one who belongs to the previous generation—that is how it has been. However, only if we go beyond this image and learn to see her as a person in her own right, that is to say, as an individual, only then can we understand that she, too, has feelings, desires and attachments..."

"Let Amma have all the worldly desires and attachments, who prevents her from enjoying them? For a mother what other desire and attachment can there be except being at home, looking after her children and grandchildren? Had I married last year, by this time Amma would have even become a grandma!"

"At the age of forty-five a woman can become a grandma, Arun, but not an old woman..."

He stared at her blankly; then got up impatiently. It was no use expecting help from Visalam Mami. She was talking irrelevant nonsense without understanding what he was saying.

Near the compound gate, Devanai and Mallika were standing and talking. What was it in Amma's hand? Was it the *archanai* basket in which she had taken the offerings to the temple? Now there were vegetables in it, and she was showing them to Mallika and saying something.

No ... He couldn't go on without Amma. He had to once again try and plead with her and say that she should not go away from here.

Amma and Mallika started walking towards the house as they chatted.

Looking up casually, Devanai saw her son and smiled—the smile flashed with a certain brilliance.

Suddenly, he couldn't explain why, as he saw Amma smiling that way, from nowhere a strange kind of sorrow burst forth from within him.

Originally published in Tamil as '*Amma pidivadakkari!*' [Amma is an adamant woman!], in the magazine *Sirukathai Kalanjiyam*, 1 October 1985.

13

A chair and a death

When she said her name was Sakuntala, *Periamma* was first surprised. The next minute she said to herself "*Asadu*!" chiding herself affectionately. Why should a servant's name be either Muniamma or Karuppayi or some such thing?

Periamma's son and daughter-in-law were good masters. Servants would work happily for them. Sakuntala was no exception. She enthusiastically laboured at the house chores with a smiling face, energetically running around. They had given her accommodation in a small outhouse at the back. She lived in it with her family. Her husband Dakshinamurthy—not Kuppan, not Madasami, Periamma remembered with laughter—too, was an honest young man. He had put up a fruit stall in the market street nearby. At any given time you could find him either at home or at the shop. No gallivanting with wastrels, consuming illicit liquor or things like that. A very decent young couple, Periamma gave a testimonial within herself, quite satisfied with them. She came to like that family, Sakuntala, Dakshinamurthy and above all, their three-year-old child, Muthukumaran.

Muthukumaran was quite dark and very beautiful, capable of captivating everyone's heart just by moving his large eyes up and down. When Periamma saw him for the first time, it was 'love at first sight' for both of them.

Sakuntala had said, "Say *Vanakkam* to Periamma!" Muthu didn't. Bashful, he hid himself behind her. "Come here, child," Periamma called out to the flashing bright eyes from behind Sakuntala's sari! Muthu would normally hide behind his mother's *mundanai* whenever he saw anyone. But now when Periamma, with her white hair and bright smile, stretched out her hand and said, "Come here, child," the shy-natured boy found it difficult to resist the call more than twice; he took a few steps forward, looked up at her once, lowered his eyes and finally let himself be touched by that outstretched hand. Periamma tapped his shoulder and gently stroked his head.

"What is your name?"

A look, a smile, then the lisping voice dripping down, "Muthukomalan."

"*Dei* Muthu! Is that how you reply when Periamma asks you? You must say respectfully, '*Muthukumaranunga*, Periamma'," Sakuntala chided him.

"What does a child know about respect and all that stuff, *di*? Let him be his natural self. Muthu, do you know what my name is?"

This time the two big eyes did not lower themselves from her face. "Uhum," the head shook.

"*Pattimma* or Periamma—come on, say it now, won't you?"

"*Peleemma*," said the child bashfully.

"Very good! Now come over and sit here!"

Pointing to the steel folding chair next to her recliner, Periamma called him. As soon as Muthu started moving towards it, Sakuntala held him back. "*Chhi chhi*! You shouldn't sit on the chair. Sit on the floor if you like."

"Again started on 'respect'? Look here, Sakuntala! You don't come between us. Muthu and I have become friends, haven't we, Muthu? Therefore you just go and attend to your work."

As Sakuntala stood there stunned, with the broom and the pan freezing in her hand, Periamma gently drew the child's hand and helped him get on to the chair and sit. Muthu looked at his mother for a moment, then smiled at Periamma. Looking at the boy who climbed up and sat in the corner of the chair, dangling his legs above the floor, Periamma said, "Lean back well and sit." At once he pressed his hands down, slowly slid back on the seat with his little feet stretched out straight in front of him, and looked at Periamma. "Very good. Intelligent boy," she said. His dark face was covered all over with pride and he put his head down, smiling shyly.

When Periamma's son and daughter-in-law came to know of the matter of the chair, they voiced their objection. They were good masters. Good people. But masters.

"*Amma*, don't ask that boy to sit on the chair. Let him sit near you on the floor, if you please," said the son.

"Why, what if he sits on the chair? Will your status go down?"

"There won't be any problem if from the beginning everyone stays in their place."

"It's a child, *da*! Two years younger than our Usha. Should we impose all these differences on him?"

"It's not that, *Atthai*. Of course, right now he is a child. But if we allow him to get used to it, won't the same habit continue when he grows up?" said the daughter-in-law.

"What if it does? Aren't all these differentiations wrong in the first place?"

"Come on, Atthai! How could that be?"

They had placed the TV set in the hall. It was the custom for all of them to sit together and watch the programmes. Periamma's five-year-old granddaughter Usha, too, would watch, sitting next to her father, whatever be the programme, as if it were her right to watch it, no matter whether she understood it or not. The child was the father's pet. When Periamma had taken her seat on her special recliner, and the son, the daughter-in-law and the granddaughter had each taken their different seats, then, the good masters that they were, they would say, "Sakuntala, you and your husband, too, sit there and watch the film." The place "there" which they pointed to would be a corner on the other side of the floor some distance away from their family. Dakshinamurthy and Sakuntala would arrive humbly, with Muthu trailing, hiding behind his mother's mundanai.

When the first time they arrived thus for watching TV, Muthu's eyes fell on Periamma's face and then on the vacant folding chair. Periamma's kind eyes enfolded him lovingly as her hand softly stroked the chair next to her and beckoned him there.

With much hesitation Muthu came nearer and stood by her. Then, slowly approaching the folding chair, drawing a line over its seat with one finger, he kept directing half glances at those around, and then looking down. The master, the mistress, and the child mistress, all three of them kept looking at him. Dakshinamurthy called out in a low tone, "Sss, Muthu, come here." Muthu lifted his head for a moment and looked at Periamma's face. She smiled at him. Feeling encouraged, he tried to get on to the chair, leaning his hands on it.

"*Patti*, Patti! The servant boy is trying to sit on the chair, look!"

"Muthu, you are a good boy, aren't you? You should not sit on this. You go there and sit with your Appa and Amma, okay? Go appa!"

"*De* Muthu, come over here!"

One after another, the voices of Usha, Usha's father, and Sakuntala rose like waves and struck his face. Frightened, Muthu gave up the effort to get on to the chair and turned to his mother. She for her part sprinted to the spot and chided him, saying, "Come here, you *kazhuthai*! Does the *dorai* demand a chair? If you do this another time, you will get a thrashing! Come over here, I say," and she dragged him away and seated him on the floor next to her.

Periamma's son looked at his mother with satisfaction. Her eyes were fixed vacantly on the ceiling.

When the movie telecast was over, the family went inside for dinner. It was customary for the daughter-in-law to call Periamma after setting her plate and serving the food. Dakshinamurthy also got up and left. Shaking her son who had fallen asleep on her lap, Sakuntala woke him and made him sit up, saying, "*De* Muthu, get up, *kannu*. I'm leaving now. You, too, come and have food and then go to sleep." And she left.

Rubbing his sleep-heavy eyes with the back of his palms and yawning, when Muthu looked before him, he could see Periamma's smiling face.

"Muthu!" Periamma called in a low secretive whisper, touching and pointing to the chair next to her, "Come and sit here."

Muthu blinked, unable to comprehend. Partly because of the dazed half-asleep state, partly because of confusion at the behaviour of the elders which changed from second to second.

"Come, there is no one else here now, don't you see? Just you and me. Come and sit on it royally, come on!"

Muthu's sleepiness at once vanished without a trace. The eyes turned bright. But the hesitation lingered. He looked here and there in fright.

"There is no one around right now. Before anybody comes, you come and sit on it!" Muthu got up. Running up to her eagerly, he climbed on to the folding chair, sat on it, and leaning back with outstretched legs, he looked up at Periamma with joy.

"Good, good! That's my smart boy Muthu!" Periamma put her hand around his waist and hugged him and smiled at him. Then she softly said, "Everyday, whenever there is no one else around, you come and sit next to me on this chair, will you?" Muthu nodded his head enthusiastically.

That settled into a routine.

There then developed a sign language of looks exchanged between the child hiding behind the mundanai of the mother and the old lady while watching TV. The folding chair next to the recliner became an important character in a drama, the third member of a secret world known only to the two of them.

Whenever the others moved away from that place once the TV programme was over, whenever some of them left for office and school and the others at home were taking rest inside during the day time, Muthu would run up with a sense of secrecy and climb on to the chair next to hers, bringing joy to Periamma's face. He would smile at her, joy and pride writ all over his face. Periamma would watch with delight the teeth and the whites of the eyes gleaming upon that small dark face like three white patches.

"What is the name of the smart boy who is sitting here royally on the chair?"

"Muthu."

"What is the boy Muthu doing?"

"Sitting on the chair."

"Beside whom?"

"Beside Peleemma."

"Where will the boy Muthu go in a few days?"

"He will go to kool."

"What will he do at the school?"

"He will study."

"Who will he come back to and report whatever he learnt at school?"

"To Peleemma."

"No *da*! First you should tell it all to Amma and Appa."

"Then to Peleemma..."

"Where will he sit and tell all that to Periamma?"

"On the chair."

"Where will that chair be?"

"Beside Peleemma."

Not that they had to be talking while sitting together. Even silence was enjoyable. Or just an exchange of looks and smiles. When the two of them were sitting together, sometimes Periamma would be reading a book by herself. Sometimes she would doze off with her spectacles on. But such things would not at all stand in the way of their fellowship. Just the fact of Periamma reclining in the chair next to his, stretching her legs, was sufficient proof of her friendship. Thus reclining, he would roll his head this way and that against the back of the chair. He would fold his legs and stretch them out again. He would twist his toes and enjoy himself. He would keep tapping the chair and enjoy the sound. If Periamma had fallen asleep, none of these would disturb her. If awake, she would enjoy these acts with a smile.

"Why do *Ayya* and Amma say that I should not sit on this chair?"

"Ignore them. They don't know anything."

"My father and mother also say the same thing."

"They, too, don't know anything."

Periamma sat up straight. She held the child's face in her hands. "Look here, Muthu, it is quite the right thing for you to sit here. Only you and I know that it is right. The others don't know. They are stupid folks."

Muthu was very pleased to hear this.

"*Ayyayyo*! There's Amma coming. I'm leaving, Peleemma..." The moment he saw the shadow of a figure emerging from inside, Muthu would get out of the chair in a hurry and run away. Still, Periamma's daughter-in-law happened to see it a couple of times.

"What's all this, Atthai? Is this still going on? Is it right for you to seat that boy on the chair next to you in this way, as your equal?"

Periamma wouldn't reply; her eyes would simply be directed to the ceiling.

The mistress tried talking to the maid, too.

"*Adi*, Sakuntala, this is not good. Of course he is a child. But do we therefore give up all distinctions? Won't it look odd to people who happen to see him come and sit on the chair in the hall?"

"Amma, I'm trying to stop him every time. The donkey that he is, he doesn't listen, what to do?"

Sakuntala complained to her husband, and one day Dakshinamurthy gave the boy a severe beating. Hearing the wails of the child, Periamma ran to the outhouse.

"Stop it, *da*! Is this the way—killing a tender child like this!"

"He doesn't listen to our words, Periamma, when we tell him, 'Don't sit on the chair, you *rascol*'."

"Wasn't it me who asked him to sit there? If that was wrong, you should beat me, not him."

"Ayyayyo, Periamma! How could you say such things?"

"If you hit the child another time, it will only mean that you beat him up because you can't beat me up."

After that Muthu's parents did not beat him. When Muthu started going to school, he would first report the daily happenings only to Periamma. He wouldn't listen even if she urged him to tell it all to his mother and father first. When he shyly said, "I like saying it to you alone, Peleemma!" Periamma wouldn't have the heart to force him to do otherwise. Tenderness could only be echoed in tenderness. When the recliner and the folding chair exchanged smiles, there existed no other world beyond. As she observed Muthu's young head showing up a notch higher than earlier over the back of the folding chair and the dark legs outstretched from the chair a little further, Periamma's heart would fill with joy. Their friendship deepened and seemed to grow stronger as the days went by.

"*Yenga*! What Tamil movie is showing this week on TV?"

"Some name was flashed, wasn't it? I forgot. Wait, I'll check and let you know. I think it is a Rajni movie."

That Sunday they all sat together in the hall as usual. Periamma, her daughter-in-law, granddaughter on the chairs on one side. At a little distance, on the floor, Sakuntala, Dakshinamurthy, and in his grip, Muthu.

"Oh my god! What fights, what fights... So boring!"

"Just a masala movie."

"Rajni has performed well, hasn't he?"

All kinds of comments were heard at the end of the movie. Except Periamma and Muthu, the rest of them got up and left the hall. Muthu had as usual gone to sleep with his head on his mother's lap. Sakuntala had shaken him, made him sit up, ordered him, "Come on wake up, Muthu, get up and come," and left.

Muthu rubbed his eyes and looked out in front. Seeing Periamma's smiling face, he, too, smiled gently.

"Muthu, everyone has left. Come over here," Periamma called to him softly, tapping on the folding chair.

Muthu got up and went to her. As he approached the folding chair, he stood for a moment. Then he sat down near it, on the floor, at Periamma's feet.

"*Ey* Muthu!"

"I'll sit here on the floor, Periamma. What shall we talk of?"

Periamma froze in her chair.

After that, Muthu did not sit on the chair next to Periamma again. Therefore Periamma, too, gave up sitting on her reclining chair. She also asked for the folding chair to be removed and kept in a corner. If you saw her eyes, they looked as though they were weeping over some death.

Originally published in Tamil as
'*Oru narkaliyum oru maranamum*' [A chair and a death],
in the magazine *Kalki*, Deepavali Special Issue, October 1987.

14

Litany

This is a story about me. You want to know who I am. Well. I am God. Who is this madman, you wonder, don't you? But you may also think who but a madman could have created a world like this. Because it is your notion that I created this world.

I have several names: Easwaran, Jehova, Buddha, Arhat, God the Father, Allah, Al Maajid ... all right, all right, I'll stop. I well know that you humans have neither the inclination nor the patience to listen to praise of others. I have many other names, too, other than those I have listed. Since I seem to be tiring you, I'll tell you those after talking about some other matters.

One of the mistaken notions you have about me is that I am 'the omnipotent He.' (Why 'the omnipotent He'? Why not 'the omnipotent She'? How do you know whether I am female, male or inanimate? Anyhow. Though some of you call me 'Devi', for the present we will use the masculine gender; because you have conjured up all the names I mentioned earlier only as masculine, haven't you?)

What was I saying? Oh, yes, 'Omnipotent.' All I want to say is that I am *not* omnipotent. No. No. If I had been omnipotent, would I have let so much suffering and injustice spread such havoc in the world? Isn't it precisely because of such suffering and other hardships that some of you have started saying, "Life has no meaning. It is just a muddle. There is no such entity called God"? Let me ask you, did I first of all say that I exist? And then did I suddenly vanish? What do I have to do with your 'theism' and 'atheism'?

It is wrong to say that I created the world. You who are of this world have created me for your comfort and to seek some refuge from your fear of death.

What is that now, a female voice wailing from somewhere?

"Oh, God, have you no eyes?"

This is what I don't like. What does it mean if you first give shape to me and then ask if I have no eyes or nose? All right. I'll go see what the trouble there is. You think I can know from here what it is. Of course not. Like you, I will know what is happening in a place only when I go there. Don't think I have powers any greater than you do. I have said already that I am your creation. How can a creation possess powers higher than those that the artist who created it possesses?

That woman may be around thirty-five years old. The loveliness of her figure was dimmed by sorrow like a rainy evening. Resembling her, like drops from her brimming and overflowing beauty, there were a fourteen-year-old daughter and a ten-year-old son.

She is not poor. She owns this small house which is worth one lakh rupees. It had been purchased when her husband was alive and in a good position. But Shanbagam is not well-to-do now. That is the problem at present.

Her husband and his brother had launched separate businesses. Elder brother Arunagiri made profit upon profit and is now flourishing as the proprietor of a motor car company. Younger brother Kanakarajan—in spite of his name (which meant King of Gold)—however dealt in sale of leather and wooden goods and, owing to lack of either luck or skill, kept burning his fingers and squandered all his possessions. The only property left was this house. But a house is an asset only when it is sold. Otherwise it is just shelter. It won't feed your hunger. You need some other source of income. Kanakarajan hunted for a job, eventually found one as a clerk in a small private company and was taking care of his four-member family.

All of a sudden a severe pain developed in his stomach. It was found that it was a major complication in the intestines. He was advised to undergo surgery which would cost around thirty thousand rupees.

Kanakarajan approached his elder brother for a loan. He got the thirty thousand rupees. The operation was performed, but the patient didn't survive. The family lost its head.

Today, eight months later, when Shanbagam was slowly recovering from her state of utter inertness, her brother-in-law has come to strike terror in her heart.

He had not given his younger brother thirty thousand rupees as an interest-free loan or even as just a loan with interest. He had exploited the crisis in his brother's life to insist that he would spare the money only if the latter mortgaged his house. The property document for the house and the mortgage deed were now securely lodged in the iron safe in his own house.

Now she had to repay the thirty thousand with interest at once. If not, she should accept the ten thousand which he was now ready to offer and she should transfer the ownership of the house in his name.

"This is atrocious!" cried Shanbagam.

"How is it atrocious? Are you in a position to pay back the thirty thousand along with the interest amount of five thousand? If you are, tell me. I will issue a receipt right away that your loan is paid up."

"Is it right to mock me like this, *Anna*? You talk like this knowing full well what state I am in! Where will I go for such a large amount all of a sudden? After your *Tambi*'s passing away, the household is running with help from some people who know us. It is only since last month that the company he worked for has given me his job on compassionate grounds. Don't we need to live with dignity? Don't I need to bring up the children and help them come up in their lives? If you take away the only possession we have, what shall we do? Where will we go? Will you at least give us a place in your house?"

"How is that possible, Shanbagam? Even if I agree to it, your *Anni* won't. Her widowed mother and unmarried sister are already with us. Moreover, don't you know our Setu has become a big officer now? He has visitors all the time. So I have given him a separate room for his office. Besides, suppose he gets married after some time, he will have his own family and the house won't be sufficient even for us. Where is the question of accommodating you and your family?"

"So you are saying you don't care whatever ruin we come to. Isn't that so?"

"What! Don't be insolent."

"Enough. I can sell the house itself, pay up your loan, deposit the balance in the bank, and my children and I can sustain ourselves in comfort."

"Don't forget that the property document for the house is with me. Moreover, how will you sell the house? Who will buy a house which is under mortgage?"

Her heart sank.

"Listen to me, Shanbagam. Take the ten thousand I offer, put it in a fixed deposit in the bank. It will earn interest and will be of help in an emergency. You have a job anyway for your livelihood. You are sure to get some small accommodation somewhere for a rent of a hundred or a hundred and fifty rupees. Very soon, if Uma completes higher secondary, I will myself get her a job. Won't I do at least that for Kanaku's child? What do you say? Tomorrow morning I'll send Setu with a cheque for ten thousand ... No, you don't have a bank account yet, I'll send him with ten thousand in cash, okay? Look, I trust you and will hand over the money first. You can then register the house in my name, saying you have sold the house to the same person to whom it had been mortgaged."

His eyes shone. How long he had set his sights on this house!

"Anna! Give me some time. I'll repay your loan little by little. It would have made such a difference if your Tambi had been alive. Don't deal me another blow even before we recover from the grief arising from his loss. Don't snatch away the only support we have. Don't drive me and my children into the street, Anna. I beg you with folded hands."

She folded her hands in prayer.

Arunagiri smiled mischievously.

"Why should you stand homeless in the street, Shanbagam? You are quite good-looking. Your daughter also takes after you. It is not difficult for women to make a living if they put their mind to it, is it?"

"Oh, you scoundrel!" she thought as her head lifted in indignant fury. Her flaming eyes dealt a savage slap on his cheek.

"All the torments of hell now will not do for people like you. A special hell will have to be created and men of your ilk thrown into it." The throbbing eyes looked above with a plaint, "Oh, Lord, have you no eyes?"

"All right then, Shanbagam. I'll send Setu with the cash tomorrow. If you take it, then the house becomes mine. If not, you'll get a lawyer's notice demanding repayment of the loan."

Arunagiri left.

What are you saying? "Here is a woman in agony, thunderstruck with blow after blow? Why don't you go and save her? If you don't, it will be quite true that you have no eyes." Is that what you are saying?

I feel like laughing. Who are you saying this to? To the empty vacant space above and all around? Isn't that all I am? I am the wind hovering in the sky of your desires, the pinnacle of your dreams, the apotheosis of all your high ideals. You are the ones who operate me. Where then do I go and what then do I do? Where do I come from if you keep calling, "Oh God, Oh God," without lifting a finger yourself? How can I see if you close your eyes?

There, the day has dawned in that house. You can see from Shanbagam's eyes that she hasn't slept the whole night.

What decision should she convey today? Take the ten thousand and throw away the house? Or say no and ... say no and...

All of a sudden her frame shook. The sound of the motorbike arriving and coming to a halt at the entrance broke into her eyes like an earthquake.

As she stood petrified, too weak to move, Seturaman came in.

He was a young man of twenty-six. Quite tall and wiry with a slim but hard frame. His handsome countenance now looked to her like the face of an *asura*.

"*Chitti*! How are you? Balu, Uma, are you okay? What is wrong, we haven't seen you at our home for quite a while. Have you forgotten your Anna?"

Shanbagam became more apprehensive at his talking to the children without looking at her straight. She somehow managed to let the word "Come" slip through her gritted teeth.

But now he looked at her with a slightly embarrassed smile. "Chitti, I came just to give this to you," he said and unzipped the leather bag he was holding.

Palpitation mounted in her. Setu, too, was feeling awkward, she thought, owing to the embarrassing mission he had come on. He had to get older before he could, like his father, wipe his heart clean of all troubled feelings.

He took out a brown packet from the bag and extended his hand with the cover towards her. She looked at it as though it was a bomb. The hand didn't move.

"Here, Chitti."

"This ... this ... what is this? Mm ... money?"

"Here in the packet is the title deed for your house and the mortgage deed that *Chittappa* had executed with my Appa for the loan of thirty thousand rupees. Take them."

She stared at him.

"Tear up the mortgage deed. Take the title deed and keep it safe inside."

"I ... I'm utterly at a loss, Setu. Your father said that I should take ten thousand rupees and part with the house."

"That's what he told me, too."

"Then?"

"It is indeed proper for younger people to respect the words of elders, Chitti. However, when the young ones grow up and attain the mental maturity to think on their own, shouldn't they look critically at the justice or injustice of what the elders say?"

Shanbagam's heart surged.

"Take this, Chitti."

"We have taken a loan of thirty thousand on the house. Today, that, along with the interest..."

"If you receive these documents, there will be no evidence to show that the house was mortgaged. And you need not repay the loan."

"No, no. I insist on repaying the loan."

"All right, I won't stand in the way of your insistence on honest dealing. But there is no need to link the house with the matter of the loan. The house will always be yours. Just tear up the mortgage deed and, without any conditions, repay the loan little by little according to your convenience. That will do. Towards that I'll also help you."

"It's not proper for you to help us with this, Setu."

"Please. Don't say no. Do I have no ties with your family? Even though my father has abjured his duty to take care of you and these children after Chittappa's departure, I have a share in that duty, Chitti! These two are not strangers to me. They are my sister and brother. Take the packet. Have no fear about Appa. I'll talk to him."

He left even before she could thank him with a faltering tongue. Even after he left, the warm smile seemed to stay before her. She sat benumbed for a long time staring at the heavy packet he had thrust into her hands, with a heart beating with mixed feelings of relief and gratitude.

Aren't you people crying, "Oh, you opened your eyes at last! You certainly are God Almighty then!" It is true that I was present there, but it was Seturaman who took me there. Didn't I say earlier that I cannot act without you? All right, all right, the story is over. You can all go home now. You must be busy with lots of things to do. After all, you are people of the jet age, aren't you!... What? "You said it was a story about you, but you have told a different story." Is that what you are saying? Although a different story came in between, didn't it end as my own story as I had said at the beginning? To that extent, I am satisfied that (unlike you) I don't tell lies.

"How was that your story? You say with feigned modesty, 'What can I do?' And then in the same breath you brag, 'I was there'. Where were you there? Shanbagam, her children, Arunagiri, Seturaman—those were all the characters we saw. We didn't see you."

My ... my ... What a hubbub! If I had ears they would have gone deaf by now. You didn't see me there, right? Excuse me. That was your mistake. If only you had let me, at the outset, tell you all my names, you would certainly have spotted me there. Don't you remember you frowned when I started with Easwaran and listed four or five names? Listen at least now. Besides the names I mentioned earlier, I have a few other names as well, for instance, mercy, sense of justice, humanitarianism...

Originally published in Tamil as '*Namavali*' ['Litany of the Lord's names'], in the magazine *Kalki Ponvizha Malar*, Golden Jubilee Number, August 1992.

15

Paths there are many

She was kind-hearted but how could she so utterly lack maturity? Yes, it was important to love but wasn't it folly to stay bound in attachments? She was fifty-six, younger to him by six years. To be pining away over children at this age? The daughters and sons had come of age, got married and gone away to live their own lives. All in the fair and natural course of life. But this woman was still pining for them. Like a young girl pining for her lover!

"Gomu, you shouldn't be so lacking in detachment. When the fledglings grow wings they will fly away. Isn't it their right?"

However much he counselled her, Gomati's sense of depression wouldn't go. She would sit immobile for hours, lost in thought. She would heave long sighs. Then suddenly a stream of memories would come surging forth.

"This is the time for Janu's second cup of coffee." "This kind of brinjal *koottu* Setu used to love; he would ask for another and another helping so many times." "I can hear the mango-seller on the street. How dearly our daughter-in-law loves mangoes! She would take it even with curd rice, saying no to pickles! Why couldn't they all have stayed with us? Why did our boys have to get a transfer?" "Our Saro's laughter still keeps ringing all over the house, doesn't it?"

Saro was the youngest of the children. She, too, had recently got married and gone away with her husband to another state. No fledgling left in the nest now.

"The house has become so bare and desolate. I don't like this at all, living all alone here." Thus she would fret.

Natesa Iyer would fly into a temper at this. "All alone! Am I not here, solid as rock? Have you decided that you are a widow already?"

"Siva, Siva! What inauspicious talk! What I meant was, does it look nice just the two of us sitting face-to-face and exchanging banalities? Some lively chat, people moving about—don't we need all that? A home is no home without sons, daughters, daughters-in-law, grandsons, granddaughters!"

"Do you have any sense? Everything in life has its place. We have lived our life with children well and happily. Now they have all gone away to shape their own lives. And that is only proper. Rather than accept this as we did the other stages of life, is it right to think of this as loneliness and vacancy and spurn it? What do we lack? There is a beauty in this quiet state. I am here all for you, and you for me. What more do we want?"

"Still ... just the two of us, looking at each other's face...?"

"Why, aren't our faces look-at-able?" Natesa Iyer laughed. "Don't get angry, Gomu! Come, join me and read the *Bhagavad Gita*. Join me when I do my puja."

"There is no greater puja than life."

"Old age is also life, you ignorant wretch! The peace and solitude you get in age is also life."

But Gomati wouldn't be comforted however much he tried. Not that she had no faith in the Divine or in puja. But as far as she was concerned, those were rites that one went through, closing the eyes for a quarter of an hour after bath in the morning. They had no relation to life. They were no substitute for life. She lived in sentiments. In ties of affection. She had found fulfillment in looking after her children and being engrossed in doing little things for them. She had been happy as long as at least one of the children was at home.

Now when the house was vacant, Gomati felt bare, like an actor who had not been assigned any role. In a house where only she and her husband lived there wasn't much to do that could be called work. The hours stretched meaninglessly. Even love had lost all meaning.

Not that Natesa Iyer's love for his children was any the less than hers. But he wasn't sunk in it. Love there was, but it had matured with discrimination into wisdom. He was able to stand apart and view everything without losing himself in it, and to find fulfillment in such a state.

From his early days he had developed an interest in books, fine arts and the beauties of nature. His familial affection was rooted in these loves. In tender moments, he would speak comparing the loveliness of his wife or his child to a sunrise or the nicety of a lyrical composition. He had started reading the *Puranas* and epics to acquire knowledge, but gradually even that motive receded and reading itself became a great and joyous experience. It became both the reason and the outcome.

"Why don't you listen to this?" he would call his wife to his side while reading the *Valmiki Ramayanam*, "What a profound thought! And what a beautiful verse to communicate it!"

Gomati had never had a taste for such things. As he sat lost in the joy of books, she would worry about his physical comfort. She would bring a pillow to support his back. She would get him a cup of coffee at the right time.

"Come, Gomu, let us read together!"

"What do I understand of all this?"

"Why don't you try reading? Forget the house for a while and come and sit here. I'll explain everything. And then you'll find yourself getting interested!"

"No, you go ahead. I'll go to the market and get some Hyderabad grapes if they are available. Vasu likes them. It seems our third-house neighbour Ramasubbu is visiting Vriddhachalam tomorrow. I am thinking of asking him to look up Vasu and give him the grapes."

A transient sign of life only when saying something about the children. Otherwise, a look of weariness and grief as though all was lost. Always. Always.

"It is wrong, Gomu, this blind attachment. We have done our duty by the children. They are all fine in their own places. To be happy about that—that is the mark of love. Whenever they come here, we will welcome them, celebrate their presence. But to pine for them in their absence—how childish! At present, you and I should live our life in quietude. That is what is proper in the evening of our life. That is how we should find fulfillment."

She would wait till he finished talking at length, and then say, "The house looks bare and desolate."

He would fly into uncontrollable rage. "Rather than talk to you, I should go and knock my head against the wall."

"There is no work for me to do. I am forced to kill time."

"Is it so difficult to spend time? Grow a garden around the house. Go and offer whatever help you can to the neighbours. Come and take a walk with me outside. Join me and read."

"Why can't you agree to our staying for a few days with each of our children by turns?"

"Don't be stupid. Instead of slowly freeing ourselves from the bonds of attachment, you are saying we should get more and more entangled—are you crazy? You know what the Lord says in the *Gita*, don't you. Man should, like drops of water on a lotus leaf..."

"*Yénna*, would our Gita remember to have her glass of milk every night without fail?"

Natesa Iyer wearily gave up, thinking, "This is a case beyond redemption." Looking at that face which had forgotten how to smile, he lamented, "Immature thing." Her grief-stricken state roused his anger. At the same time, he also felt pity. Why was she withering so, like a plant that had been denied sunlight? Why was she sitting thus, sunk in emptiness as though life had lost all meaning? How could he enlighten her? How could he lift her to the heights that he himself dwelt in?

Suddenly everything changed.

One evening, as he returned home after his walk, Gomati, her face radiant and enthusiastic, ran towards him with a letter in her hands.

"Did you hear this? Great news! Our Setu has written. His company is sending him to Japan for two years for some special training. He is taking his wife along. But he is not taking the children as their education will get disrupted. He is going to obtain the transfer certificate from the school and leave the children here for two years...!"

The words tumbled out in a flood of enthusiasm. The eyes glowed. She spoke excitedly as though her frame had received a new lease of life.

"From now on, all joy and radiance will return to the house. I should immediately look for a maid. Shouldn't there be someone to attend to the household chores while I am tending the children? ... I will make *murukku* and *seedai*. The elder one likes them. He needs something to munch all the time. Oh, I forgot! I have to tell the flower girl to deliver two *muzhams* of jasmine every day from next week. The younger girl simply loves flowers. I will ready the small room for the children to keep their things. But of course they won't sleep there. They will sleep safely by my side. Do at once arrange for an extra packet of milk. Yénna, shall we have the compound fenced? The little one, poor thing, shouldn't go out into the street while playing! What do you think...?"

She went on and on. What a transformation! Her whole frame was now all aflutter with joy! It was like a glow taking human shape and turning music into words. What a woman! Was there no end to this folly? Such ignorance born out of attachment?

"What, did you hear? What a happy day it is today! Here is the end to loneliness and emptiness. There will be life in this house again! There will be joy and cheer. Children will laugh. We will hear little feet frolicking around..."

Natesa Iyer swallowed his anger and went to his room without replying. He opened the *Bhagavad Gita* to find peace. The Lord says: Don't bind yourself to life. Perform your duty, but stand apart and do it.

But here? It was not out of a sense of duty that Gomati was looking forward to the coming of the children. Rather, she was finding happiness in turning love into a bond. Would she ever attain maturity of mind?

He started reading the exhortations from the *Gita* to overcome his anger and bitterness. The body is only a piece of clothing ... the soul casts off the torn clothing and puts on a new piece ... the soul has no death. ... The one who sees Me everywhere and sees everything in Me, he never loses Me.

As the higher wisdom and philosophy radiating from the printed lines slowly and gently took hold of his consciousness, a profound peace spread over the mind. The anger receded little by little. The mind engrossed in the content, he felt a joy; for a moment he raised his eyes.

The full-length mirror fixed to the almirah in front reflected his figure—he was startled to see the expression on his own face. How strange! The rapture that brimmed and overflowed from Gomati's countenance when she broke the news of the grandchildren coming, the same rapture now radiated on his face?

Then?

The kind of fulfillment that high philosophical truths gave him, did she find the same fulfillment in those little ties of affection? Was the state called 'joy' ultimately the same for everyone? That everyone attained it in the way that accorded with their mind and taste—was that the only truth? If that was so, who could say which of these was higher and which lower? "Whatever path one chooses to seek Me, one attains Me in the same path" was the Lord's saying. Did that same dictum apply in the matter of happiness, too?

His face flushed with the sharp stab of humiliation that he felt thinking of himself. Looking down on her with derision from a high pedestal, wanting to be her mentor and shape her in his own mould...

He bowed his head.

As he sat in that attitude of humility, there seemed to ring in his ears another kind of teaching from the *Gita*: "True maturity lies in accepting everyone for what they are."

Originally published in Tamil as '*Vazhikalpala*'
[Paths many], in the magazine *Pudiya Parvai*,
Deepavali Special Issue, November 1993.

16

Must prop up this crumbling edifice

The same tiled house. But she didn't remember the plaster having fallen off so extensively earlier. Wouldn't they have got the house painted even once during these past ten years? Or they did, but the paint didn't hold?

Indu got off the auto, dismissed it and entered the compound, opening the wooden door of the barbed wire fence. Noticing the closed front door, she hesitated. Even the plastic basket of fruits that she was carrying seemed to weigh rather heavy. A closed door and a smileless face are the same, both unwelcoming.

Should she go back?

But then, when was the front door of this house ever open? It was always like this, always closed. Both the front and the back doors. The tightest security. With both Ratnam *Mama* and Kantimati *Mami* as the warders holding their three daughters in rigorous imprisonment. In the end, one by one, all three somehow broke through those doors and left the house in the darkness of night.

Who then were these closed doors now meant to guard? It was like locking the door after the horse had bolted.

That was all in the past. Now, how were they doing, those poor parents who had lost their three children alive?

Indu passed her eyes over the wall. There was no calling bell to be seen. Everything was the same. They had not changed anything.

She knocked on the door. The door opened after three or four knocks. Standing at the door was Kantimati.

There wasn't much change in her after these ten years. Mami had always been thin. And her hair, ever since Indu had come to know the family, had always been gray. "We don't know what the problem is," Mami had said, "One of my younger sisters and I are the only ones in our family to have this. Our hair turned gray even at thirty." Indu watched with relief that Mami still had *kumkumam* on her forehead and in the parting of her hair. The keys fastened to the *thirumangalyam* with safety pins flashed through the blue cotton sari that Mami was wearing.

Mami did not say, "Who is it?" The familiarity was reflected in her eyes and in the smile that appeared the moment she saw Indu.

"Come, Indu, come in," she said in the most casual way, as though they had met and parted just the previous day. Mami was always composed. Else she couldn't have lived with a tyrannical husband from the age of eighteen till she was sixty-three.

As soon as Indu entered the drawing room, Kantimati closed and bolted the door again.

"Why, Mami? Why not keep it open? We are here. And let there be some breeze."

"No, Indu. Mama doesn't like it. Moreover ... well, you know ... after all that happened, his severity has only increased. 'Shut the door. This is our penal imprisonment for begetting such children,' he says. Let that be. Tell me, how are you? Come and sit here. What if your husband got transferred and you left the place? Haven't we been neighbours and friends for so long? Was it nice not to look us up these ten years?"

"Don't be cross, Mami. Yes, it was quite wrong on my part. What do I do? In these ten years he got transferred three times. We have moved around quite a lot in north India. All that business of settling down in each place, the problem of children's education, getting servants, adjusting to the local climate, don't you see? Something or the other all the time. We could never make it this side. Just now my brother-in-law's daughter's wedding came up. That was a good excuse for a visit to Chennai. And a chance for me to look up all my relatives and friends. Here, I brought some fruits for you. Please take them."

"Why all this? I am so glad you came."

"I got the apples as Mama likes them very much. Do accept them."

"He has no teeth now to bite into apples."

So there has been some change in the last ten years!

"You eat them then."

"Certainly. You got them with so much love. And I will make some apple juice for Mama. Sit, Indu."

"Let me first go in and say hello to Mama."

"He is resting."

"Oh, yes, one to two in the afternoon is his sleeping time, isn't it? Nothing seems to have changed, Mami?"

"Nothing—including his anger."

Nor would Mami's sorrow have changed. But Mami didn't show it. How would it be for her now, poor thing, dwelling in this house where she had lived with three daughters? She would have been spared the sorrow if she had got them properly married and sent away. But when each one of them chose her own path and ran away in stealth...

Indu looked at her keenly. There was no visible disturbance apparent. But what lay contained in the depths behind those eyes could be guessed.

"Have you had any news about your daughters, Mami?" she asked as she sat down on the chair.

A roar broke out at that moment from the room inside.

"Who is talking in this house about those runaways?"

Startled, Indu stood up. Kantimati rushed inside, flustered.

"Nothing. Please don't get tense."

"Haven't I said there should be no word spoken in this house about those *moodevis*? Who was it that spoke?"

"Don't get upset. Our Indu has come from her place to look us up. She was just asking casually about them."

"*Namaskaram*, Mama!" said Indu, as she quickly stepped into the room, not wanting to let that exchange go on. "How are you? Have I disturbed you in sleep?"

"Come," he said as the old frame pulled itself together and sat up on the bed. Though the anger stayed, civil and courteous words did come forth. "Are you well? How is your husband? Sit, isn't it quite a few years since you moved up north?" Puffs of air came out with the words as he spoke. The rose-tinted dentures were floating in water in the glass on the table beside the bed.

Indu was shocked to see that form. Had all the changes that had taken place only come upon him? Was the toothless state a sign of his decline? A toothless lion? Ratnam Mama was a man with a well-built physique. Now reduced to a skeleton, hair lost, the face and the eyes sunken ... even the height seemed to have diminished ... What kind of shrunken state was this? Was it sorrow over the loss of the daughters? But the sorrow didn't seem to have been caused by affection. He had always exulted over the hegemonic power he had exercised over his wife and children. The exit of the three daughters breaking that power had been a blow to the tyrant's vanity. Was this sorrow and anger because of his inability to take that blow? All the three girls had been scared even to speak loudly in his presence. "Don't do that"; "Don't talk like this"; "Don't stand there"; "Don't laugh like that." It had always been strict controls and taboos. If anyone ventured to talk back, he would, never minding that it was a girl who had come of age, just take off his leather belt and swing it at her brutally. The revolt would vanish without a trace.

Indu remembered even now how the eldest girl Kamala had come to her and cried.

Kamala was then twenty-eight years old. Ratnam's sister's son was working as a clerk in some small place somewhere far away. In the hope that the young man would one day, after marrying off his sisters, come forward to tie the *mangalsutra* round Kamala's neck, Ratnam had not looked for any other alliance for her. Kamala neither hated marriage nor longed for it. But she was bored sitting idle at home for years together after finishing her education with just schooling. One day she had gone to visit a friend. There was a standing order from the father that wherever they went they should be back home by six in the evening. Kamala's friend took her to a women's association that she knew of. Kamala felt drawn to the social welfare activities that those people were engaging in. She also relished the prospect of mixing with people and helping them. By the time she returned home after going back to her friend's house and chatting with her enthusiastically about the association, it was eight in the night. Ratnam was waiting at the gate. When he saw her, he said nothing, but simply dragged her inside and shut the entrance door. That night the leather belt was cracked until it snapped. "*Akka, akka* ... what can I do, akka? I should either get married or engage my mind and attention in something. It is better that I kill myself rather than die dreading *Appa* and taking his beatings and suffering this living death every minute." The tears didn't stop however hard Indu tried to comfort her.

Exactly ten days after that, Kamala was at home through the night. The doors were locked as usual. When the day dawned, the front door was open. Kamala was gone. There were some words found in a bit of paper.

"I am leaving. Don't look for me."

How did she muster that courage? With a father gripping his leather belt even while sleeping. And a mother who slept light, waking up at the slightest noise. How did she get past them, open the door and go out?

"You have two children, don't you?" Ratnam abruptly asked.

"Yes, Mama."

"Girls?"

"One."

"Brand her in the foot."

"Indu, let him rest for a while. Let us go and chat," said Kantimati, intervening quickly.

Indu got up instantly, saying, "All right, Mama, you..."

As if ignoring her very presence, Ratnam turned to his wife and said, "Get me some water to drink and then you can sit down to gossip."

Indu followed Kantimati out of the room. She saw Kantimati entering the room again with a tumbler of water. The next moment she heard Ratnam shout, "*Saniyané*, can't you hand me the tumbler without spilling water on the bed!" This was followed by the noise of the stainless steel tumbler hitting the floor and rolling.

"Pardon me ... it just slipped..."

"You want me to lie soaking wet and die of pneumonia? If you don't want me, why do you wait for me to croak? Why don't you, too, like the three vipers you bred in your womb, open the door and walk out?"

"*Siva, Siva*. Don't say such things. I am a lowly creature who has taken refuge at your feet. Just get up for a while and I'll change the sheet. First I'll get you another tumbler of water to drink."

"Pour it on your own head."

Indu sighed. No wonder those three girls wanted to flee this kind of ambience. She looked around the house searchingly. Both the front and the back entrance doors were shut. Though this was quite a common practice in the afternoons in all houses in view of security, somehow in this particular house it looked like a blockade imposed with some relish.

How did they escape from this prison-house? It would have been understandable if they had left home in the daytime on some business and vanished without ever returning. But, as if it was all preplanned, all three of them had opened the door in the night in a gesture of defiance and got out, leaving just a note behind. How did it happen?

Not that she didn't have her own guesses about it. Still...

Kantimati herself had told her that, after Kamala went away, the surveillance turned even stricter. The second daughter Vimala had taken up a job after finishing her M.Sc. Kantimati would herself escort her to the office bus in the morning. When she returned in the evening, Ratnam would wait at the bus stop, pick her up and bring her home. The third daughter Amala, who was studying B.A. Economics, could only go to college with a friend. In the evening, Kantimati would wait for her, standing at the college entrance, and bring her home. After the doors were shut for the night, Ratnam, who couldn't easily go to sleep, would get up every now and then in the first part of the night and patrol the house like the night security guards in the streets. Kantimati, of course, didn't need to patrol the house as she always slept very light and would wake up at the slightest sound. Still, since it was her assigned responsibility to keep watch in the later part of the night after Ratnam went to sleep around one, she would get up two or three times to check if the girls were safely in bed.

Kantimati carried out these security instructions unquestioningly. She could, of course, never act against her husband's decrees. Besides, as she told Indu, "You know, Indu, how people said all sorts of things after Kamala left the house. Isn't it fair on his part to insist that we shouldn't give the other girls any chance to make a fool of us? The times are bad. We do need to be vigilant till we marry them off."

And yet they got away!

The third daughter Amala was the next to leave.

She said that her heart was not in the consumer market and the law of diminishing returns, and that her soul yearned to paint. One of her college friends was the daughter of the principal of a college of arts. She had shown some of Amala's paintings to her father. She said, "Father says you have a great talent, Amala. He says you can grow into a major artist if you join his college and get formal training in art."

"Please let me join the College of Art immediately after I finish B.A.," Amala begged. It was three years after Kamala had gone away.

"I will knock your teeth off. You want to paint pictures? That is the pastime of idlers. You must take up a job and save up for your dowry. What can we do with just the five-sovereign jewellery that we have made for you? What do you mean, talking of painting and stuff?" shouted Ratnam, taking off his leather belt.

The story repeated itself. After two months, the day after she finished writing her B.A. final examination, Amala opened the door and vanished. Gone with her were the five-sovereign worth gold bangles and chain which had been made for her as well as Kantimati's antique gold bracelets, also worth five sovereigns.

Amala had left a note saying she was going away to seek liberation.

Ratnam turned into Lord Siva in a fire of rage. But there was no *Manmathan* before him to burn and destroy. Anger and humiliation tossed him about. How dared she defy him and walk out? How was that possible? Did she pull a fast one on Kantimati? Did she mix some sedative in her mother's food that night? Kantimati was equally dumbfounded. "Oh, the wretch! However did she get out? Oh, Lord Muruga, why are we being tested over and over again like this?" she lamented, utterly devastated.

They found the address of Amala's classmate, the daughter of the fine arts college principal, and enquired there. When it turned out that they knew nothing, the only thing left was to complain to the police. When the first daughter had disappeared, they hadn't made a complaint for fear of ignominy. This time they did file a complaint, but to no avail.

"Why has she done this to us? Why...?" Ratnam grieved in despair. He must also have been worried over any harm that might have befallen his daughter, but he didn't show it. It was days before Kantimati started eating properly again.

Two years passed.

Vimala fell in love. It was a colleague in her office. He loved her, too. His parents also gave their consent and came to Ratnam's house and formally asked for Vimala as the bride. They said they wanted just the bride and no dowry or gifts with her.

Kantimati entreated her husband, "Look here. Two girls deceived us and left. Why can't we perform a proper wedding ceremony for this one and send her away ourselves? She is thirty now. We haven't been able to get any other alliance. She wants this. The boy and his family are good people. Just say yes without a word. After all the shocks we have had, let something auspicious happen in this house."

Ratnam jumped up in rage and fury. "What nonsense are you talking, you stupid fool! Is marriage something she can decide on? Am I dead and gone? Have we run out of bridegrooms? After those two tarts defied me and ran away, this one at least must obey me and marry only someone I find. You keep quiet."

He insulted and shooed away the boy's parents.

Vimala gazed at their backs with tears in her eyes. She was crying late into the night. When dawn broke, she was gone. It was the front door which was open.

But this time there was no mystery about where the daughter had gone. She had left a note saying she was going to marry the man she loved. She came back after a couple of weeks with her husband, with garlands round their necks, to seek the blessings of the parents. Ratnam insulted and shooed them away even at the doorstep.

A month or two after this development, Indu's engineer husband was transferred to Lucknow, and she moved out of Chennai with her family.

Kantimati got Ratnam another glass of water, persuaded him to get up, and changed the sheet on the bed. After he went back to rest, she entered the kitchen with a heavy sigh, as if she had climbed a rock.

"Come here, Indu. He will sleep undisturbed if we sit here and chat. We can talk in peace."

When Indu came and sat beside her, Kantimati asked her about her welfare.

"By God's grace, there is nothing we lack, Mami. Tell me about yourself."

"Well, what is there new to say?"

"You haven't changed much. But it seems to me that you are frozen inside. It is Mama who looks shattered even outside."

"Is it some mild shock he has had? Poor man. Three blows one after the other. Will you have coffee or tea, Indu? We'll have it with the fruit you brought."

"Maybe after sometime. Is Vimala okay at her in-laws' place? Do you have any contact with her?"

"None whatsoever. Your Mama's rage at all three hasn't abated one bit. Vimala and her husband are now in Chengalpattu."

"So you are in touch with her."

"No, no. It is all hearsay. What do I have to do with those who defied him and went away."

Kantimati washed two apples, brought a plate and a knife, and started peeling them.

"Do you have any news about the other two? Poor Amala, the youngest of them. She had taken some jewellery, too. I hope she is safe. It was her I was worried about after I left this place. In fact, I had even sent you a letter asking about her. But you had sent a curt one-line reply, saying you didn't know. It was in the style of a message saying, 'Are you okay? I am okay'."

"What could I do, Indu? There was indeed nothing known at that time."

"But there was some news later...?"

"Mmm, just hearsay. It seems that at first Amala went and hid herself in the house of one of the relatives of the principal of the arts college. It was, of course, arranged by her friend. After some time passed, when she thought there would be some let-up in the efforts to find her, she went directly to the principal's house, stayed with his family and studied at the college. It seems she sold the jewellery she had taken, put the money in a bank, and handed over the interest every month to the family towards expenses on her account. When she finished her training and got the diploma, she got a job on the principal's recommendation as an art teacher in a private school. I heard that she is earning a salary as a teacher, and she is also painting. It seems that a few of her paintings were on display at some exhibitions."

Indu sat looking at her keenly.

"She had completed her B.A. Did she take the degree certificate?"

"She seems to have taken it later, by post. If she had come here for the convocation, we would have come to know, wouldn't we? That is why."

Indu's eyes were still fixed on her.

"And what about Kamala? Have you heard anything about her?"

"Kamala is in Madurai. Well, it seems that she is in Madurai. It was said that at first she joined some women's organisation and took part in social welfare activities. Seeing how enthusiastic and caring she was, they appointed her warden in a children's hostel that they run."

A gentle smile formed on Indu's lips. "Your younger sister is also in Madurai, isn't she, working as secretary in a women's organisation?"

Kantimati looked up, met Indu's eyes for a moment, then bowed her head again and vigorously resumed the peeling.

"Not bad, Mami, you do have quite a bit of news about the three girls—of course it's all hearsay!"

"Done. Here, take it," said Kantimati, pushing the plate of apples towards her.

"You have some, too, let's eat together. I have always wondered about something, Mami."

"What is it?"

"All three of them got out in the night. Mama used to go around the house with an eagle eye the whole night. However, he would slide into deep slumber in the later part of the night. But you! You always slept so light that the slightest movement anywhere would wake you up. And, without you knowing, not one, not two, but all three—how did they open the door and go out? And the jewellery, too—I know the key to the iron safe was securely tied to your thirumangalyam. How did Amala take it out from your neck, and put it back there, without disturbing your sleep?"

Indu looked keenly at Mami without batting an eyelid. Kantimati looked back at her for a few moments. The smile on Indu's lips seemed to infect her, too. And then she laughed aloud.

"You are very smart, Indu."

The laughter soon stopped and the next moment the look on her face turned intense—as if she were delving deep into the heart and its innermost motives.

"It's not enough to beget and bring up children. One should also pave the way for them to be happy. You are a mother, too. You will understand."

There was silence for a while.

"Does Mama know that they are fine?"

"Yes, he does. I told him in the course of time, bit by bit, saying this is what I had heard."

"It must have given him comfort?"

"No. The anger still predominates. He still talks of them as renegades. He still can't digest the fact that they rebelled against him and went away."

"Can I ask you something, Mami, if you won't get offended?"

"Ask."

"You were the one who made it possible for them to defy him and leave. So, your behaving as if you are still in fear of him and your submitting to his authority—is it all a mask?"

"Not a mask, Indu. It is just being human. He is excessively hegemonic by nature. That disposition has taken a severe blow because of the daughters. If nobody feeds his ego, he will be completely shattered."

Kantimati's face was clouded in thought.

"I pray to God daily that his anger should subside and that he should forgive his daughters. If that doesn't happen, some day I may have to disclose the truth. His rage might then get diverted towards me and he might be reconciled with the girls. That's just a fond wish."

They both remained silent. A bee was circling the plate with the pieces of apple and was trying to alight. Kantimati mechanically shooed it away with her hand.

Ratnam's thunderous voice boomed from the room inside.

"*Ei*, where did you get lost? Come and switch on the fan here. You want me to sweat and die?"

"*Aiyo*, don't get angry. Here I come!"

Kantimati got up with a start and rushed into the room.

Originally published in Tamil as '*Kavalaimeeri*'
[Breaching security], in the magazine
Pudiya Parvai, 16–31 January 1994.

17
Grandmother

From this side of the window the child on the verandah could not be seen. But the voice came permeating the wall like a spirit. The song brimmed and flowed through the verandah, touching the ears and cajoling, "Look at me, look at me..."

There is a price one pays for becoming a grandmother, with rheumatism, a bent back, cataract of the eye. But there is a big gain, too—that you are able to listen to your grandchild lisping a song. A fair bargain altogether.

"*Amma*, have you eaten?"

The son came and enquired. He was fifty-six, but still a child when with the mother. He never left for work without asking about her welfare.

"Yes, *da*, I have."

When she put on the eyeglasses and looked up at her son, she felt the same fullness of joy that she had experienced when she had held him, her first-born, against her breast. After the first-born, another boy, then two girls. For all of them she was even now the adored goddess. When Appa died, this man had firmly declared, "Amma will be with me hereafter." The younger brother was upset of course. "Why, isn't she my mother, too?" But the reply came with a smile: "Well, wasn't I the one who first taught her what it was to be a mother? Therefore, she is more a mother for me than for you three."

Besides coming down from Delhi once a year, the younger son also sent her a cheque every month to assert his right. The two daughters would also visit every now and then, bask in the affection of the brother's family and exchange endearments with the mother.

There were no problems in this family like generation gaps or lack of mutual understanding. Not sorting people into old and young and making them mutual strangers, they mixed freely together, weaving a strong fabric of love. For the children, *Patti* was a friend. For the mother-in-law, the daughter-in-law was a daughter. As for the men, as son, husband, father, brother, they were all sweet people who took on various roles to spread mutual affection.

Right now, Patti's younger daughter had come from Salem with her two children to spend the summer holidays. It was her second child, the three-year-old Babu's music that was filling the verandah.

When the voice rose to a higher octave, it broke into a screech. The breath would come heavily. The face would flush. But the voice didn't give up singing.

"The music sounds grand, doesn't it?" said the son, his very voice a smile.

"Yes."

"But it's all just lisping still. Can you make out any words?"

"Why should we make out anything? He is singing. That's the child."

"That a song?"

"That is a song. That is joy. A lusty proclamation to the world: Here I am, look at me, look at me."

"It's beautiful, just the way you look at things," he said, coming close to his mother and holding her hand. "If there is a soul like you, we need not worry about anything. That's why I am certain that Manju will be comforted if you explain things to her."

Manjula was his only daughter. She was married three years earlier. Six months ago a child was born, but died the same night because of some strange complication relating to the blood. Manju had sunk into grief, and hadn't come out of it still. He had written to his son-in-law to send her here for a month so that she could have a change. So Manju was arriving from Bombay the next day.

"What a stupid girl, Amma. If the child had grown up and died, grief would certainly have been understandable. What is there to miss if the child passes away even before you realise it has arrived? After all, she is only twenty-six and there is a lifetime in which she can have children. I, too, was apprehensive for a while when she was in such agony, whether there was some complication completely ruling out any future childbirth. However, when we talked to the doctor, we learnt there was no such problem. Why then this unrelenting sorrow? You put it across to her and see that it goes home."

Patti was looking out through the window.

"What, Amma, what are you thinking about?"

"Hmm ... I'll talk to her."

The son went out, relieved.

"*Pathi*!"

Through the curtains of the window, a little head could be seen as a shadow. Patti parted the edges of the curtain, bent and looked down. A crown with hair like a bunch of black beetles. Below it, two blazing black spots. Nothing below them. Even for this the child should have been standing on tiptoe.

"Oh, *kuttippayalé*."

Babu leaped and vanished with a laugh. The laughter kept ringing like an astral voice even after the little figure had disappeared.

Patti closed the curtain and waited. The laughter inside her also waited.

After a while...

"Pathi!"

Once again the curtains parted. “Oh, kuttippayalé.” The leaping and vanishing crown.

This game went on for some time. Patti got up slowly and walked through the main entrance and into the garden. The next time the child stood on tiptoe in front of the window, looked inside and cried, “Pathi!” there she was, laughing and saying, “Here I am, right behind you!” and Babu threw his arms round her stomach and hugged her. Patti’s arms were ready for the reciprocal embrace, too.

“Pathi!”

“Hm?”

“Why do you always bend and walk? Why don’t you stand straight and grand, like me?”

“Oh, there are seventy-four years sitting on my back and pressing it down, *kanna*! That is why.”

Babu released himself from the hug, went behind her and looked at her back.

“There’s nothing sitting here.”

“You can’t see it with your eyes now.”

“Can I see it if I put on eye glasses?”

Patti laughed and said, “Shall we go in? It has started getting hot.”

“Pathi, I heard Manjookka is coming tomorrow?”

“Yes.”

“Amma told me. Who is Manjookka?”

“Your uncle’s daughter.”

“Have I seen her before?”

“When she got married, you were a two-month-old baby. After that you two haven’t seen each other.”

“But I saw her when I was a baby. I do remember.”

He got to like Manjookka the moment he saw her. Manju, too, as soon as she stepped into the house, went straight to him saying, “Oh, it is Babu, isn’t it?” and hugged him. The soft flesh pressed against her and her body shook silently.

"All right, all right, have your coffee first and take a bath to wash away all the dirt from the train," said Manju's mother.

The past days rose and sank one by one. Manju floated on them with her feet never touching the earth. How lovely she had been then! Flowers would bloom from the very space she stood on! Now, lean and emaciated, this is Manju's shadow. Just a facial sign reminding them of her.

Manju did now speak and laugh casually with her parents, Patti, aunt, the children. The legs did move around to render help to the elders. The hands did fondle the babies. The voice did join Babu in singing. But ... Manju was lost somewhere.

"Why this long face all the time? Shall we go to the beach?"

"Shall we see what is showing on Star TV?"

"Or shall we go to the cinema and watch *Mahanadhi*?"

"That is sob stuff. Why don't you think of something light, right, Manju?"

All the talk slid over her without sticking, like water over oil. Eyes that roamed around, pecking and pecking at the space ahead. Faces in front of the eyes. Voices dropping from those faces. Amma, *Atthai*, Appa.

Patti hadn't yet gone beyond saying things like "Have you eaten, Manju?" "Anything special in the papers, Manju?" "It's rather chilly today. Maybe it will rain tonight, don't you think so, Manju?" and she hadn't moved any closer to her. Manju's father frowned at his mother secretly. It was two weeks since Manju had arrived.

"Why haven't you given her some sensible advice yet? See, she is sitting and brooding all the time, the very picture of woe."

Patti didn't reply.

"Aren't you going to speak to her?"

"Yes, yes, I will, *da*."

For her part, wary of the counsel that Patti would give her, Manju tried as far as possible not to get close to her.

Despite being in the midst of so many, the feeling of loneliness never left her. It seemed to her that they all spoke a different language. She couldn't even cry her heart out here. Everyone was ready with some response at the tip of their tongue to bring her round.

In the mornings her eyes would be red.

"Were you crying all through the night? What a fine girl you are! Don't you know the proverb, *kuzhippillai madiyile*? The child buried in the pit will soon be in your lap, reborn. Another will be born in quick time. All this petulance about such a small thing! And after six months!"

Should she fly back to Bombay?

But even there.

In the beginning the husband displayed much sympathy. He cried with her, and both gave and received mutual comfort.

Then, little by little...

"Shall we go to a movie, Manju?"

"We will if that is what you wish."

One day his patience ran out.

"How long are you going to be like this, acting the crybaby? Don't I, too, feel the grief over the loss of the child? Is it as though we will never have a child again? As if our whole life has come to an end ... *Chhi*!"

She put on her guard. She learnt to smile. She pushed the tears behind the eyes, and they seeped inside and rusted the heart. When, however, he came to see that the smile on her lips was fake, he said, "Your father has written. As he suggests, go to your parental home and stay for a month. When you come back, you should come as my cheerful Manju of old."

As though seeking that cheerfulness, Manju was now looking intently at the guava tree and the jasmine creepers. The fragrance of the jasmine filled the night. She touched and stroked the soft petals. This softness, this fragrance, the memories that secreted and oozed from those empty hands...

Even as she began to feel the first stirrings of the flood from within getting ready to gush out, she heard footsteps behind her, and the sob instantly died a premature death, like her infant child.

"Manju."

Lucky Patti couldn't read her face in the darkness.

"Haven't you gone to sleep yet?"

"I'm not getting any sleep, Patti."

"Neither am I. That's why I thought I would come out and get some fresh air. Come, let us sit on the verandah steps."

Manju hastily said, "No, Patti. I'll go in and lie down. I think I am feeling sleepy now."

"It's okay. Just sit down for ten minutes."

She sat down near Patti hesitantly.

Now, the golden sayings will begin to drop one by one like leaves from a tree.

—The Lord gave and the Lord has taken. What can mere mortals do?

—This was what was destined for us. Comfort yourself.

—Time will heal all sorrows.

—That was a blessed soul. It played out all its *karma* within a day. Should we grieve over it?

—The child in the pit will be the child in the lap. The dead one will soon be reborn. When you get another within a year, you will forget all this.

—You have all the time in the world to get a child. Are you an old wretch of a woman? Wipe your eyes.

—How could you feel close to a child who didn't live for even twenty-four hours? It's absurd grieving over it and crying all the time.

—You are getting on *mappillai*'s nerves. Beware.

—Look here, dear! Stop crying, okay? Go, freshen up and pay obeisance to the deities in the puja room. Everything will be fine.

She closed her eyes and waited for Patti's voice to emerge, like a prisoner getting ready to face gunfire.

"Manju."

No response.

"Manjumma."

Manju could hear Patti's sigh, but still didn't open her mouth. She checked the impulse to run away from there.

"Your father asked me to comfort you..."

Her frame stiffened.

"But what can I say that will comfort you? I can see you are in grief. But I don't comprehend what kind of grief it is. I cannot. My words will carry no meaning. All the four I brought forth are alive. I have not known the sorrow of a child's loss."

Her head turned quickly. In the darkness her eyes sought Patti's.

Patti caressed her head and held her cheeks in both her hands. Manju could feel the bony fingers quivering over her face.

"Weep. Cry your heart out. I am nothing before your sorrow. All I can do is to pray that *Easwaran* will take your part..." Patti moved closer and held her tight against her chest, "... and this."

The comfort and consolation that this embrace gave ... how did Patti understand?

There was no voice for the feelings that burst from the heart. Her head buried itself in the old woman's lap. The grief that had descended on every corner of her heart now surged upward and outward and flowed and drenched the face of the night in torrents. As the frame shook and the wordless sobs sprang from the heart's founts, far beyond, there was the faint stirring of a heaviness lifting.

Originally published in Tamil as '*Patti*' [Grandmother],
in the magazine *Dinamani Kadir*, 11 September 1994.

18

Mr Outlet

He was a *yogi*. In the eyes of others.

One who has lost the use of his legs is a yogi. That is how the world sees him.

One who has lost the use of his legs should also lose all desires and attachments. He should just be a log of wood, an embodiment of patience and composure, an ascetic without saffron robes.

"Oh, Ravi? Poor thing! He had an attack of polio at the age of three and is confined to his wheel chair. But so what? Just as *Easwara* said about *Vallalar*: 'Ramalingam will attain realisation without chanting prayers', this man, too, is a born genius. Just staying at home, there is no book he has not read. Everyone in this colony holds him in high esteem. He discusses threadbare matters of high philosophical import. Oh, he is a true sage, that's what he is. A greater sage at the age of thirty than sixty- and seventy-year olds."

If he was a sage, there was no need to worry about his feelings. What feelings did a sage have? And even if he did, what did they matter for one who looked upon joy and sorrow the same way?

Who would think that he would burn with inner rage watching his father as he left the house after bullying his mother, his mouth red with betel nut juice, singing an erotic film song, holding up the end of his peacock-eye-bordered dhoti?

His mother would describe to him how intimate her husband had been in the early days. "There was a time when your father would always address me as 'My sweet little parrot'! If, after finishing all the chores that my mother-in-law had set for me, I was late even by a quarter of an hour in entering the bedroom, he would jump up and down, shouting, 'Why so late?' And now, at this age, he is running after..." Thus she would confide her sorrows without in the least stopping to think that she was speaking to a grown-up son. Because he was a yogi. One could say anything to him. He was just an outlet.

An outlet he was for lots and lots of people. The world was a huge mouth as it were, and he was its permanent ears. "Captive audience! I can't exactly get off the chair and run away, can I?" he thought.

"What Ravi, what are you doing? Reading a book as usual? Real genius you are!"

It was *Appa*'s bosom friend. It was difficult to believe that this man, bald and thin, and Appa, a six-footer still retaining the sheen of youth, were close friends. But why did friendship need physical similarity? It was enough that both went to the Gymkhana club and liked to play billiards.

"Please come, *Mama*. There's no genius here. I read just to pass the time. Please sit," said Ravi, putting on a smile for courtesy's sake.

"When you laugh, it is exactly like your father's. Your build is the same, too. If this polio attack hadn't happened, you would just be a xerox of your father," he said looking at the shawl that covered Ravi's legs.

"Why don't we talk about something else, Mama? What's the matter? Appa is not at home."

"When was your Appa ever at home at six in the evening! It would be eleven in the night by the time he leaves from 'there'." He lowered his voice. "Have you seen her? She is so sumptuous, like a *laddu*."

"In this book, Pudumaippittan..."

"My heart feels so heavy, Ravi. I thought I would pour out my sorrow to you and cry on your shoulders. You know my business partner, Narahari, don't you? Goes about calling himself a big film critic. You know what he has done? All the profit in the business he has cornered and he has bought houses and shares in the name of his brother-in-law, and left me with nothing! It is brazen betrayal. I don't mind telling you this, I have already met with huge losses in the last bank scam. And now this second blow like a thunderbolt. I don't know how I can bear it. What am I going to do...?"

He had no doubt whatsoever that what he was saying would interest Ravi. No one who spoke to Ravi ever entertained any such doubts.

"It is good to be like you, Ravi. You are a yogi. These things are nothing to you. That rascal..."

Sitting in the balcony outside his room, he could have a view of the compound opposite with a tall cannonball tree and its dense foliage covering the house behind like a curtain.

Once after strong winds when the tree had shed all its leaves and stood with just bare crisscrossing branches, he had spotted in the window the bright face of a girl.

The first time, the faces withdrew with a start. After a few more times, the expression on the faces seemed not to change. Still later, when the last few leaves had made way and the two faces clearly emerged, they were ready to wear smiles of familiarity. When someone called from inside the house, "Santha!" and her face disappeared from the window, it struck him that Santha was a beautiful name.

One day when Ravi was sitting in the balcony and reading a book, his friend Gopalan came. He must have been the same age as Ravi. He was one of those from the neighbourhood who called themselves Ravi's friends and came to visit him. To all of them, Ravi constituted a great facility: they could unburden whatever was passing through their minds.

"What, Ravi? Reading?" Gopalan asked as he sat on the floor beside the wheel chair.

"I suppose that's what people generally do when they have a book in their hands." Ravi sheathed his rage in a smile.

"How well you talk! Intelligent fellow! That's why the heart feels so light after talking to you. Do you know what is happening in my house? This fight between my mother and my wife day in and day out, it's just getting intolerable. She tells me one day—and I don't mind telling you—'If you are a proper man, either take me with you and set up a separate establishment, or divorce me'. That's what she says. Now how do you like that? Can I, for my part, ask, 'You have this doubt whether I am a proper man after five years of married life? You ask me to abandon my mother. Will you ditch your mother?'"

It was Ravi's cousin Sundaram who had come another day. "Ravi!" he said, "I don't like anything here. Wherever you turn, there's corruption, poverty, caste discrimination. There's no scope for talent here. After finishing my MBA, I have applied to a few American universities for higher studies in management. Even my parents don't know about this. But what's the problem in telling you? If I get admission somewhere there, I will slowly get a foothold with studies and a job, and finally get citizenship and settle down there. Keep this to yourself. But who are you going to tell? Poor fellow. You live like a saint, keeping away from all gossip and unnecessary talk."

It was as though he got a fresh spurt of energy when Santha became friends with his mother and started visiting their house.

She spoke and moved with him with natural ease. She borrowed books from him. She wheeled him to the balcony, sat on the floor and discussed the books she had read. She had a cheerful and radiant face and a well-proportioned physique. She acted and spoke with tenderness.

Ravi found himself eagerly looking forward to Santha's visits. He took the mirror from the stand and checked his face. A regal and fair complexion. Curly hair. A broad forehead (a sure sign of intelligence?). Large eyes. Lips rather thick, but that fault vanished with the gleam of the neat white teeth when he laughed. There was a radiance in him, too, a touch of majesty...

The withered legs covered by the shawl notwithstanding, some woman might still ... like him ... Maybe.

Some care now went into applying cream and grooming his hair, wearing bright-coloured shirts.

He was sitting in the park one day. One of his maternal uncles had come by car and brought the entire family, and also Ravi's wheel chair, to the park. He had left Ravi seated in the wheelchair near a concrete bench, and gone for a walk.

An old man came and sat on the bench. He cast a curious intrusive look at Ravi.

"Poor boy! What is the problem?"

Silence.

"Is it polio? Or some accident? Didn't you take treatment?"

Silence.

"You came alone? Or did someone bring you? Is your house close by?"

"Those flowers in front look beautiful, don't they, sir?"

"Yes, chrysanthemum."

"Dahlia."

"You know everything! If the Divine takes away something, He also gives something in return. Hmm. Why can't He grant me something good? So many family problems. Son who has finished studies and is roaming around unable to get a job. Daughter who has lost the use of her legs. No problem if it is a boy like you. But she is a girl! Shouldn't I entrust her to someone's care? I've gone bankrupt taking loan after loan for her treatment. The yellow thread around my wife's neck is the only thing left." He dabbed his eyes lightly with his upper cloth. "And no peace at the work place either. I have been a clerk in my office for fifteen years now. And some fellow half my age sits as my superior in an AC room and lords it over me like a white master. Shouldn't he show some respect for age? I don't mind telling you, sometimes I feel like killing myself..."

"Am I an outlet for rank strangers, too? Is it written on my face: 'This is a Garbage Bin. Empty All Your Worries Here'?"

"Come, Santha! We haven't seen you for a week now."

He heard his mother's words spoken in the hall downstairs. Ravi sat up straight in his chair. He ran his fingers through his hair. A smile formed on the lips ready to welcome her.

"I had some work, Mami, that's why," Santha's voice came through.

What work it was he came to know when they sat in the balcony and talked.

A gentle breeze wafted through the warmth of the golden light of dusk. Ravi's heart was filled with ardour.

"No praise is too high for Tirunavukkarasar who compared the joy one finds at the Lord's feet to the gentle south wind. Don't you think so, Santha?" he said.

They had just been talking about Tamil songs, old and new. His heart was still bubbling over with lyrical joy. What he said was just a continuation of that joy. The golden evening light and the lyrical touch coupled with her closeness enhanced the sweetness.

"Absolutely, Mr Ravi. Today I can truly enjoy and discuss poetry as before. Do you know why?"

"Why?"

"Because today I am so very happy!"

"So gratifying to hear it."

"For the past one week, just worries, arguments, objections and explanations," she smiled. "But I have no problem telling you: I am in love with someone. He's an Assistant Lecturer in our college. His name is Palanivel. He loves me, too. But there is opposition from both our families. Caste is the issue, of course, what else? He is a very good man, Mr Ravi! I generally don't move in an uninhibited way with anyone. Can I move without fear with all men as I do with you?"

Ravi's face shrank sharply.

"But Palani is different. He struck me as a noble being the moment I saw him. We have got to know each other. We wish to marry. Over the last one week we met secretly several times and discussed the matter from several angles as our parents don't agree to the match. Finally, we have decided to elope if we don't get our parents' consent. We will try for another week or ten days, entreating and arguing with our people. If it still proves futile, a runaway marriage it will be."

She sighed with a smile.

"The heart feels lighter the moment I confide in you, Mr Ravi. You are a man of deep knowledge. Someone who understands everything the right way..."

"Get up and get out!"

Dumbstruck, Santha looked up at his flushed face contorted by fury. Ravi was panting. Fuming words burst through the quivering lips and were spat out along with spurts of saliva.

"Why do you come and tell me all this? Am I Father Confessor to everyone? You fall in love with anyone you like. Marry him. What is it to me? Am I fated to carry everyone's secret burden? I don't want anyone to come and tell me anything! I am not a log of wood! Just get up and leave!"

"Mr Ravi..."

"Go! Go! Get lost! Mr Ravi, Mr Ravi indeed!"

Even after Santha, terrified and confused, reached her house, looking back every now and then, the shouts of "Go! Go!" kept sounding in the air like a frenzied wail.

Originally published in Tamil as '*Vadikaalan*'
[One who is an outlet], in the magazine
Amudhasurabhi, Deepavali Special, October 1997.

19

Insecurity

The skin looked as though it had been coated with a blend of rose petals and snow. Light brown hair with golden streaks cut rather long. Blue eyes. Long blue skirt with a below-the-knee hemline, as though it was a concession to the South Indian sartorial code. White blouse. Though the sandals were not high-heeled, for a moment it looked as though she was as tall as Gopi. However, when they were both asked to stand side by side for the *arti* ceremony, it was seen that Gopi was a full inch taller than his wife.

Gopi's elder brother Sundaram was standing aside. He had received them at the international terminal of the Meenambakkam airport. After they had got off the flight and completed the immigration formalities, he welcomed them with a "Hello, Gopi! Hello, Sylvia! How was the flight?" and brought them home to Chetpet in father's Maruti Suzuki. Mangalam, the mother, and Janani, the elder daughter-in-law, were doing the circling of the arti for the couple. "*Sita kalyana vaibhogame ... Rama kalyana vaibhogame...*" Janani sang softly.

"What are they doing?" Sylvia asked her husband.

"They are welcoming us," said Gopi and stood respectfully.

The bride looked at her sister-in-law with a friendly smile and said, "Hi, Jenny."

Two years earlier, Sundaram and Janani had gone to Florida when the wedding took place. So Sylvia had some familiarity with her. In the midst of mostly unpronounceable Indian names, 'Janani,' sounding rather like the Western 'Jenny,' had been rather easy for her to say. 'Janani' had thus become 'Jenny.'

Janani smiled back, carried the arti plate outside the gate, emptied it there and returned. Sylvia paid her respects to her mother-in-law with folded hands, proud to have learnt the Indian mode of salutation.

Mangalam was pleased, too. Though Sylvia didn't prostrate like "our girls," she was cultured enough to greet elders with folded hands.

"*Nannayirumma*," she said in Tamil but immediately corrected herself and said, "I mean, my blessings to you." There were curious faces at the neighbouring windows on both sides. Mangalam felt proud, thinking they would have seen her welcoming her American daughter-in-law with arti and speaking to her in English.

"Come in, Sylvia; step in with your right foot first," she said in English and went in with a stately gait, but not without glaring at her elder son who was whistling a Tamil tune, "*Manamahale, manamahale, vaa, vaa, un valadu kaalai eduttu vaittu vaa, vaa*" (Enter, oh bride, enter, enter, put your right foot forward and enter).

It was a golden evening and the entire family had arrived at the Marina beach and were sitting on the sands. Sylvia didn't tire of gazing endlessly at the sea and the people who were selling conches beside the advancing and receding waves. Every now and then she and Gopi would rise, walk some distance on the sands, stand in the midst of the waves and return with their trousers and jeans dark with the wetness.

"Fantastic sunset! I have shot it all. I wonder how it has come off," said Sylvia beaming. She always had the flash camera in her hand. She had taken snaps of everyone at home. When she went out anywhere, everything that drew her attention would find its way into the camera.

There was nothing on the beach that she missed shooting. The people who went round selling *sundal*, the beggar woman with a naked child in her arms, the boys in shorts who were cheerfully taking a dangerous bus ride, hanging on to the ladder at the back, the children sitting heroically or nervously on horseback and taking short rides, the tomb of *M.G.R.*, the girls who ran round selling flowers...

"Oh, how nice! How interesting!"

Janani was slightly annoyed. Was everything in India just a showpiece for her? Was this all the value that the motherland carried for foreigners? Typical tourist attitude.

As the days went by, the rock temples at Mahabalipuram, the Kapaleeswarar temple tower and many more like them became the targets of Sylvia's photographic ardour.

Once on the Elliots beach she looked curiously at the *narikkurava* couple they had run into. The man in just a loincloth, the woman with half her body exposed, wearing a green skirt and a yellow blouse, chains of beads of all colours in her hands and a basket on her waist. A monkey perched on the man's shoulder.

"How colourful!" exclaimed Sylvia and promptly stored them in her camera.

As curiously as she stared at them, they were also gazing at her. Janani didn't like this either. Wherever Sylvia went, all passers-by unfailingly stared at her, as though they had never before seen anyone with a white skin. The curiosity seemed all the greater if a foreign woman was seen in the company of a few Indians. It was sad to think that Sylvia was just a showpiece for these people.

Janani felt angry when she saw young urchins and girls following Sylvia and pestering her with "Missie, good morning missie, take this chain of beads missie, just fifty rupees missie!" and trying to dump on her, for fifty rupees, something which was worth hardly five rupees. These people thought that all foreigners had fat purses and could be easily duped! She felt humiliated at the idea.

At home, however, Sylvia was by no means a showpiece. Sambamurti as well as Mangalam had accepted her as an individual, and as a daughter-in-law.

True, they had been shocked when Gopi had first written to them that he wished to marry an American girl. True, how great it would have been if they had got as bride one of "our" girls, exquisitely perfect in all features, looking stately like a *kuttuvilakku*, draped in an ample-folded sari coming down to the floor, a *tali* dangling from the neck, and speaking clear and sparkling Tamil! Instead, for them to unite in some registry of a far-away place, signing as Sylvia Mary Harrison and Aattur Sambamurti Gopalan...

But when your boy, now a grown-up man taller than you, and more a friend than a son, goes abroad for higher education, graduates and settles with a job as an electronics engineer, when he says, "This is what I wish to do," is it possible to stop him? Even if you do, can you bear to look at his hurt countenance?

At the personal level, there was no fault they could find with Sylvia. A nice girl. She had wholeheartedly agreed to stay with them here rather than stay in a hotel. With a radiant face, she had herself handed to her mother-in-law, father-in-law, brother-in-law and sister-in-law the gifts she and Gopi had got for them from America. When they were worried that she would want non-vegetarian food, she didn't even ask for eggs. Except for the fact that she preferred wheat to rice, she went with the others saying that what the others took—vegetables, curd, milk—would do for her, too. They had, on their own, stored for her things like bread, butter, jam, fruits and sweet corn. She drank with relish the coffee they made and paid a lavish compliment: "After French coffee, I find the best flavour only in the one made in this house, Jenny—delicious!"

When she had first got acquainted with Gopi, she used to address him as "Mr Gopalan." With Western practices of naming in mind, she had thought that in "Aattur Sambamurti Gopalan" the first name was his individual name, the second a middle name and the last the family name or surname. In her culture, only people who knew one well and relatives or friends were free to call one by the first name. When, therefore, after they got to know and love each other, she called him "Darling Aattur," with the tender intent of communicating intimacy, Gopi was shocked and explained to her the naming conventions of South India. It was thereafter that she started addressing him as "Gopi." All this the family came to know from Gopi.

This was the first time after their marriage two years earlier that Gopi had come to India with his wife, taking a month's leave, and the first time her mother-in-law and father-in-law were seeing her. When they showed her to the room upstairs that they had readied for the couple's use, she said, "The arrangements you've made are excellent, but why did you take all this trouble? Whatever place you had here, I would have adjusted to it." Even during the first week, while getting used to the differences in the East-West time zones and fighting the jetlag, as she dozed off in the daytime and sat sleepless in the night biting into bread loaves, even during that time she wasn't remiss in mixing sweetly with them.

But still...

There was that "But still" somewhere...

It was the day of *Varalakshmi nombu*.

Mangalam finished her bath and, for the occasion, draped herself in a *madisar* sari. As she was looking after the arrangements for the puja, Sylvia was watching her. She had seen some women dressed in this fashion as she was driving through the streets. But now here, in this house, her mother-in-law was dressed in the same way for some special occasion! She ran upstairs and fetched her camera. First she shot a picture of the *kalasam*, representing the goddess, decorated with flowers, *kumkumam* and a new sari. She then asked her mother-in-law, "Can I take a snap of you in this traditional dress?"

Mangalam felt annoyed. It was shooting pictures of gypsies one day, and now the mother-in-law in madisar! What was this, a fancy-dress show? Was she going to return, show all these to her American friends and add explanatory footnotes like, "These are a nomadic tribal couple, and this woman here is my husband's mother. This is the orthodox mode in which Brahmin women from Tamil Nadu wear their sari on special occasions"?

She tried to decline saying, "Why all this?"

"For my sake, *Amma*! Please!"

That was the only Tamil word Sylvia had learnt to say with an American lisp. The special concession she had made for her husband's mother.

"All right, as you wish."

As Janani, too, entered clad in madisar, Sylvia's enthusiasm doubled. "O Jenny, this is great!" After taking a picture of her mother-in-law separately, she shot one with them together, and then retired to her room upstairs.

"Janani, I have a wish."

"Tell me, Amma."

"I wish to see her dressed in a sari at least today."

"Amma, she's not used to it. What if she trips and falls?"

"Why don't you show her?"

"Well, she may say, 'Why should I dress myself in a sari when your own girls wear only churidars and salwars?'"

"Only for today! That, too, only till the puja is over. From the day she came, have you seen her wearing a sari even once? Skirts, jeans, trousers and suits—all the time. After all, isn't it an Indian she has married? Wouldn't she want to please his mother and father at least once, standing before them dressed in a sari?"

Janani felt pity for her mother-in-law. "I will try asking her," she said. Then, hesitating for a while, she said, "You said 'Indian', didn't you? Gopi may not stay 'Indian' for long."

"What do you mean?"

"He's going to become an American citizen in a few years. He was telling his *Anna* and me. It seems that is Sylvia's wish."

Mangalam's face paled. Janani, too, felt heavy in her heart, but she tried to comfort her mother-in-law.

"Come to think of it, there is nothing to feel bad about in this. Just think, Amma. Gopi has a good job there, and recognition for his talent. Will he get the same satisfaction, opportunities and salary here? He is in any case going to settle there. An American wife, too. Naturally, American citizenship will be next! Can that be avoided? That will be the most convenient thing in the future, when the children arrive."

Mangalam sighed and held Janani's hand. "Well, you and Sundar are here with us, in our last days."

"Absolutely. Please don't worry. And Gopi, too; will he ever lose his affection for you? He will give us whatever help we need. He will come and look us all up at least once in a few years."

"Yes, on an American passport!"

When Janani talked to Sylvia about the sari, she politely but firmly refused.

What was her problem in wearing a sari just once to satisfy the wishes of her husband's parents? What did she fear she would lose by giving in to this? Why this intensity in insisting on her difference, although superficially she seemed to mix well with them? Was she making the wearing of a sari a metaphor for the Indian woman, and affirming: "I have a different identity"?

At the time of the wedding, Sambamurti and Mangalam had sent, through their elder son and daughter-in-law, some gold ornaments for the bride and two silk saris with broad *zari* borders. Janani now recalled that Sylvia had said that she had cut the two saris, made pretty dresses out of them and worn them for parties.

Some relatives visited them in the evening. Ever since they came from America, there were visitors almost every day. Mangalam introduced the younger daughter-in-law.

All the visitors displayed a special interest in looking at "the woman from the other place." Since it was a love marriage, they thought on the lines of "What did he find in her?" and sized her up within themselves. Those who knew English felt proud speaking to her in English. They pretended to follow her American accent when in fact they didn't.

Sylvia was sitting slightly apart and observing everyone, her husband in particular. How cheerful, how happy he looked as he sat there with his family, chatting with the visitors! To those elderly women who couldn't speak in English he spoke in Tamil. In fact, except when Sylvia was spoken to, it was Tamil by and large which was being used in the conversation. Sylvia just sat there watching without comprehending anything. Gopi must have said something very witty. Huge laughter broke out and echoed across the room. Sundaram said something in response, laughed and affectionately slapped his younger brother on the back. When one of the visitors translated the joke Gopi had cracked for Sylvia, no smile came to her lips.

Janani made coffee for everyone and brought them in two plates one after the other. Sylvia helped her in serving everyone. Gopi was one of those that she handed the coffee to. He took the tumbler from her and continued chatting with his aunt who was sitting next to him. Sylvia waited for a few seconds, her face lightly flushing. When Gopi had finished drinking the coffee, she bent as though to pick up the empty tumbler and said to him in a low but tense voice, "Say 'Thank you' to me." And Janani distinctly heard this as she passed by behind them.

Gopi quickly looked up at his wife; there was a touch of panic on his face. "Thank you, Sylvie ... Thank you very much."

He would have a job to do that night making up to her, thought Janani.

Wasn't the husband-wife relationship one of intimacy, going beyond the need for these small civilities?

Evidently, Gopi didn't quite succeed in the night. The whole of the next day Sylvia stayed with a long face. Gopi kept himself busy attending to her. At mealtimes he brought her plate and filled her tumbler with mineral water. He arranged the chair in the right position for her to sit. He brought the coffee for her and handed it to her. When all of them were sitting together and she said, "Excuse me, I'll go up and rest for a while," and rose and left, he followed her upstairs.

When the power supply went off that evening and the house was shrouded in darkness, Gopi was in agony. He made phone call after phone call ("O hell, what kind of phone is this! Goes on strike at such an awkward time. Appa, throw this away first thing and get a cell phone!") and called in the people from the Electricity Department. Even as they opened up the metre box and were examining it in the light of the torch that Sundaram was shining, Gopi kept rushing and annoying them, "Is it done, is it done?"

"Show a little patience, Gopi! They are at the job."

"But can't you see Sylvia is in distress? She is not used to these things. She is sweating profusely without the fan."

Sundaram laughed, "Well, everyone sweats if the fan doesn't work!"

Gopi climbed up and down the stairs restlessly. Every now and then he went up the stairs with a chimney lamp in hand and reassured his wife, who was sitting in candlelight, "The power supply will soon come back, don't worry." He breathed normally only when the power was restored.

"Oh, my god, what a fuss he makes, as though he is the only one in the world with a wife!" said Sambamurti to his wife and laughed. There was a sadness mingled with the laughter. Most of these young Indian men, when they marry girls from the West, seemed to think that a celestial being had deigned to descend to the earth to wed them!

Sylvia was her normal self again in four or five days. One day she and Gopi visited the USIS library using Sundaram's membership card. In the evening, as they were driving through Pantheon Road on their way to the beach, they saw a notice at the entrance of the Museum Theatre announcing a play to be performed by the Madras Players. The next day, when they returned home after watching the play, Sylvia was indeed quite happy.

There was a bakery in the next street which sold square-shaped biscuits, and Sylvia used to eat them with relish, exclaiming, "Oh cookies!" One evening Gopi had left with his brother around half past five to get a pack of those biscuits, and they didn't return for quite a while. It was a quarter past seven, and Sylvia's eyes were fixed on her wrist watch even as she was sitting in the hall talking to Janani.

"Jenny, they have never taken so long for this! What do you think has happened?"

"They would have run into some friend on the way and lost count of time in the midst of their chatting. They will be back. Don't worry."

"Most irresponsible."

It was around eight when the cheerful voices of the brothers were heard at the entrance. They came in together.

"Why so much delay?" Sylvia asked her husband.

"Maybe you caught hold of some old friend," said Janani, laughing, and Gopi laughed, too.

"Right you are, *Manni*!" Gopi responded instinctively in Tamil, and bit his tongue at once and switched to English.

"We ran into an old friend on the way. In the course of our chat he mentioned that our old school principal, Mr Arunachalam, had been troubled with arthritis for some time now and wasn't able to move about much outside. When we heard that his house was quite close by, we didn't have the heart to miss looking him up."

"He was very happy that we went to see him! He made us sit, asked his wife to get us coffee and kept talking to us," said Sundaram.

"It seems nobody visits him these days. He simply wouldn't let us leave. Luckily we had the pack of cookies that we had just bought, so I handed it to him, saying, 'This is for you, Sir'."

"Mr Arunachalam is a good man," said Sundaram.

"Won't you say that? He was quite his pet student, Sylvie," said Gopi laughing and gave Sundaram a playful jab in the arm.

"Me his pet? You know, Sylvia, what this fellow used to do? Terribly naughty he was! Once in the maths class he carelessly said, 'Two and two makes five'. When the maths master sternly demanded, '*De*, what is this? How much is two and two?' Gopi put on an innocent look and replied, 'Don't you know even this much, Sir?' The master flew into a rage. Finally, a complaint went to the principal that here was a cheeky boy. In all justice, shouldn't the principal have called in this fellow and given him a dressing down? Instead, he called me and said, '*De*, Sundar, you are the elder one and you are studying in a higher class. It is your responsibility to see that your younger brother behaves himself.' Now you tell us. Who was his pet?"

"Don't go by what he says, Sylvie. He is just exaggerating. We asked our principal about his health. He is better now. He talked to us very fondly and enquired about us in great detail."

"He was very proud that Gopi is in America, employed in a high position."

"We had a very sweet time with him, didn't we, Anna?"

"Definitely."

"One of his sons is in Mayavaram..."

"Jenny, I don't feel hungry. I won't have food. I am going upstairs," Sylvia said, rising abruptly, and went away.

All three of them felt the sudden jarring note that had halted the sweet music of the conversation. Gopi stood frozen in shock for a moment and then ran upstairs following his wife.

Around nine in the night, when Janani put two *chapathi*s, cooked carrots and a cup of Sylvia's favourite yogurt on a plate and took it upstairs, anxiously hoping that she would eat at least now, she found that the note of discord had taken a clearer shape. The altercation had evidently been going on for some time. Janani halted outside their room.

"... That's what I'm saying. After coming to India you have become an Indian out and out. When I served you coffee the other day, you failed to say 'Thanks'. When any of your people come to the house, you simply swell with joy. Today, without me, without even telling me, you went out with your brother and came back after having a great time together. Both of you are beside yourselves chatting about this and that. What do I have to do with all the things that you described? Weren't you dwelling with your brother in a separate world from which I was clearly excluded? Are you after all the typical Indian male who shows no regard for his wife?"

"Sylvie, look, when I come here once in a long while..."

"Gopi ... Gopi..." her voice choked, "I am scared that your roots will pull you back again, Gopi..."

"You should never think so. Nothing can pull me away from you, Sylvie."

He must have embraced and comforted her. After moments of silence, her voice was heard, this time very gentle.

"Gopi!"

"Yes, honey?"

"If ... If you had married a Tamil girl, would you have been happier? Do you have any regret that you didn't?"

"What a stupid question! The only girl I want is this girl. I love you, Sylvie! Don't you know that?"

Janani went back down quietly. Her heart was heavy.

Didn't that girl have faith in the strength of their mutual love? Why did she see it as something so fragile, so insecure, so vulnerable to threat all the time? Was she pressing him to become an American citizen just to reaffirm that he was hers and hers alone to possess?

After that, till the time they returned, Gopi never went out anywhere without Sylvia. Wherever he went, she went, too. Even when he went to the street corner to drop a letter in the post box. Even when he went to the salon for a haircut. ("Only I can say what hairstyle will look nice on him.")

Not that they didn't go out with the others. The whole family together, or sometimes just the two young couples without the parents, went to movies, exhibitions or on tours. Still, it seemed to Janani that it was the occasions when Gopi and Sylvia went just by themselves that Sylvia most liked.

Sylvia looked very happy indeed when they both went shopping and bought presents for their friends and relatives in the US. She looked even happier when one night at dinner time she said to her sister-in-law, "Next Wednesday this time we will be in Florida. Not the same time, of course; it will be morning there."

At the airport, while taking leave of everyone, she invited them all to the US. "Don't worry about food, Amma. If you come, I will learn how to make *rasam* and *sambar* and serve you everything myself," she said to her mother-in-law wholeheartedly.

"I am so pleased even by your saying so, amma! We wish both of you well," said Mangalam. The parents' eyes moistened as they looked at their younger son—when would he come back again?

"Jenny, all the pictures I have taken, I will make copies when I reach home and send them to you."

Hanging from her shoulder was the camera which held all the pictures she had taken: the one in which all of them posed sitting together after asking the boy next door to click the camera; the ones she had taken earlier; the ones she had taken just a few days ago like those at Valluvar Kottam, Gandhi Mandapam, and pictures of the Triplicane temple elephant.

The family, which had come to see them off, had to halt once the couple went into the security zone.

They watched as the plane rose into the sky, grew small and faded away.

Mangalam checked a sob. The four of them walked back to the car.

"Poor Gopi. He is so scared of his wife," said Sundaram as he was driving them home.

"She is scared, too," said Janani.

"Sylvia? Of whom?" asked Sundaram.

Janani made no reply. She was lost in thought.

Originally published in Tamil as '*Amerikkavirundali*'
[The American guest], in the magazine
Ladies Special Deepavali Malar, November 1999.

20

Identity and amnesia

Even as she was entering the house, her eyes fell on a name-board at the outer gate: S. SUGANDHI. Rama raised her eyebrows and smiled to herself. Gold-coloured, strikingly bright letters inscribed on a black marble slab. Since when does Sugandhi *Mami* have a name-board? It wasn't there when she had come two months earlier and presented a gift to Mami on her sixtieth birthday and touched her feet. Does Mami feel that she is now sixty and so is entitled to show off a bit?

"Mami..." she called as she entered the house.

"Come, Rama, come. At long last!" said Sugandhi as she came from inside. For a moment the words sounded rather odd to Rama. Something you say to welcome people who haven't visited you for a long time—to say that to someone you had met just two months ago?... The next moment however she got over the surprise and said cheerfully, "How are you, Mami?" Sugandhi held her hands and they sat together on the sofa.

Rama noticed that Mami looked a little tired, and physically reduced, too. And the eyes ... was there a shade of fright in them? Mami afraid? That would be surprising. Sugandhi Mami was a person full of self-confidence, never giving room for fear of any kind. Rama had heard that Mami's mother had died when she was a child. The father had lived long but had been struck with a fatal disease in old age and died. And before Mami was barely forty-five her husband had also died, leaving her a childless widow. But Mami had never ever lost courage. That was what Rama's mother had told her. After she had come to know and respect Mami through her mother, Rama had herself become her friend and looked her up whenever she could.

Sugandhi's moderately fair-complexioned face was marked by clear, neatly drawn features. She was tall and plump, with a shapely neck and a majestic gait. That stateliness you would have thought was just a reflection of her inner self. She didn't shut herself off and sit at home when her husband passed away. On the contrary she threw herself into social service. She lent support to consumer rights movements. She embraced abandoned children with her service, saying, "Aren't these our children, too?"

She read a lot. And whatever she read was sculpted in her mind. A countenance always radiant. An ebullient woman in harmony with life.

That kind of person now looking tired and frightened? What had happened to Mami?

"Aren't you well, Mami? You don't look all right!"

Sugandhi sat for a while staring ahead of her, then shook her head and smiled.

"Oh, it's nothing. The heat is unbearable, isn't it?"

"Wait, I'll switch on the fan."

Rama got up and switched on the fan. Hanging on the wall next to the fan switch was the calendar. And at the bottom of the calendar, the letters: S. Sugandhi.

She turned and looked at Mami. What do we make of this? On the one hand, there is this frightened look. And on the other, this sense of ego, making one's name all-important. Wasn't there some inconsistency here?

She came and sat down on the sofa again. The fan was blowing hot air.

"I am fine, Rama. How are you? How are the children? Is your mother okay?"

They chatted for a while.

"Wait, I'll go make some coffee for both of us."

"But isn't Annamma around? I'll go and tell her. Please sit, Mami."

"It's okay. I made some *rava kesari* this morning. I'll get some of that, too."

Mami spoke cheerfully and with her usual exuberance as she got up and went in. Mami frightened? No way!

"What, you stupid girl, why are you scared to death like this? Will your Miss chop off your head? But you must of course get the song by heart and recite it properly. Come on now, let's hear you recite it."

That is what Sugandhi Mami had said to her once. Rama was fourteen years old then. There was a competition in the school for the recitation of *Saint Vallalar*'s songs. And she kept forgetting whatever she had memorised. The teacher had thought of her as a bright pupil of Tamil. Which she generally was. But get things by heart she could not. Rama was afraid that "Miss" would be quite disappointed if she didn't win the contest.

"You shouldn't get scared about anything and everything, Rama. Come on now, let us see, recite it to me."

Rama began, "*Unnai marandiduvena? Marappariyen. Marandal ... Marandal ...* I can't get it, Mami!"

"Nice indeed! You keep forgetting even as you say *Marappariyen*. Smart girl! Now I will recite, and you repeat it after me."

"Wait, I'll go get the book."

"Why the book? I know it by heart. *Marandal uyir viduven...!*"

"*Uyir viduven!*"

"*Kanandariyen...*"

"*Kanandariyen...*"

"*Un anai idu...*"

Mami recited the entire song, with Rama following after her. Sugandhi completed the song with "*Idu tarunam arutjyoti enakku viraindarule*" and said, "Now, you recite it in full."

"*Unnai marandiduvena? Marappariyen ... Marappariyen ...* Can't get it after that. Sorry, Mami."

"The first time you were at least able to remember the next word. Now it is just the story of '*Ottakkoothan pattukku rettai thappal*'!" Mami laughed, and Rama's mother laughed with her. Then Amma said to her, "You know something, Rama! Both Sugandhi and I learnt this song when we were in class seven. See how well she recites it even now! Our teachers used to praise her power of memory even in those days." Rama just stared wide-eyed.

"Don't worry. I will teach you the whole thing. You are going to win that contest, you will see," Sugandhi said encouragingly.

Mami was always a courageous person, Rama smiled as she mused.

Was she still making the coffee?

There was an almirah of books standing before her. Was Mami still reading Vallalar? Who else was she reading? Are these Tamil books or English?

There were both. She took out one of the Tamil books and opened it on a page in the middle. Thank god, it was prose, not poetry! She read a paragraph, and found it to be written in a good style. Who was the author? She turned to the title page. Sure enough, she found the title and the name of the author, and above them, written in ink: S. Sugandhi.

Nothing surprising about people writing their names in books. Most people do that. But Mami never had that habit. On an impulse, Rama took out the books at random one by one and looked. In each of them was written in Mami's own hand: S. Sugandhi.

She put the books back and closed the almirah. The day's newspaper, neatly folded four times, had dropped from the stool to the floor. She picked it up and put it back on the stool. On the top corner of the paper she saw: S. Sugandhi.

Rama was now troubled by a fear she could not define.

"The milk had gone cold. I had to heat it and make the coffee. And then find the plate and the spoon for the *kesari* ... That's why it took time."

Rama looked at Mami thoughtfully as she ate the kesari and drank the coffee.

"Why do you look at me like that, Rama? There's nothing wrong with me. Don't worry. Where did you buy this churidar? It looks so nice on you. Have you read any good books recently?"

She could see Mami was trying to sidetrack. "You see, Mami..." As she was speaking, the sound of a car was heard arriving and stopping at the gate. The door was heard being banged shut, following which Sankar entered. He was Sugandhi's elder sister's son. He was dressed in a *dhoti* and shirt and had a rose-coloured polythene cover in his hand.

"Come, Sankar!"

"Hello, *Chitti*. Who is that with you? Oh, Mrs Rama? How are you?"

"I'm fine. How are you, Mr Sankar?"

"Oh, life goes on. Last week I ran into your husband at Luz Corner. We chatted for quite a while."

"He told me. It seems both of you went at Indian politics hammer and tongs."

He laughed.

"You look quite like a bridegroom, glittering in a silk dhoti. What is the special occasion?"

"Very smart, Chitti! You ask as if you don't know. Isn't today my *Chittappa*'s daughter's wedding? I have just come after attending it. Why didn't you come? It seems they had come and invited you in person, and you had said you'd attend it without fail. They were quite upset you didn't come."

Sugandhi stopped sipping the coffee, put the tumbler on the table and stared at him.

"What? Wedding? Was Visalam's wedding today?"

"Not Visalam. Vimala. Yes, the wedding was today. You knew, didn't you?"

"I just forgot!" The voice sank low. "I forgot..."

"Here, the *tamboolam* bag. Sent by my Chitti, that is my Chittappa's wife, to my other Chitti, that is my mother's sister!" He placed the bag on the table in front of Sugandhi. She looked at the bag mechanically: red letters on the pink bag, "Wedding: *Soubhagyavathi* Vimala, M.Sc., and *Chiranjivi* Sridharan, M.Sc., MBA."

"I came just to deliver this. I must leave in a hurry now. Shall I? Why, Chitti, aren't you well? You don't look all right."

"Oh, it's nothing..."

"Okay. I'll get going then. See you, Mrs Rama."

Rama went with him to the car and saw him off. When she returned, Sugandhi was sitting on the sofa, head bowed. Rama couldn't bear to see her sitting thus with her index fingers pressed on the sides of the head. She sat down close to Mami and touched her on the shoulders. Sugandhi looked up—her face was pale.

"I forgot the wedding date. And I have known the bride's mother for so long. ... A very good friend ... So frequently these days ... I forget things..."

Words coming out with a stutter. Panic writ large in eyes which had always been marked by clarity and courage.

Question arising from forgetfulness: "Did you find your way at last?"

Sankar's correction: "Vimala, not Visalam."

"Don't worry, Mami. There's nothing unusual about forgetting things as we grow old. Don't be scared." Rama smiled.

Mami recovered and managed to smile back with an effort. She did look shrunken. The few strands of gray here and there in the dark hair—were they new? They didn't seem to have been there two months earlier.

"Sit back and relax, Mami. I'll put the plates and tumblers back in the kitchen. Shall I also keep this tamboolam bag in your room?"

"Mm."

With the utensils in one hand and the polythene bag in the other, Rama first went into Mami's room. As she put the bag down next to the writing pad on the dressing table and turned back, she noticed something. Letters written on a piece of white paper and pasted on the wooden frame of the mirror: S. Sugandhi.

She moved. Again, on the wall: S. Sugandhi.

She felt a sharp stab of apprehension. What was happening to Mami?

Young lovers etch their names with a knife on barks of trees. She had heard that prisoners who have lost all hope of release write their names on the prison walls out of helplessness and desperation that there should be some sign of their ever having lived. Which prison was Mami frightened of?

She went to the kitchen. As she passed the door, on the wall opposite, in black ink: S. Sugandhi.

As she was about to wash the dishes in the kitchen sink, Annam, the cook, entered and said, "Here, Amma, let me do them." Together they washed the utensils.

"How are you, Annamma?"

"Okay, Amma, and you?"

"I'm fine. I am only worried about Mami. She was always so cheerful, so full of life. What has happened to her? Isn't she well?"

"Oh, that, don't ask me."

"Why, what's the matter?"

"It's not fever or headache or anything like that. About a month and a half ago, the seven-year-old daughter of one of Mami's friends underwent a surgical operation for some problem in the gall bladder. It was Mami who arranged for a good hospital and a doctor through her contacts. The child was kept in the hospital for a week after the operation. She was a timid child and the mother had to be by her side in the night. The mother did stay with her; but after four days, there was news of some death in a relative's family, and she had to be away for the night and could return only after the cremation the next morning. It seems she asked Mami whether she could go to the hospital for that one night and stay with the child. Mami agreed at once and said she would certainly go."

Annam was silent for a while.

"Then ... she forgot."

Silence again for a few moments.

"I only came to know later. Otherwise, I would have reminded her. It is from that time that Mami has become as if she is terror-struck. We are even scared whether her brain has been deranged. She writes her name all over the house. Look at this wall. She was never like this earlier."

"Hmm ... That child ... Did something happen to her...?"

"No, no. She fully recovered and was discharged after a week and she went home."

Rama returned to Mami. She sat close to her and held her hand comfortingly.

"I'm getting more and more forgetful, Rama..." she murmured.

Again that fixed stare.

"Let it be, Mami. This is a problem that so many people have. Why do you make so much of it? Is it a big crime to forget a wedding date?"

"Not just that. There is something else ... much more serious. I had said I would keep a child company..."

"I know. Annamma told me. Don't fret yourself thinking about it all the time, Mami."

"It seems the child was very scared and kept crying..."

"Mami, Mami..."

"Luckily, the night nurse acted sensibly, hugging her, comforting her with soothing words and putting her to sleep with mild sedation. The child had got over her fright by the morning. And the mother also returned by noon."

"So everything ended well. Then why do you keep tormenting yourself? Let us talk about something else, Mami."

Sugandhi's eyes fluttered in distress. "Children are like flowers ... How could I forget a child's need? Hereafter what will I not forget? I am scared, Rama, very scared..."

There was an unfathomable fright in the eyes that looked up. With melting sympathy Rama stroked her back. "Don't be frightened, Mami. Aren't you the one who gave me courage and told me never to be frightened?"

Sugandhi's face was pale. The voice came through as though with a slight revival. "I am scared that what happened to my father will happen to me, too."

"What happened to your father?"

"It seems it is a disease which comes with brain debility in old age. On account of that father was gradually afflicted with mental decay, disorder and forgetfulness. Has something like that begun for me, too? Will I also be struck with the same disease? I am very scared, Rama ... Your name is Rama, isn't it? Not Vimala?"

"No, it is Rama, of course. See—you haven't forgotten anything! Don't worry."

"Appa would wake up at midnight, saying, 'I must have a bath now' and take off his clothes. Once, oblivious of everything around him, he stepped into the street and walked on and on for nearly twelve kilometres, and went and sat in a cremation ground. Someone who saw him by chance asked him who he was and why he was sitting there. He could give no answer. When they asked, 'Tell us your name at least,' he couldn't even tell them that and just kept staring ahead, and then he started singing some nursery rhymes. Then someone who knew him happened to see him and brought him home."

Mami stood up, looked at Rama and spoke like someone possessed, "My forgetfulness shouldn't be the beginning of that kind of state. The Divine should take me before I forget my own name. I must have my name. I must have my identity. I am Sugandhi. S. Sugandhi. Lest I forget that, I write my name everywhere in the house."

And I thought that she wrote her name everywhere from an excessive sense of ego, Rama mused. On the contrary, she is doing that fearing a loss of ego.

"As I stand before the dressing table mirror combing my hair, I get a sudden fright that I may forget whose face it is. That is why I have written my name on the frame, so that I can see it every time I look at the mirror."

She took hold of Rama's hand impulsively, dragged her into her room and pointed to the frame of the dressing table.

"Did you see?"

"Yes, I did."

She sat before the mirror and looked at her image in it. The voice had now lost its passion and sounded gentle. She spoke looking at the image.

"Do you know there is a song by Vallalar which starts with 'Will I forget you? (*Unnai marandiduvena?*)'. It goes on with things like, 'I will give up my life if I forget you, I won't live even for a moment (*kanandariyen*)'. Of course, it was sung by Vallalar addressing the Divine. But, whenever I see my face in the mirror, my heart looks at it and wails, for me: 'Will I forget you?'"

Tears started flowing from the anguished eyes. Rama held her face to her bosom.

The covering sheet of the letter pad kept on the table fluttered in the wind and opened. On the first sheet, in line after line, like '*Vél Murugan Thunai*' or '*Sri Rama Jayam*,' was written:

S. Sugandhi
S. Sugandhi
S. Sugandhi

Originally published in Tamil as '*Adaiyalam*' [Identity], in the magazine *Kalki*, Deepavali Special Issue, October 2003.

Glossary and notes

adai: a kind of thick *dosa* made with a paste of coarsely ground rice and pulses.

adei/da/dei (masculine) */adi/di* (feminine) */ey*: vocative/ suffix, sometimes affectionate, often showing disrespect, used while addressing children, younger people or social inferiors.

adeyappa: expression of wonder.

aiyo/ayyayyo: used to express shock, alarm, fright.

akka: elder sister; any girl or woman older than oneself.

amma: mother; mistress of the house; also used as a suffix, more polite than *di*, while addressing a woman or girl.

ammadi!: ouch!

anna: elder brother.

anni: elder brother's wife in non-brahmin dialect.

appa: father; also used as a suffix, more polite than *da*, while addressing a younger man or boy.

appada: expression of relief.

archanai: ritual puja performed at the temple.

arti: plate of water mixed with turmeric and lime waved before newlyweds while welcoming them.

asadu: stupid.

ashramam: hermitage.

asirvadam: blessings.

asura: demon.

atthai: father's sister; mother-in-law.

ayya: master; also used as vocative.

chhe/chhi: used to express disapproval, contempt, anger, revulsion.

chiranjivi (abbreviated in writing to 'Chi.'): one blessed with a long life; traditionally used by elders before names in letters and invitation cards, referring to younger males, bridegrooms.

chittappa: father's younger brother.

chitti: mother's younger sister; father's younger brother's wife; stepmother.

(a) coconut sapling or a squirrel!: a common expression in Tamil while referring to ungrateful children, meaning that, instead of begetting such offspring, the mother (or the father) could have as well planted and reared a coconut sapling or brought up a squirrel. There is a pun here on '*pillai*' which can be used as a word meaning a human child, or as a suffix attached to the name for a coconut, '*tennampillai*' (a coconut sapling), or the name for a squirrel, '*anippillai*' (a baby squirrel).

Devi: goddess.

dorai: one who puts on lordly airs.

Easwara/Easwaran: the Divine, especially Lord Siva.

gramsevika: a woman employed to advise and assist villagers in matters of community welfare and development.

Hamsadhvani: name of a raga in Carnatic music.

Jaganmatha: Mother of the Universe.

jamukkalam: thickly-woven carpet-like fabric, laid on the floor to sit or sleep on.

janmam: birth; life.

kalasam: metal pot. See note on *Varalakshmi nombu*.

kanna: vocative form of Kannan, a Tamil name for Lord Krishna; used to address children lovingly; also used as a suffix to names.

kanné/kannu: literally, 'eye', used as a term of endearment.

karma: consequences of deeds in previous births.

karmayogi: one who performs her/his enjoined duty without expectation of reward.

kartha: doer; one ordained to perform ceremonial rites.

Karthar: God the Creator (in Tamil spoken by Christians).

kazhuthai: donkey; used affectionately or indulgently; also used as a term of contempt.

keerai: spinach.

koottu: semi-solid vegetable dish cooked with lentils, coconut, etc.

kumkumam: vermilion or violet-coloured powder worn in a circular shape on the forehead by women, especially married women.

kuttippayalé: little fellow; used as a term of endearment.

kuttuvilakku: a pedestal oil lamp.

laddu: ball-shaped sweetmeat.

madisar: sari measuring nine yards worn in the traditional mode by married brahmin women.

Mahanadhi: National Film Award-winning and critically acclaimed 1994 Tamil film, directed by Santhana Bharathi, starring Kamal Haasan (who also wrote the story and screenplay). A powerful drama full of disturbing and violent incidents, it has been described as one of Tamil cinema's most depressing films.

mama: mother's brother; any elderly man.

mami: maternal uncle's wife; also used to address or refer to any married woman.

Manmathan: God of love in Hindu mythology, also known as Kama. Lord Siva burnt him to ashes in rage when he shot a love-dart at him, disturbing his penance.

manni: elder brother's wife in brahmin dialect.

mantra: ritual prayer or utterance.

mappillai: son-in-law.

Masi: the eleventh month of the Tamil year.

M. G. R.: M. G. Ramachandran (1917–87), the legendary and iconic Tamil film actor-turned political leader, and former

Chief Minister of Tamil Nadu (1977–87). His tomb, on the Marina Beach in Chennai, is a popular tourist spot.

moodevi: female deity believed to cause misfortune; used as a term of abuse.

mundanai: loose end of the sari hanging behind the shoulders of a woman; *pallu* in Hindi.

murukku: crunchy fried salted snack made from rice dough.

Muthukumaranunga: *-nga* is a suffix indicating respect.

muzham: cubit.

namaskaram: respectful greeting.

narikkurava: gypsy.

Ottakkoothan pattukku rettai thappal: The first words of a Tamil proverb '*Ottakkoothan pattukku rettai thappal pottadupola*' (literally: like bolting the door doubly against Ottakkoothan's song). The nearest English expression would be 'to make matters worse' or 'to do something (annoying or unacceptable to the other person) with a vengeance'. The proverb is typically used when a person is displeased/angry with, or sorry for, something that has happened, and somebody tries to soothe him, but only succeeds in irritating him further.

The story that the saying originates from is provided by Rev. Hermen Jensen in '*Vinodarasamanjari*' on p. 271 of his *A Dictionary of Tamil Proverbs* (originally published as *A Classified Collection of Tamil Proverbs*, London, 1897; reprint New Delhi: Mittal Publications, 2005). A king had a favourite poet named Ottakkoothan; his queen had another. The king's poet was jealous of the queen's poet, and had him imprisoned. On hearing this, the angry queen went into her room and bolted the door. When the king came to see his queen, she said she would not let him in until her favourite poet had been released. The king sent Ottakkoothan to sing outside the queen's door so that she might think that her request was complied with. But the queen knew at once that the song she heard was not by her favourite, and grew even angrier with the king and bolted the door with another bolt. Thus the king's ploy to make amends only made matters worse.

pachadi: semi-solid dish made of pieces of cucumber, onion or coconut mixed with curds, seasoned and served raw.

panchayat: local self-governing body of a village.

pathi: *patti*, in the child's lisping voice.

patti/pattimma: grandmother; any old woman.

pavi: sinner; wrongdoer; wretch.

payasam: sweet porridge.

periamma: mother's elder sister (as in 'Fear and trembling'); also elderly lady of the family (as in 'A chair and a death').

puja: prayers recited, chanted or read.

Puranas: mythological stories.

raja: king; also used as a term of endearment.

rasam: watery soup made with tamarind juice and other ingredients, usually taken mixed with rice.

rascol: colloquial, illiterate pronunciation of 'rascal'.

rava kesari: a sweet dish made of wheat semolina, also called *kesari*.

Saint Vallalar's songs: See note below on *Unnai marandiduvena*.

sambar: highly seasoned thickish soup-like dish made of lentils, tamarind and vegetables, usually taken with rice.

saniyané: vocative, term of abuse; wretch.

seedai: tiny ball-shaped snack made of rice dough, coconut and sesame seeds.

Sita kalyana vaibhogame: song in celebration of the marriage of Rama and Sita, usually sung during the *arti* ceremony.

Siva, Siva: invoking Lord Siva's name to express shock and disapproval.

soubhagyavathi (abbreviated in writing to 'Sou'): one blessed with good health and prosperity; an auspicious way of referring to a girl, bride or married woman, traditionally used by elders before women's names in letters and invitation cards.

Sri Rama Jayam: 'Victory to Lord Sri Rama', often written in notebooks as a form of invocation.

sruti box: a musical instrument which provides the drone, used while practising or performing Indian classical music.

sundal: boiled and spiced pulses served or sold as snacks.

suryadarsanam: ritual viewing and worship of the sun, performed at sunrise.

Swami: God; also master.

talam: (in music) beat; keeping time by striking with the hand.

tali: See note on *thirumangalyam*.

tambi: younger brother; any boy or younger man.

tamboolam: betel leaves, areca nuts, coconut, etc. usually put in a bag and offered to visitors during festivals and wedding guests when they leave the celebration.

thatha: grandfather.

thirumangalyam: *tali*; gold chain or turmeric-smeared cord with holy pendants worn round the neck by married women; Tamil equivalent of Hindi *mangalsutra*.

Unnai marandiduvena? Marappariyen: Song No. 3806 from *Tiru Arutpa*, a collection of 6000 songs composed by Ramalinga Swamigal (1823–74), also known as Ramalinga Adigal or Vallalar, a loved and revered Tamil mystic and saint. The Tamil song excerpts in the story 'Identity and amnesia' are from this song. The song, addressed to the Divine, is as much a prayer to God never to forget the devotee as it is an ardent vow taken by the devotee that he will never forget God. Ironically, the fear of forgetting that haunts the protagonist in the story is one that relates to her own identity. A translation of the song is provided below:

Will I ever forget You?
I know not how to forget You.
Should I ever forget You, I will not survive,
not even for a moment. It is Your command.
Will You forget me? If You forget me, what will I do?
Where will I go? To whom will I speak?

Oh, Mother! Even if You, more compassionate than the mother, do forget me,
Your divine grace endowed upon this entire universe will not forget me.
Knowing this, I remain in joy. This is indeed the moment.
Oh, Light of Grace, make haste and bless me here and now.

(Translated by C. T. Indra and Prema Jagannathan)

vaa: come; enter.

vadai: South-Indian savoury, round or doughnut-shaped, made of seasoned lentil paste and deep fried in oil.

Vallalar: See note above on *Unnai marandiduvena?*

vanakkam: term of respectful greeting, like *namaskar* in Hindi.

Varalakshmi nombu: ceremony performed by married women (*sumangalis*) in most parts of South India to propitiate Goddess Lakshmi—also known as *Varalakshmi*, meaning one who grants boons—and for the welfare of the family, especially the husband. During the ceremony, performed in the month of Sravana (July–August), the *kalasam* or metal pot representing the Goddess is decorated with a sari, flowers and jewellery, and fruits and other offerings are placed in front of it.

varnam: a type of composition in Carnatic music, usually sung at the beginning of a concert.

'Vél Murugan Thunai': literally, 'May the spear-wielding Lord Murugan be my support', written as a form of prayer.

Yama: God of death.

yéndi: vocative, used while addressing girls or younger women.

yénga: literally, 'What/Why,' used as an opening while addressing elders instead of using their names, and also by non-brahmin women while speaking to their husbands.

yénna: vocative used by brahmin women while addressing their husbands instead of using their names.

yogi: saint, ascetic.